Author's Note

This book is a work of fiction. It is based on true events
that occurred from 8 December 1930 to November 1931.
I have knowingly taken liberties with the chronology of
historical events and mixed them with fictitious ones. The
Devenish family and the named Political Officers are entirely
imaginary as are all thoughts, actions and opinions of any
character, historical or otherwise, who appears in this book.

To Ch. N. N.

Tell Me, Apollo, for thy Daphne's love,
What Cressid is, what Pandar, and what we?
Her bed is India; and there she lies, a pearl.

William Shakespeare, *Troilus and Cressida*

CRESSIDA'S BED

Desmond Barry was born and brought up in Wales. He works in Tibet during the summer and is presently an External Fellow at Glamorgan University. He is the author of two previous novels, *The Chivalry of Crime* and *A Bloody Good Friday*.

ALSO BY DESMOND BARRY

Desmond Barry

CRESSIDA'S BED

VINTAGE

Published by Vintage 2005

2 4 6 8 10 9 7 5 3 1

First published in Great Britain in 2004 by
Jonathan Cape

Vintage
Random House, 20 Vauxhall Bridge Road,
London SW1V 2SA

Random House Australia (Pty) Limited
20 Alfred Street, Milsons Point, Sydney
New South Wales 2061, Australia

Random House New Zealand Limited
18 Poland Road, Glenfield,
Auckland 10, New Zealand

Random House (Pty) Limited
Endulini, 5A Jubilee Road, Parktown 2193,
South Africa

The Random House Group Limited Reg. No. 954009
www.randomhouse.co.uk/vintage

A CIP catalogue record for this book
is available from the British Library

ISBN 0 099 47196 5

Papers used by Random House are natural, recyclable
products made from wood grown in sustainable forests.
The manufacturing processes conform to the environ-
mental regulations of the country of origin

Printed and bound in Great Britain by
Bookmarque Ltd, Croydon, Surrey

PART ONE

BOMBAY, LATE NOVEMBER 1930

CHAPTER ONE

NOTHING BUT A BAND OF SKY WAS VISIBLE ABOVE THE NARROW alley where garish signs written in the entwined letters of formal Hindi and misspelt English were fastened to the façades of the red-brick buildings of the Murarji Gokaloab Bazaar. Christina Devenish read the movements in the visible clouds – fierce with reds and purples – that contorted and deformed themselves in freak winds above the rooftops. It was as if battle raged in heaven between deity and demiurge – dreamt into being by one of this country's gods, some Brahma or Shiva or Indra – and she was convinced that this display of half-hidden forces was magically moving mortals towards some parallel clash upon the Bombay streets. The last rays of the dying sun shafting sideways into the narrow street caught her slightly sunburned and freckled face, causing her to squint, the skin around her eyes to wrinkle, and she turned her head away from the contorted clouds and glanced back over her shoulder at the flickering torches and dipping placards of the protest march about seventy yards behind her. Rowdy chants filled the space of the cacophonous evening market. She brushed away a strand of red hair that had come loose from her braid, pulled up the skirts of her green and gold sari and rushed on through the crowded bazaar where the textile stalls cascaded delirious colour: gaudy reds, suffocating yellows; and the tiny eyes of mirrors sewn into those embroidered brocades from Rajasthan that winked as if to mock her hurry. Brown faces, irritated at her clumsy, intrusive passage, stared at her as she pushed through the crowd.

She was alien among these people. No matter how she dressed, or whatever she believed, she was marked by her skin, her voice, her family, her long, light body and her copper-red hair that swayed above the heads of everyone around her in the street. But she was an outsider too, among the Bombay British: an unmarried woman of thirty-one; a disciple of Annie Besant; and a woman who ran a birth control clinic, a sari-wrapped Englishwoman.

A roar erupted from the marchers behind her and drove her into a near-panic. But she could thank whatever God she believed in, for the bazaar-wallahs would slow the marchers more than they slowed her. She had to get the staff and patients out of her clinic before the demonstrators arrived. The violence was worse every day. Gandhiji in jail and nothing to stop the religious fanatics. On Tuesday, it had been just slogans outside the clinic. Then, yesterday, the horrible bang of half a brick as it hit the door, the cascade of broken bits of terra-cotta tea cups and half-rotten vegetables that had made a shambles of the veranda. It had been terrifying. The birth control clinic was a symbol of the Raj for them: a British plot to stop Indian reproduction and to destroy the moral fabric of Indian society, Hindu and Muslim alike. Every torchlight procession from the Buleshwar District to the Town Hall on Elphinstone Circle had to pass by the clinic.

The air was suffocating her, thick with the smell of frying oil from the food vendors, and of turmeric being spooned from a tin to be weighed, and the stinky tang of asafoetida. It all caught in her nose and throat. She pulled up the shoulder fold of the sari so that it would not drag on the ground and slipped between a handcart and a market stall piled high with bright sweetmeats coloured orange and white and the delicate green of pistachio. Fat black dots of flies swirled up around her face and then resettled upon the sweetmeats like foul currants. Women in saris and men in *khurtas* yelled at her and gesticulated as if the violence of the approaching march was already infecting them.

She broke free of the crowd at the end of the bazaar, hitched up her sari and jumped over the foetid sewage ditch on the north side of the street and onto the open courtyard of the clinic. She hurried towards the steps of the building whose grand title, the All India Women's Health Clinic, belied the tiny, tin-roofed and mud-walled hut. She had received some small financial help from Marie Stopes in London in order to buy the plot and to build and equip the clinic. Margaret Sanger from America had also sent her a generous donation. Christina had added to that capital some money of her own from a small trust fund, which had been set up for her by her Irish grandfather. She still had some of her grandfather's endowment in reserve should she need it. Christina's staunchly Catholic mother had been aghast at the use to which Christina had put her trust money and had immediately cut off all communication with her. Just as she had refused to speak to Christina for three years when she'd discovered that her daughter had taken to Theosophy. Having enemies, she thought, was a sure way of knowing that she'd really made an impact on the world.

She stumbled momentarily on the rough wooden steps of the veranda and caught herself on the twisted tree trunk that held up the porch roof. The clinic's white-painted door was open. No one was in the tiny reception cubicle. The single desk, too big for that space, was cluttered with files and loose papers on the ink-stained blotter as if the staff had left in a hurry.

'Lakshmi,' she called.

Her high voice seemed to be swallowed by silence. She waited. Listened. Heard a shuffling sound off to her right. Lakshmi appeared from the examination room. She was a lot shorter than Christina's five feet ten and she stooped slightly, giving her broad upper back a domed shape under the drape of her purple and white sari. Her grey-streaked hair was pulled back in a tight bun and the hard eyes behind the horn-rimmed glasses seemed to be appraising Christina. She gripped the handle of a large black umbrella as if she were brandishing a sabre. Christina had first seen that ferocious look at a conference of the All India Women's Federation where Lakshmi was a formidable presence on the Bombay branch committee. Lakshmi was an expert midwife. Her husband had died before she had had any children and she was without any living relative that Christina knew about. Lakshmi had been enthusiastic about the clinic, and so alike to Christina in her isolation from family and society that it was inevitable that they had formed a deep friendship. And Lakshmi guided her through the India that Christina was rediscovering since the long years away through childhood and early womanhood.

'I have sent them all home, madam,' Lakshmi said.

'You sent them . . . ?' Christina said.

'Something very bad in the air. They're out for trouble. You can feel it.'

'You can go, too, Lakshmi. They won't dare do anything while I'm here.'

Lakshmi's lips pursed. The eyes were contemptuous behind the thick lenses of her glasses.

'Memsahib, is it? I'm afraid that they might not care about a memsahib. I think I'd better stay with you.'

'Lakshmi, this is my responsibility.'

Another look of contempt.

'*Ah chaa,*' Lakshmi said.

'Let's get the shutters up, then,' Christina said.

She squeezed between the wall and the desk and opened the cupboard behind it. The shutters were made of rough pine and not at all heavy. Lakshmi leaned her umbrella against the door jamb of the examination room. The chants of the marchers sounded near and clear now.

Coming from the middle of the bazaar, Christina guessed. Only a few minutes left before they were outside the door. She slid the first shutter between the wall and the desk. Lakshmi carried it towards the door. She stopped at the threshold.

'Oh, too late, madam,' Lakshmi said.

Christina turned to the front window.

Like skirmishers out in front of the main march, a group of protesters – about thirty-strong, she guessed – already stood close to the ditch beyond the courtyard. Shaking their placards, they yelled slogans in Hindi, unaware of her at the window.

'Let me get by, Lakshmi,' Christina said.

Lakshmi shook her head but Christina stepped out onto the veranda to face the mob, convinced that they would be afraid to hurt a white woman.

Above the bazaar, the air was thicker and smokier now over the demonstrators who were gathered in ever greater numbers behind the ditch. The wild-eyed young men were but fifteen yards away and she could look into the faces of each individual and each one she looked at avoided her eyes and waved his placard with its Hindi slogan as if to ward off the embarrassment that he seemed to feel at confronting her. The main body of the march inched ever nearer and the noise of the chanting grew louder. The marchers had cleared the confines of the bazaar. They swelled out towards both sides of the street and filled the whole area between the buildings. A placard flew across the courtyard, its pole a shaft, its sign the flight of an oversized arrow that thudded to the ground close to the clinic's bottom step.

Christina was suddenly and acutely aware of the frailty of the human body: her own human body; strong as it was with no excess flesh, its tight muscles on a slender frame, used to riding and shooting when she was only a little younger. But now she could easily imagine those long bones snapping and her flesh bruising and her head cracking under some flailing club. She had lost her advantage, that sense of intimidation which she had held for a moment as she glared at the vanguard of the marchers. A tall young man in a brick-coloured turban jumped across the

7

ditch. He began to yell at her in Hindustani what she assumed was a stream of abuse. She was suddenly mute. Despite herself, she retreated into the shelter of the office. Immediately she regretted it. Now something awful would happen and she had no way to make it stop.

'What the hell do they want with us, Lakshmi?'

Lakshmi shook her head.

'It's time we were going.'

'Is the medicine cabinet locked?'

'I'll make sure.'

Lakshmi disappeared into the examination room again.

The files. She had to put the files away. If they broke in, she didn't want the demonstrators stealing the records and persecuting her patients. She gathered up the brown cardboard folders in the crook of her arm, dodged around the desk and ran into the tiny and claustrophobic medical records office with its one grey metal cabinet. She always felt too big for this room. She pulled the top drawer open and pitched the folders into it. She could alphabetise them when this was all over. She took her bunch of keys from the peg behind the door and turned one quickly in the cabinet's feeble lock. That lock would keep no one out.

'We should get out of here, now,' Lakshmi called from the reception area.

Christina clutched the keys tightly.

'Come on, then,' she said.

The sound of the chants hammered almost palpably against the aged building in waves of noisy religious and political outrage.

'Oh God,' Christina said. 'They won't let us through, will they?'

Lakshmi shuffled across the room and put her hand on Christina's shoulder, a tender gesture, maternal, at odds with her fierce expression.

'The police will come, certainly,' Lakshmi said. 'This crowd, it could easily turn against the government offices. The police won't like that at all.'

'I hope you're right.'

The front window shattered, jagged glass in the frame, shards and slivers on the desk top.

'Oh Lakshmi!'

'Come on.'

The chants were louder without the glass. There was something bestial about the noise. Christina pressed the keys into her palm to get herself under control. She and Lakshmi would walk out onto the veranda, lock the door behind them and then face the crowd. She would take Lakshmi's hand and they would walk across the courtyard and the demonstrators would see that they were two women; and then they would part like the Red Sea before Moses and let them through to the bazaar. Right was on her side. That was how it would go. She couldn't predict what the demonstrators would do to the clinic but she prayed that they would march on to Government House, once they saw that the women had locked up and left and there was no one left to hear their slogans.

'Let's see if the police have turned up,' Christina said.

She turned towards the door.

Within the outline of the shattered window frame, she caught a glimpse of a dark object trailing flame. She lifted her arm across her face and, as if time had suddenly slowed, the object grew larger in its arc and then there was a crash and tinkle as more glass broke and a low roar as the flaming bottle disappeared behind the desk and a loud 'whump!'. Fire exploded upwards into the room in front of the wall and the window frame and filled the air with a stinking heat against which Christina instinctively ducked, bumping into Lakshmi. Coils of black, unbreathable smoke, lit up orange from below, twisted thickly under the tiny room's ceiling. An intangible assault raked at Christina's lungs. Heat seared her skin. Bright flame flickered

9

within the thickening smoke. She lost sight of Lakshmi. Flames cut her off from the only door out of the building and the fire was sucking all the air from the room.

Christina twisted away from the heat to see Lakshmi leaning against the door jamb of the examination room. She was curled over the handle of her umbrella, one hand raised as if to hold off the fire and the smoke's assault. Christina clutched at the waist of Lakshmi's sari and pulled her to the floor. She pushed at her to get her through the door and into the examination room. Lakshmi scuttled on her hands and knees like a turtle, almost comical, the broad back and fat behind in front of Christina, the umbrella still dragging along by Lakshmi's side.

Christina retched. Her eyes burned and streamed. She crawled rapidly after Lakshmi, the keys gone out of her hand, and she swung the examination-room door shut behind her. For a moment, she could breathe, but her nasal passages down through her oesophagus were raw. Smoke seeped beneath the door, making her retch again just at the sight of it. More grey smoke drifted in a layer over the examination table. A low roar raged behind the pine barrier. Lakshmi knelt beneath the closed window and gasped for air, retched and coughed, too. Her hair had come awry. She gripped the umbrella as if for support, its point between her knees, the handle curled above her head.

'How will we get out?' Lakshmi said.

Her voice was a croak.

Christina stood up. The room seemed to tilt and it wanted to spin. The glass-fronted instrument cabinet floated on the right of the six-light window whose white-painted panes held a preternatural brightness. The window was nailed shut. There was no means to open it other than to smash it. She gripped the edge of the examination table in the middle of the room to steady herself. Her knee joints had come undone and didn't want to hold up her swaying body. The air that burned her nose and throat was disgusting – filthy with burnt pine and varnish. She clawed the air, desperate for a clean fresh draught of breath in her lungs. She focused on a chair, gripped it and marched with it towards the window. Christina swung the chair up above her head and the room swam and she swung it down hard at the blind panes. The opaque glass shattered and she was in a frenzy, smashing the glass until the six small frames were gone. She pressed her face against the metal mesh beyond the jagged frame and let fresh air stab into the dry burned membranes of her lungs and throat. Her head cleared. Behind the bent wire were faces and heads, turbans and bodies swaying in the shifting red light.

'You bastards,' Christina whispered. 'God help us.'

Christina clawed at the mesh, her fingernails scraping against the tight metal loops. She began to laugh. It was so absurd. After all, it was *meant* to be thief-proof. Christina put her broken fingernails to her dry lips. She wanted to scream against the terror of burning, or suffocating, that gnawed at her consciousness, but the fear was lost in the rush of adrenaline.

'The table,' Lakshmi said.

What on earth did she mean?

Christina turned to face the smoke-filled room. There was a bright inner glow to the walls, the cabinets, the table and the chair that lay on its side among the white-painted broken glass. Smoke drifted in layers from the ceiling and almost to the floor. An ethereal beauty to it. Lakshmi leaned against the table, more bent than ever, breathing in shallow pants.

'We'll use the table,' Lakshmi said. 'To break the wire.'

The table's edge jutted out at least a foot beyond the legs.

'Yes,' Christina said. 'Yes.'

Lakshmi was too strong for a woman over fifty.

Christina glanced at the door. Smoke was drifting from under it and there was a deep roar behind it. It wouldn't hold for ever. She forced herself to walk away from the window and into the smoke while her muscles and bones seemed to be in revolt, trying to force her back to the window and fresh air. Lakshmi's mouth hung open, her eyes were bloodshot and watery and her smudged face was tracked with tears. Christina's legs wobbled as she lifted the front end of the table. She felt the back lift and the table tipped and she almost lost her grip.

'I'm ready,' Christina said.

She focused on the jagged-edged window frame. The tin roof began to ping loudly and small sparks spat down into the room from above. She was so hot.

'One,' rasped Lakshmi. 'Two. Three!'

Christina lurched towards the window and lunged at the mesh. The table bounced back off the wire, twisted her arm muscles and threw her back into the smoky room. But she kept a strong grip on the table. She sucked in hot and thick air that made her gag. She glanced back at Lakshmi, who still held up her end, tottering in the depths of the smoke. More smoke was cascading into the room like a dark grey waterfall oozing from a crack between the wall and the tin roof.

'Again,' Lakshmi said.

Christina gripped the table tighter. They backed away for their run-up.

'Once more,' Lakshmi said. 'Come on. One, two, three!'

Christina lunged forward again and the table bounced off the dented mesh and twisted out of her hands, scraped down her shin. The table crashed to the floor and Lakshmi fell to her hands and knees. Christina gasped, bent over and a wave of darkness blanked her vision for a second and then the room swam and she was lying on her side. Her hands were bleeding and stung a little but she could hardly feel a thing.

It can't finish, she thought. Not like this.

She used the wall to help herself to her feet. She was hot and dirty and greasy in the folds of green and gold silk. Her red hair hung in wisps about her face.

'Oh God. Please,' Christina prayed.

'Again,' Lakshmi said.

How was Lakshmi on her feet?

Christina began to cough. Her eyes blurred with tears. She straightened up, gripped the table and lifted it. Behind her, Lakshmi was breathing in sharp gasps.

'One, two, three!' Christina croaked.

They charged again and the table jammed up against the mesh. Christina held on this time – Lakshmi, too – but she didn't know how.

'Yes,' Christina said. 'Again.'

They backed away. Bells rang in the distance. Shots cracked out.

'Police are coming. And firemen,' Lakshmi whispered.

The heat in the room increased all of a sudden. Christina glanced towards the door. Its varnish had begun to blister and smoke. A loud crack and a shower of sparks came from a split in the panel. Tiny orange and blue flames formed in the jagged line, and a little flare roared at the bottom of the crack.

'Once again,' Lakshmi said.

Christina lifted her end of the table. Her hands were filthy. She had just to stay on her feet. She could hear Lakshmi wheezing behind her.

'Come on,' Lakshmi said. 'One, two, three!'

Christina stumbled forward, the table hit and the mesh tore. Just like that.

'Oh!' Christina said. 'Again. Again.'

'One, two, three!' Lakshmi called.

A great rent opened in the mesh and Christina could have screamed for joy but Lakshmi's end of the table suddenly thudded down behind her. Lakshmi was sitting on the floor holding her chest.

'Oh God, no,' Christina begged. 'Hang on, please, Lakshmi. We can get out. Look! Look!'

She had to get her out. She dragged the table beneath the window sill and turned to pick up Lakshmi. With a deafening crack, the pine door exploded in bright orange light and a shower of fiery splinters. Christina ducked, shielding her eyes, her muscles contracted, all instinct. She batted at the burns in her smoking sari and turned to face the roar of a seven-foot wall of flame that raged in the shattered door frame. Heat seared the room, air rushed in to feed it from the broken window and the fire flared out and swallowed Lakshmi who was suddenly on her feet, engulfed in a twist of orange flame that clung to the raw silk of her sari.

'Oh God! No!' Christina howled.

Lakshmi in a mass of orange light staggered past her. Christina beat at the flames on Lakshmi's body with her own bare hands. Lakshmi's arm swung up and back and her hand smacked into Christina's nose and Christina hit the floor. Above her, a blurred Lakshmi, like a saint enveloped by holy fire, mute, clawed herself up onto the table, flames rising from her curved back. The rushing air made the fire swirl up higher around her. Lakshmi toppled towards the gap in the mesh. Her heavy body hit the metal and ripped it apart and then there were only her scratched brown legs and sandalled feet and then nothing at all but a hole in the mesh beyond which light flickered.

Christina pulled herself up by the table edge. She retched, sucked heat and no air into her tortured lungs. The torn metal dug into her palms. She put one sandalled foot on the bottom end of the rent and thrust her head through the broken mesh into fresh air. The rush of blood to her head made her see everything in a deeper red than firelight. Behind her the room roared. She fell forward and the mesh split yet more, tore at her foot, and the ground rushed up and slammed the rest of the breath from her body. She rolled in the cool broken glass, whooping, as her lungs tried to drag in air and her whole being was in a state of panic, wanting breath. Black forms swam through the garden. Voices yelling in Hindustani. The shiny helmets of firemen. Men all around her. She fought off a wave of suffocating darkness and sucked at air that refused to enter her parched lungs. She failed to push up on her elbow and the sky and the men above her and the earth beneath her spun out of control and her head dropped back onto the hard ground and the next wave of darkness engulfed her.

CHAPTER TWO

I

A TERRIBLE WEIGHT PRESSED DOWN ON HER CHEST AND A
bright light blazed through her shut eyelids. She could hear a
sucking sound. Her mouth and throat were forced open by
something firm but Christina was too weak to fight against it
and she thought perhaps it was an iron lung pumping her chest
full of breath and emptying it again to keep her alive. The light
was so bright that she couldn't bear to open her eyes. Her eyelids
were too heavy anyway. This bright light held her down like a
stone crushing a beetle and it was useless to struggle, to try to
lift her body against it. Where was she? An operating theatre?
Coming out of a coma? Was she breathing? She tried to lift her
body in a sudden stark panic, her throat and mouth wanting to
moan to let them know she was coming awake, but nothing
would come out around the obstruction. What were they doing
to her? Was there anybody there? She was terrified of what she
would discover as the anaesthetic wore off, or was it an anaesthetic? Were they going to amputate a part of her? Where was
she? She couldn't lift her shoulders. She sank, too exhausted to
struggle, and her mind, her senses, were in a thick fog. It was
all a thick fog. A greyness all around her and she couldn't feel
her body any more. The weight was gone off her chest and she
was sure that she had lost control of her bladder, and she was

drooling around the tube, just a horrible draining sensation with all the struggle flowing out of her, no matter if she wanted to struggle or not, and there was this terrible confusion of whether she should be reaching upwards towards the light or letting herself sink back into oblivion as the anaesthetic took her down. If that's what it was. No one was speaking and there were no instruments that she could feel but perhaps they were prepping her for the op. No! No op! What are they doing to me? Little sparks in the fog now. Sharp little scintillations that lit up. It was awfully cold. Cold sparks. Little shards of bright ice, more and more of them swirling like a frightening ice storm. It was so chilly. She struggled to wake up, to get back to the surface through the cold. But it was useless. She just couldn't breathe, and she was twisting upwards or trying to twist upwards but it was useless and she couldn't remember where she was, and all she felt was a huge empty hole and then a great dark nothing.

2

The starkness of the hospital room put Christina in mind of a cell. There were even white-painted bars on the inside of the window. The top halves of the walls were painted white and the bottoms green, and reddish-brown *pan* stains marred one corner where a copper spittoon had been left unemptied. She was keeping vigil beside Lakshmi's bed and the straight-backed wooden chair had become positively penitential. Beside her, on the white-enamelled bedside cabinet, Lakshmi's horn-rimmed glasses lay next to a clear and untouched pitcher of water that was covered with cheesecloth to keep out the flies. Two unused glasses stood upended beside it. A drip bottle hung from a metal tree, its shiny needle in a vein of Lakshmi's gauze-wrapped arm, and a black oxygen mask had been fitted over her face with a corrugated tube that connected her to a green tank. The tank had two clock-like gauges, and a valve that hissed softly. It seemed as if Lakshmi's soul was held to the earth only by this hellish machine made of green metal and black rubber. No doubt she, Christina, had been connected to something such as that. She still had terrible gaps in her memory. Great areas of blackness. Of course, the fire. Even now, she had no idea how long she had been beside Lakshmi's bed. Christina's breathing came in no more than shallow sips and even that small effort inflicted sharp pains on her parched mucosa and the damaged cartilage of her ribs. But at least she had all her sense faculties and her limbs. Dr Forbes had assured her that her lungs would recover, but in her blackest moments she doubted him to the point of panic. She was so desperate for a deep draught of cool, filling air. Absurdly, she had a sudden urge to smoke a cigarette as if each cell in her body craved tobacco to calm her, soothe her, make her feel normal again, because nothing was normal any more. She leaned forward with her elbows on her knees, and stared at Lakshmi from between her bandaged hands, desperately willing life into her.

Dr Forbes stood at the foot of the bed marking a chart. His grubby lab coat hung open over a wrinkled white shirt that bulged above the belt of his white ducks; the big round face was waxy and colourless, a pockmarked moon with a heavy grey moustache and topped with a thick bush of grey hair.

'She looks terrible, doesn't she?' Christina said.

Forbes glanced up at Christina, then continued to make marks on the chart as if he hadn't heard her. She gave her attention back to Lakshmi. The injuries sickened and fascinated Christina: those puckered, pale and taut patches of scar tissue on the once brown skin of Lakshmi's face and arms; and the unpigmented bald spot above her shrivelled ear. Under the tented sheets, the upper body was covered in gauze and ointments. Regular shots of morphine kept Lakshmi virtually comatose.

'She just needs time to heal, Dr Forbes, doesn't she?'

'I think you should go home, now, Dr Devenish.'

She shifted in her loose cotton frock so that it didn't rub against the stitched cuts on her right arm.

'I really don't think so.'

Her voice was little more than a hoarse whisper.

Forbes fidgeted with the long tube of the stethoscope that dangled from the right-hand pocket of his lab coat.

'You need rest, Dr Devenish. I discharged you on the understanding that you would go home.'

'She is going to get better, isn't she?' Christina said.

'I'll be honest with you, Dr Devenish,' Forbes said. 'Her lungs are in terrible shape. I don't know if there's enough live tissue to support her. You do understand that.'

She nodded. She tried to think of this as a purely anatomical affair. She could picture Lakshmi's pulmonary tree and the damage that the heat and smoke must have done.

'Please, Dr Devenish. Let me get you home. I've had the driver bring my car around for you.'

'That's very kind of you,' she said.

She knew how Forbes felt. How many times had she forced relatives or friends to leave their loved ones in an unfamiliar hospital bed? This was a scene out of a bland and customary nightmare in the profession that she, too, had chosen. Sooner or later, she would have to leave the hospital and face herself.

'All right,' she said.

Forbes looked relieved. He had been especially kind right after the disaster. He had wired her family about the fire and had taken care of the flurry of telegraph messages back and forth to her mother in Cork and to her father who was nearer. But not that near. Colonel Devenish was in Bhutan, a Political Department man. She saw him so rarely. More often than not, he spent his time on the Empire's frontier, among the Himalayan kingdoms, and even when he did get back to India, he was based in Calcutta rather than Bombay. When she thought about it, she had really seen so little of him in her life. And mostly that had been his fault, not hers. And now that she had come so close to losing her life, she both resented her father's distance and wanted to get closer to him. She really didn't know him that well.

'Shall we go?' Forbes asked.

Christina leaned forward in order to come to her feet. A spike of pain jabbed through her torn ribcage. Lakshmi's closed eyes were like smooth brown eggs above the curve of the hideous black mask. She let her bandaged hand hover over Lakshmi's shoulder then turned away from the bed. Forbes picked up her striped bag, woven from highland wool.

'I'll help you with this,' he said.

All the bag contained were her nightdresses, toiletries and a ruined sari. She flushed as she became overly conscious of her wrapped hands.

'Oh, yes. Thank you,' she said.

Forbes turned to the door and Christina looked back once at the bed and the unconscious body attached to the hissing machine. Then she followed Forbes down the ward where dirty bandages lay in tangled piles next to some of the doors and the corridor was scattered with various pieces of litter: flattened and dusty cigarette packets, crushed *beedees*, a wad of chewed and soggy *pan* leaves.

Forbes held open the door to the stairs. She took each step carefully so that her ribs wouldn't ache. Forbes helped her through the hospital's side door at the bottom of the stairs. His long grey Healey idled on the tarmac outside. The evening sky was cool and blue but even that muted light was too bright for her. She shaded her eyes with her ugly bandaged hand. The Indian driver, a small, wizened man in a pale khaki uniform, held open the rear door for her.

'You need plenty of rest,' Forbes said.

'Oh. Yes. I think I'll go straight to bed.'

With only her elbows to help her balance, she slid awkwardly onto the back seat of the car. The shady interior smelled of old leather and stale tobacco. The driver slammed the door and she heard him open the boot for her bag. After the next slam, Dr Forbes waved once and she nodded back, keeping her hands in her lap. It was dark in the car. She leaned her head back on the seat and closed her eyes. The Healey set off towards her bungalow in the European haven on Malubar Hill.

3

A narrow strip of morning light infiltrated the room from behind the rattan blinds, lighting up only the edge of the bookshelves that darkened two walls of the room. She had no will to raise herself from the bed. She stared at the rows of books that had once defined her but now seemed like so much dead paper. She had bought them in her student days at University College Hospital, on Gower Street, or on the Charing Cross Road, in London. It had cost a fortune to ship them to Bombay. Books on gynaecology, pharmacology, anatomy and psychiatry. And then there was Blavatsky's *Secret Doctrine* that she had bought in Bloomsbury. That, and the *Bhagavad Gita* translated into English by one of the members of the Theosophical Society; and *Varieties of Religious Experience* by William James. And Madame David-Neel's *Journey to Lhasa*, which was a real inspiration – a woman who had defied British and Tibetan prohibitions and had journeyed in disguise to the city of the Dalai Lamas. Those four books were still a comfort. Back in 1922, Christina had scandalised her medical student colleagues by keeping a copy of HPB's masterwork on the desk in her study at UC. She had been the only woman among all the interns of that year, and the others had always teased her about Theosophy. But studying karma and dreams and reincarnation at the Theosophical Society's

London branch had been her link to her father back in the Himalayan kingdoms. The Society's Mrs Besant was still something of a heroine for Christina: a political radical, a birth control pioneer, Blavatsky's heiress, and even president of the Indian National Congress for a while; someone about whom Christina could have impassioned arguments with her father by letter. For years that had been her only contact with her father. She, Christina, was a radical. The suffragettes had gained votes for women over thirty in 1918, and Christina had taken to the streets since whenever Mrs Pankhurst's militants had marched for their rights. And through this political action, Christina had come to understand the nature of the struggle of the poor and the oppressed throughout the world, although she had far less sympathy for godless Marxism. The experience of working in a clinic with poor women in the East End of London, trying to lighten their load of constant child-bearing and child-rearing, was a solid foundation on which to build her Indian vocation. She was defiant about her beliefs, political or religious. Perhaps she had inherited that trait from her mother's fanatical Catholicism. Christina's approach to religion was as radical as her politics. She had even dabbled in the extremes of Theosophy's more bizarre offshoots. Oliver Haddo, the infamous magician, had initiated her into the Order of the Silver Star. She still missed the theatrical rituals – the robes, the incantations – and the sex in the magical circle had shaken the remains of her Catholic upbringing to the roots. She had drunk brandy and claret with the Bloomsbury set and recited poetry and danced with Florence Farr and slept with Oliver Haddo and even slept with Florence Farr. And then there were the powders and potions that Oliver had given to her. She had never seen any contradiction in her interest in the medical and occult sciences.

She had even sought to bring an analytical approach to her drug-taking. Her journal was full of the experiments she had done with hashish, opium, cocaine, heroin, tiny mushrooms gathered in Wales. Each plant or powder connected with one of the Sephiroth on the Tree of Life that she had carefully categorised according to its planetary characteristics: opium for Saturn, hashish for the moon, cocaine for Jupiter, the colourful visions conjured up by the mushrooms for the sun. Now, it seemed like so much delusion, but at the time she was completely convinced of the scientific nature of her experiments upon herself. Medicine helped her discover the miraculous constitution of the human body and the awesome nature of disease, while Theosophy opened up to her the superhuman dimensions of being. She had studied the mind scientifically, too, through the works of Dr Freud and Dr Jung, and even its more abberant psychologies through the works of Sacher-Masoch, de Sade and George Sand.

From outside came the tinny ding-ding of a bell and the rattle of a bicycle interrupting her distracted thoughts of the past. She heard voices speaking Hindustani: Madhan's, her *chaprassi*, was one; and perhaps the postman. She had been inundated with messages of condolence over the clinic from her patients. And from hundreds of members of the All India Women's Association, who had read about the fire in *Shtri Dharma*, their monthly magazine.

The bicycle rattled away. She twisted on the cot and was surprised to find that her body was tense with anticipation. The floorboard in the passage squeaked and there was a light tap on the door.

'Yes?'

Madhan's muffled voice came from beyond the door.

'A letter, madam, from your father. Express dispatch.'

Her father?

'Yes. Just a moment,' she said.

She made a brushing movement with her heavily bandaged right hand in order to push back the sheet, raised herself up by leaning on her elbow and then eased her legs over the edge of the bed. The dressing picked and itched at her fingers. Even though Bombay was in its late November cool, her white cotton nightdress was still wet with sweat and clung to her back. Her long red hair hung loose and disorderly around her face. Madhan always managed to see her at her worst.

'Oh, just come in,' she called.

The door creaked and a narrow parallelogram of light shafted into the room. Madhan slipped through the gap between jamb and door edge, his thin, dark body blocking some of the unwanted light from the passageway. He held up the slim envelope between the thumbs and index fingers of both hands.

'Shall I open it for you, madam?' he said.

He waggled his head on his shoulders, an Indian interrogative.

'Thank you, Madhan. Please do.'

He crossed to the desk, picked up the brass letter knife off the blotter and slit the top edge of the envelope. He laid the thin sheet of rice paper on the blotter. Then he lit the kerosene lamp.

'Would you care for anything else, madam?' Madhan said.

'Not just now. Thank you.'

He nodded, walked over to the door and closed it behind him without another word. Christina sat down at the desk. She could rest her elbows on the arms of it and her near useless hands on the blotter. She stared down at the familiar cursive:

Dearest Chrissie,

I received the telegram from Forbes. It is so frustrating that I can't see for myself how you are recovering despite the assurances that you are. Please do rest and recover as quickly as possible. I am devastated by your loss of the clinic. You must be too. But really, Chrissie, I am just so happy to know that you are alive. Up here, I'm quite well. I'm at Talo, the court of the Shabdrung – Bhutan's version of a Dalai Lama. He's a sort of religious king who shares power with the political Maharaja. If you are able to travel, why don't you join me here in Bhutan?

The Shabdrung has said that he would send you a letter of invitation. It would serve as a pas partout for the entire kingdom even in the area governed by the Maharaja, Jigme Wangchuk. I think it would be far better for you to leave behind the political heat of India for a while and join me here to convalesce. I would love to see you.

Bhutan? He was inviting her to visit him. The idea of leaving Bombay certainly had its appeal. Get away, yes, have a holiday. As soon as Lakshmi was better. After Christmas, perhaps. Christina would be fit to travel by then. Lakshmi might have recovered enough, too. That's what she hoped. Rest in the mountains. And not just in any hill station but in Bhutan. Bhutan was a closed kingdom. And her father was such an expert on the place, too. Her father. Christina had never really forgiven him. He had abandoned her and her mother so that he could travel among these remote mountains and glaciers. Perhaps this was a chance to make her peace with him, before one or the other of them died. The way things were in India now . . .

These kings have grand titles but accommodation in their dzongs or fortresses, is very rude, I'm afraid, but don't worry, I'll arrange for your comfort here. Wire your cousin Richard Parker and ask him to put you up. I usually stay with him when I'm in Calcutta. Come by train to Calcutta, and from there Richard should be able to arrange a car and an escort to the border of Bengal and Bhutan. Have him wire me when you are ready to come and I will arrange everything this end for permits, escort and accommodation en route.

She'd stayed with Richard in Calcutta the last time she had seen her father. He was another Department man. He had been very sweet to her and would probably arrange what her father was asking. She turned to the second page.

The escort is essential. Bengali terrorists are very active of late.

At the border, I'll have you met by a Bhutanese escort and brought to Talo on horseback. I am sure that you will find the Shabdrung fascinating. He has a veritable treasure trove of ancient texts that I have been translating which I'm sure will delight you. Your Madame Blavatsky should have studied with him. He's the real thing.

But above all, Chrissie, I'm terribly worried about you. I think a rest from India will do you the world of good. No country is without its political tensions and Bhutan is no exception but I am sure that you will be safer here away from the agitation in India for a while.

Come soon. I beg of you.

Love,

Daddy.

Love? Beg? He really did want to see her, she was sure of that. 'The real thing', he had written. That was a backhanded swipe at Madame Blavatsky. He had always been extremely cynical about Theosophy. But he *was* an expert on Himalayan religion – not to mention the geography and politics of the border kingdoms. He was ideal to act as the eyes and ears of the Political Department, up there. The real thing. She would have to dictate a reply. It would be at least another few days before her healing fingers and lacerated palms were recovered enough for her to hold a pen. As if she had dreamed up the sudden sound, the soft purr of a Healey's engine approached from down the hill. The car stopped outside the bungalow. Forbes had a Healey.

She ran to the door and fumbled with the knob, oblivious to the pain in her fingers. Madhan had the front door open. Bright morning light cut a swath into the house. Forbes was coming up the path with that waddling gait of his. His face was set. He stopped on the threshold of the bungalow. She knew what he was going to say and then he said it.

'I'm sorry, Dr Devenish. She died last night.'

The corridor and the door frame all shifted hideously; her eyes blurred with tears and she drew in breath through her nose to bring herself back under control. She couldn't break down in front of Madhan.

'How did she die?'

'Her lungs,' he said. 'They just packed up.'

'Just packed up.'

'May I come in a moment?'

'Oh, yes,' she said. 'Madhan, take Dr Forbes into the garden. I shan't be a moment.'

Lakshmi dead. All her fault. It was. She, Christina, had sent her to lock up the medicines. Held her back to put away the patients' files that had all burned to ash anyway. She waved a hand at him. She stumbled back to the darkness of the study. Closed the door quietly against the light. Her breath came in short stabs. Her ribs hurt terribly as she staggered across the carpet. She fell to her knees beside the bed and pushed her face into the mattress to stifle her sobs, then she banged the edge of the bed frame with her bandaged and useless hands until all she could feel was the searing and purifying pain.

CHAPTER THREE

SMOKE ROSE FROM THE BURNING GHAT. ALL ITS STEPS AND terraces were black with soot. The very stone was impregnated with human fat and the residue of cremations from uncounted years, a gateway to some dark netherworld. Already three pyres blazed upon it and yet another dark pile smouldered; it must have been burning throughout the night. Tree trunks and dry branches stood in great heaps upon the blackened steps. Squarely cut sandalwood logs for the richer cremations were piled on the upper terrace of the ghat. Corpses wrapped in white linen lined the terraces close to the pyres while male mourners in white knelt by the waterside and barbers with straight-edged razors stood behind them and shaved the mourners' heads.

Lakshmi's wrapped and shrouded body lay beside a newly prepared pile of corded faggots and straw and branches and sandalwood. Beside it stood the Brahmin whom Christina had paid to organise the cremation. In this setting, he seemed like a creature out of a sordid Hell with his bony face and stubbled cheeks and his skull shaven, apart from a small tufted scalp lock. Madhan squatted on the stone steps some ten feet above them and smoked a *beedee*.

Lakshmi had no relatives in Bombay. Christina was determined to see that she had a proper cremation. The idea of the already burned body being totally consumed by fire was enough to turn Christina's stomach but Lakshmi was a devout Vishnavite.

Madhan had found the Brahmin to take care of the formalities of transporting the body and performing the rituals, even down to buying the sandalwood. Now, with the cremation about to begin, Christina slumped down on the steps and watched as the two bearers lifted the linen-wrapped body and laid it on the pyre. The Brahmin lit the kindling and flames began to crackle. Through the blur of her tears, she saw the straw catch and set light to the faggots and then she caught the first fragrant whiff of aromatic sandalwood. The linen wrap began to burn and the fire to spit and spark. Within another few minutes the smell of roasting flesh was every bit as fragrant as the sandalwood; the fire tenders stoked the blaze with their long bamboo poles, lifting piles of faggots and branches and trunks so that the air rushed into the blaze, causing the flames to roar. Christina could see the room in the clinic again. And Lakshmi lit up in a halo of flame and Christina was powerless just as she was powerless here in the face of death. Fat from Lakshmi's body dripped into the fire and caused the flames to crackle and leap and flare. Christina watched in fascination as the fire did its work. Lakshmi's blackened skeleton popped through the split and roasted meat but one absurdly unconsumed foot stuck out beyond the heat of the flames. One of the fire tenders raised his bamboo pole high above his head and swung it down hard. The kneecap cracked and, to Christina's horror, with one end of the bamboo pole the fire tender flipped the fleshy foot and the skeletal shin back into the depth of the blaze. Even here on the ghats – especially here, she thought – the body was nothing but carrion from which the soul needed release. And then she heard the skull pop.

The heat of the flames prickled Christina's skin. She swayed over the stones of the ghat and the sparks spat and Madhan's face appeared before her and his fingers dug into the flesh of her arms and dragged her back from the fire, across the stones. And then the Brahmin's face was in front of hers, as if he would exorcise some dire spirit that had taken possession of her body; but she twisted away. She stared into the flames. The whole horrible unchangeable past was like a vast hole that could swallow her. When the tears had all drained out of her she squatted on the steps of the ghat, Madhan and the Brahmin on each side of her, close to the fire.

'Are you all right, madam?' Madhan asked.

She nodded.

He stood up and went down the steps to join two bearers who sat smoking their *beedees*, close to the water. The Brahmin was still reciting some prayers. She sat and watched, hour after hour, her mind numb and blank until the fire was nothing but a few smouldering coals and white ash and the day faded to dusk. The fire tenders took heavy cane brooms and swept the remains of the spent fire into the stream so close to the indifferent sea. The crowd had gone. A new pyre was burning fiercely on the ghat above her. The last remains of Lakshmi floated on the water in front of Christina, and they were caught by a current and swept away beyond further mutilation. Christina was exhausted. She stood up shakily and Madhan was at her elbow gently holding her.

'We should get you home, madam,' Madhan said.

'Yes,' she said. 'Yes. I'm all right, now.'

She moved her arms so that Madhan let go of her elbow. Her ankles and knees seemed rather wobbly on the stone steps of the ghat. The empty sky was a steely blue, the far shore in darkness. She was nothing but an animated sack of skin that enveloped flesh and nerve, bones and organs. At this moment, it seemed that her consciousness could almost quit the flesh and follow Lakshmi into the unknown. But, it was just as impossible for her to quit her body as for Lakshmi's ashes to reform and her spirit reanimate the dead flesh. Christina had no clinic, no Lakshmi. Like some perverse affirmation of life, she suddenly felt the desire for a man: someone who would go to bed with her, give her warm and fleshy pleasure, and then leave her alone and expect no more than that from her.

'Madhan,' she said. 'Would you find us a *gharry*. And tell the Brahmin we can settle up in the morning.'

'You should rest now, madam.'

She allowed him to take her elbow again and to lead her away from the cremation platform. She ascended the blackened steps of the ghat through the fragrant smoke of sandalwood and roasting flesh while above her the stone façades of the European section of city faded into the smoke of night.

PART TWO

CALCUTTA, DECEMBER 1930–JANUARY 1931

CHAPTER FOUR

AT FIVE PAST NOON ON 8 DECEMBER 1930, MAJOR OWEN DAVIES, Political Officer for His Majesty's Government of India, fastidiously wiped his hands on a clean white napkin. He had just finished a plate of *pot au feu sanglier* for which the Great Eastern Hotel was justly famous, its kitchen supplied with boar shot in the Ganges delta and brought to Calcutta by lorry. Rich living had somewhat softened Davies since his soldiering days in the Great War. He'd grown accustomed to all that food and claret and gin. But he still kept himself fit even if he was over forty. Still a rugby player, Davies was proud of his shape: just under six foot, he had broad shoulders and heavy arms, but he was a bit too heavy around the hips these days. Got his physique from his father – the Reverend Wyn Davies, who preferred the pulpit to the playing fields – and the soldiering had done it no harm either. But since joining the Department, it was the day-to-day attrition of the office, sitting at a desk, poring over those files on the independence-wallahs, that had taken its toll. The muscles of his abdomen were no longer so well defined under their fleshy layer. His oiled dark hair had slightly receded from the temples. Women still noticed him when he came into a room. And on the rugby field younger men thought twice about trying to bring him down if he was running full tilt for the try-line. It would be a sad day when he gave up playing.

All around Davies, the dining room of the Great Eastern

clattered and rattled with cutlery and porcelain and buzzed with garbled conversation. The fourth glass of claret had softened the hard hissing edge of that numbing and dreadful emptiness that had been present within him for weeks, and would continue to build over Christmas and the New Year. It was two years almost to the day since his wife, Emma, had died of malaria – a Calcutta commonplace. The dark sense of constriction that gripped him was a sickening reminder of the unalterable fact of her death. She had hated India. And he felt so terribly guilty at bringing her here to die.

Coloured festoons hung from the chandeliers to the picture rails two feet below the high ceilings. These twisted streamers were like a set of oppressive multi-coloured spider's webs waiting to drop on everyone in the dining room. For the next month, he was going to have to endure this appalling Anglo-Saxon joviality that had happily transplanted a Christian feast into the hothouse of India like some ghastly hybrid. He felt as if he was being strangled, suffocated. No one around him could fail to notice the symptoms – his irritability, his distraction, the sudden rages. That was why his assistant, Richard Parker, and Charles Simpson, His Majesty's Inspector of Prisons, had invited him out to the Great Eastern for a mood-lifting lunch. Both Simpson and Parker knew all about Emma.

'Want another?' Simpson asked.

He waggled the almost empty second bottle.

Davies shook his head.

Simpson was as broad and as tall as Davies was. He had that English lobster look. His carroty thatch was clipped short, military style. He had a well-trimmed ginger moustache and his chin was a little weak. He had made his reputation in Ireland as an officer in charge of the Black and Tans. Simpson used the same methods against the Bengalis as he had in the fight against the IRA. The terrorists hated him with a passion. But Davies, too, believed in polarity, especially in war, and, in Bengal, the

Government and the terrorists were certainly at war. The Nationalists used guns and bombs here. They didn't give a damn for Gandhi and his non-violence. It made Davies's job easier in a way.

'Well?' Parker asked.

Parker always looked that little bit unshaven, dishevelled – but he was never so far gone that you could reprimand him about it. His sandy hair was just a bit too long and curled over his ears, his off-white cotton suit was a bit grubby and slack on his wiry body, the tie slightly loosened. Even the rosebud that hung on his lapel was almost wasted away. Davies liked Parker. Parker was a Cambridge man and had that pukka bloody accent that used to irritate, even intimidate, Davies at one time. But Parker was loyal and intelligent and had become something of a protégé of Davies's.

'No more for me,' Davies said. 'We've got work to do this afternoon.'

The truth was that he was afraid that more wine would turn his mood even blacker. He wanted to go back to the office. They had invited him out to help him forget Emma but the wine had done something to his liver. If he didn't get out of the restaurant soon, then he would do, or say, something stupid or bitter.

'Rather fancied a brandy myself,' Simpson said.

'We should go,' Davies said.

Parker looked resigned.

'A big case?' Simpson asked.

'Devenish,' Davies said tersely.

'Ah yes. Colonel Devenish. I hear he's been a bit . . . ah . . . ?' Simpson waved his hand.

'Troublesome,' Davies said. 'Up in Bhutan.'

'You don't expect it from an old hand, do you?' Simpson said.

'Nothing predictable about Devenish,' Davies said.

'I've nothing but respect for the chap,' Parker said.

Parker and the Colonel were related somehow. Simpson drew a silver cigarette case from his jacket pocket, lit one and returned the case to his pocket.

'Devenish was involved in the Connaught Rangers mutiny, wasn't he, back in 1920?' Simpson asked through the smoke.

After all his years fighting the IRA Simpson would be doubly interested in the Connaught Rangers mutiny.

'Not the Colonel,' Davies said. 'The Department investigated him because his wife was from Cork. She'd left him to run off to Ireland in 1905. A bit of a Fenian certainly, but she did put the daughter through college in London. She was the one, his wife, who put the Colonel under a bit of a cloud . . .'

Davies tapped his nails against his wine glass.

'She just wanted any excuse to leave him,' he said.

'She didn't like India?' Simpson asked.

'Colonel Devenish lives for the Himalayas,' Parker said. 'Always was a bit of a loner even before the separation. Sometimes he'd go missing for months up there. Even the Department didn't know where he was.'

'So the wife got sick of him?' Simpson asked.

'I think so,' Davies said.

'Bit of an eccentric?' Simpson said.

Parker waggled his head like an Indian.

'A brilliant man,' he said. 'He studied Sanskrit and Classics at Cambridge. Speaks Hindi, Bengali and Tibetan fluently. Even Dzongkha.'

'What the bloody hell is Dzongkha?' Simpson asked.

'The language of Bhutan,' Parker said.

'Where the Colonel is now,' Davies said.

It was important to be good with languages in the Department. Davies had made Parker learn the local languages, just as Devenish had done with Davies when *he* had first taken a post with the Politicals. Davies spoke Welsh and English from childhood. He'd learned French and a bit of German during the war. Learning the local languages had been difficult at first – the scripts were so different – but he had grasped the value of it immediately. Half these bastards in the Department only learned enough to order their servants about. Parker was an exception. He even seemed to share the Colonel's interest in Himalayan religions. The last time Davies had seen Devenish had been at Emma's funeral. He had looked completely alien in his formal suit and black tie, awkward by the graveside.

'He's been a genius at ensuring the loyalty of the petty kings and abbots who control the passes into Tibet,' Davies said. 'A little glib diplomacy backed up by strategic gifts of livestock and rifles.'

I'm trying to convince myself, Davies thought.

'But now he's in trouble with the Department,' Simpson said.

'The Department recalled him to Calcutta,' Parker said. 'But he's refusing to leave Bhutan until he clears up a bit of a sticky situation up there.'

Yes, he flatly refused a direct order, Davies thought.

'Sticky?' Simpson asked.

'Devenish sided with a one-time ally of his,' Davies said. 'The Shabdrung, a sort of religious king. The Shabdrung's family are Tibetan . . .'

'Tibetan?' Simpson asked.

'Reincarnation business. Like the Dalai Lamas. The Shabdrung was born in Tibet but is recognised as the reincarnation of the previous religious king.'

Simpson shrugged. He was familiar enough with the peculiarities of Himalayan Buddhist kingdoms for it not to seem unusual.

'It seems that the Shabdrung's family fell out with the secular Maharaja of Bhutan,' Davies said. 'Over grazing rights for a herd of bloody yaks. And the conflict went from bad to infinitely bloody worse.'

'It's completely out of hand,' Parker said. 'The Maharaja made it all into a bloody sovereignty issue. We're pretty sure he wants to get rid of the Shabdrung. The Colonel's at the Shabdrung's court. He's having none of it.'

'But the Maharaja has become an ally of the Raj,' Davies said, 'while the Shabdrung is a bit of a Gandhi-wallah.'

'I'd have thought Devenish's loyalty to the Department would have come first, then,' Simpson said.

Yes, thought Davies. Simpson was right.

Davies stared at the red bead in the bottom of his glass as if to divine the afternoon's portent. Not good at all. Not at all. His fingertips squeezed the bowl of the claret glass.

'Well, are you two ready?' Davies asked. 'The Devenish files await us.'

He eased his chair away from the debris of their rich meal and led the way out of the dining room into the gleaming lobby. The plants looked obscenely healthy as if the swamp had encroached even into this neo-classical extravaganza with its marble floors and brass doorknobs and panelled walls. A cockroach skittered across the dark mouldings which were arched over the half-door of the cloakroom where an ancient and grey-stubbled orderly handed Davies his panama.

Davies let the hat dangle from his fingers and when he stepped out from under the shadow of the Great Eastern's massive portico, the bright December sunshine struck him hard in the eyes. He settled the light hat on his head.

'Let's walk,' Davies said.

'Digestion?' Parker asked.

'Exactly,' Davies said.

On Old Court House Street, clerks in white *khurtas* and *dhotis*, some hand in hand, strolled along outside the Central Telegraph Office. Davies led the way across the road through the ox-carts and rickshaws to the crowded promenade between the traffic-cluttered eastern thoroughfare on Dalhousie Square and the watery stillness of the Lal Dighi tank where the practical and the supernatural shared the same flagstoned pavement. Barbers and astrologers squatted under makeshift awnings next to sandal-makers and silversmiths and a group of Shaivite yogis clothed in nothing but grey ash and face paint. Davies had got used to it in the seven years he'd been in India but the country was rotten with all sorts of bloody strange religions: gods with elephant heads, four arms, snakes and God knows what. Unlike his father, Davies was no missionary out to convert the heathen, but neither could he make any sense of it all. No matter how well he knew the language or lived in the culture, his world and theirs, the Indians', ran on parallel lines. Never met. Impossible, he thought, to step over into that other world of gods and demons, even for a moment.

Striding into the crowd, he deliberately distanced himself from Simpson and Parker. He could feel his mood getting darker and fouler by the second as the alcohol worked on him. Davies slipped his hands into the side pockets of his jacket. He played with the few coins he kept in there for the beggars and let his little finger slip into a small silver ring, which he twirled with the tip of his thumb. It was one of Emma's. Not anything expensive. Just Nepalese silver. It was an unseen reminder of her that he could play with as he walked. He *had* thought about other women but all the women he met at the club, or some dinner evening, would always fall far short of what Emma had been to him.

Davies stepped off the pavement among the *gharries* and ox-carts and man-drawn rickshaws and a beige Austin Seven that clogged the road on the north side of the square. It was dangerous for a Department man to walk the streets. Two Bengali terror-ists had attempted to kill Sir Charles Teggart, the Chief of Police, right here on Dalhousie Square, not a month before. The bloody fools had stood on opposite sides of the road and each lobbed a bomb. They'd missed Teggart's car and had blown each other up. Could always depend on that story for a laugh. The laugh that had everyone in the Department carrying a revolver these days. That was why Davies carried the Webley .455 under his jacket. Heavy on his ribs. He had never had to use the Webley – or any gun since the war, other than in target practice – but ten British officials had been killed in the last few months. The revolver was reassuring.

On the other side of the congested traffic rose the red stone walls and verandas and balconies of the Writers' Building. In the distance, in front of the seated statue of Lord Eden, the accusatory marble finger of the Halwell Monument, erected as a reminder of the Black Hole of Calcutta, appeared to be entangled by the trolley lines and wires that crisscrossed at the opposite end of the square. Davies passed through the arched entrance of the Writers' Building into the cool interior of the main hall and waited for Parker and Simpson to catch him up. The name of the building always called to mind a great labyrinth of novelists scribbling away but all the writers in the offices were only clerks in the pay of the Raj.

'Such a hurry to get back to work,' Simpson said.

Davies shrugged. Allowed them a brief smile. He led the way across the hall through the administrators and clerks in suits, aides-de-camp in the dark blue uniforms of the Politicals, and turbaned orderlies. He took the marble stairs two at a time to the first floor and turned into the somewhat threadbare-carpeted corridor with its rows of doors. On the wood-panelled walls hung stuffy portraits of deceased bureaucrats in all their gouty aplomb.

'Well, don't work too hard,' Simpson called and he left Davies and Parker at the door to their office.

Simpson's office was four doors further along the corridor, opposite that of the Judicial Secretary. Three tall young Indian men in European suits passed by as Davies waited for Parker to unlock the door. Simpson waved, key in hand, before he disappeared from the corridor. Parker had the door open and went in. Davies stopped when he saw the three young Indians follow Simpson into his room. Clerks? They weren't bloody clerks. He heard the first shot. Then a staccato bangbang, bang.

'Simpson!' Davies yelled.

Two more explosions, hard and metallic, from inside the office. The three Indians reappeared in the corridor. They all had pistols in their fists. He drew the Webley and leaned in close to the door jamb. Simpson first? Of course. Inspector of Prisons.

One of the Indians still had his revolver pointed towards the door of Simpson's office. The other two had that jerky movement of men who anticipated physical danger that might come from any direction around them. Davies lined up the Webley's sight on one of the Indians and a door opened on the opposite side of the corridor.

Walker. The Judicial Secretary.

'Stay back, man!' Davies yelled.

One of the Indians fired at Walker. Point blank. Walker screamed and disappeared from sight.

'God damn you!' Davies shouted.

The Webley roared in his ears and bucked in his hand. Once, twice, three instinctive shots. Missed with them all. All three Indians swung in his direction, levelled their pistols at him. Davies ducked into his office before a volley crashed out and great divots of wood sprang out of a door panel and the door slammed back into the wall.

'Jesus Christ,' Parker said.

He had a revolver in his hand and lurched towards the door.

'Stay back,' Davies said.

He grabbed the edge of the door and pushed it to. Shouts now. Three rifle reports. .303s. More pistol shots. The sound of running in the corridor. Coming his way. He eased the door open, glanced through the gap and fired. More wood splintered off the door jamb and he ducked back. Three more shots came from down the corridor. Davies pulled the door wide open and a stronger stink of cordite wafted into the office. A clatter of boots came from the stairs and a squad of red-turbaned policemen, each with a Lee Enfield rifle, appeared on the landing.

The voice of a Sikh police sergeant said: 'Where the hell did they go?'

Davies came out of the office. Parker was right behind him.

'Get a doctor up here,' Davies said to him. 'Simpson's office, have a look.'

'Yes, sir.'

Parker moved quickly up the corridor.

Duty, Davies thought. It was his job to take command. His job. But he knew that it was really over. He had fired four shots and missed with each. He had to get back to the range. Get some bloody practice in.

A door was open to one of the offices at the eastern end of the corridor. The panelled walls of the corridor were lit as if from within themselves and each curlicue of the gilt frames of the portraits on the walls stood out sharply as he passed by. Davies stepped close to the door jamb. He risked a glance through the opening.

A bang and he jumped back. Another bang. Nothing had hit either the door or the opposite wall.

'Here,' he called to the police squad.

He raised the Webley, crooked his elbow around the jamb and fired blind. His arm jerked back and his wrist and elbow twisted with the recoil.

'Damn this bloody thing.'

He rubbed his elbow, the gun still heavy in his fist. He slid out from the cover of the jamb and fired again, arm straight but poorly aimed at the terrorist sitting at the desk. Then he ducked back behind the wall again.

'Throw down your weapons,' he yelled, his voice cracking. 'Let's have them. Come on.'

What a bloody shambles. He hadn't got one clean shot off.

The young Sikh sergeant ran past the door and took position at the other jamb.

'Sir. They're down, sir.'

Davies didn't believe he could have hit anything with two blind shots. He risked another glance. Two of the Indians were slumped on the floor, pistols still gripped in their hands, but their bodies had a slack look as if muscle and nerve and ligament were no longer connected. Both men had a powder-burned, bloody hole close to the right temple. Their cheeks were covered with blood that glistened on their brown skin. Their dark hair was matted with it. The room was like an abattoir, blood all over the walls and the floor.

'Topped themselves,' Davies said. 'By Christ.'

The Sikh sergeant shouldered his rifle and stepped into the doorway.

'Keep still,' the sergeant called in Bengali. 'Don't move.'

Davies followed him into the room.

The third terrorist was indeed at the desk, head bowed, his hands in his hair. His revolver lay near his right elbow. A glass phial lay on the blotter in front of him. Whatever had been in it was spilled out all around it. There was some on the boy's lips. His chin. He reached for his revolver and Davies swung the butt of the empty Webley. It cracked against the side of the jaw and the boy flipped backwards out of his chair. The body felt light as a feather but it crashed against the wall and slid to the floor. More policemen crowded into the room.

'See to those other two,' Davies called. 'Keep them alive if there's life in them.'

Davies holstered the reeking revolver under his jacket.

The phial on the blotter was clear glass. The spilled crystals had a pale yellowish tinge to them: potassium cyanide. Two of the policemen grabbed the boy by his arms and the scruff of his neck and dragged him to his feet. The sergeant was kneeling next to the two who had shot themselves.

Dear Christ, he thought. These boys'll be bloody heroes all over Bengal. The Writers' Building. The heart of the Raj. In broad daylight. Davies rubbed his smooth face with his palms and ran his fingers back through his hair. He had been sweating and now the perspiration cooled on his body under the sweep of the weak electric ceiling fan that batted the air above his head. He turned quickly back into the corridor. It was crowded with clerks and secretaries and aides. He spotted Parker. His face was white. Blood stained the bottom part of his jacket below the left side pocket.

'He's dead, sir. Simpson is dead,' he said.

Davies started up the corridor towards Simpson's office. Parker stayed at his shoulder.

'What about Walker?' Davies said.

'Got it in the hip, but I think he'll be all right. Doctor's with him.'

'Anybody else?'

'A number of clerks. We've rushed them off to hospital. I'm not sure of the names.'

'Get me a casualty list,' Davies said. 'Bring it to the office.'

Davies turned into Simpson's office. Two orderlies, one with a stretcher, stood near the window. A young doctor knelt close by the body. Simpson's white suit was soaked through with a deep rose red. A pool of already congealing blood spread out around the body on the varnished wood of the floor. There was a ragged hole in his cheek. The wiry red hair was matted with blood.

'Oh Simpson,' Davies said.

'We should take him down to the morgue, sir,' the doctor said.

'Yes. Yes, of course,' Davies said.

He would have to tell Elizabeth, Simpson's wife. Let her tell their kids. He would have to do it this afternoon. Duty. His duty. The corridor still stank of cordite. So crowded. More stretcher-bearers came up the stairs. Davies pushed his way through the chaos. He ran his fingertips over the gouges in the wood of his door. He drew the Webley from its holster, clicked out the cylinder and took the six spent casings from the chambers. He would clean the gun later. He opened the right-hand drawer and took out the box of .455 calibre bullets. His fingers shook as he reloaded the empty chambers. Davies clicked the fully loaded cylinder back into the Webley. The gun wobbled in his hand. He set it down on top of Devenish's file on his desk. Why was the Colonel causing all this trouble in times like these? Simpson had been right. They should all be sticking together. Looking out for each other. Devenish should stop all this bloody nonsense and get out of bloody Bhutan. A shooting in the Writers' Building? The heart of the Raj. They had to stick together – stick together – or they would all be swept away on a bloody brown tide.

CHAPTER FIVE

I

PARKER PASSED A POORLY PRINTED NEWSPAPER ACROSS DAVIES'S desk. Davies thumbed through the flimsy rice-paper pages. He knew the publication well enough: *Basudhara*, the Nationalist rag.

'Dinesh Gupta got a letter out to his relatives,' Parker said.

'And?'

'Best read it,' Parker said.

The headline was simple enough:

LETTER FROM REVOLUTIONARY HERO TO HIS MOTHER.

This, he knew, was going to be another bloody propaganda coup for the terrorists. He started reading.

You have asked me as to how to find the path to mental peace. We are Hindus. We know that death is not the end; it is the body that dies. The soul is indestructible. I am that soul and that soul is God.

You may say, 'This is a cliché which I know but it does not bring me peace of mind.' The path to that is absolute surrender of self to God. This is the only way to mental peace. In spite of all our worships and chanting of mantras and marks on the forehead, can we say that we love Him? To one who loves Him, death does not exist. Remember Nimai of Nadia when you think of love of God, remember Jesus Christ and remember the boys of our country who have faced death with a smile on their lips.

You may remember that I used to make dolls with your hair and make them dance. The puppets used also to sing songs and as soon as a puppet finished its part, it did not have to appear again on the stage. As soon as we have done our parts, we shall have served our purpose and He will remove us from the stage. There should not be any room for regret in this.

Davies put the paper down.

'Do you ever think we're going to lose it, Parker? Lose it all?'

Creases appeared around Parker's eyes and a smile played nervously around his lips.

'They'll never win it like this,' he said. 'Shooting one or two, here and there. Only makes us more determined, doesn't it?'

'It inspires them, though, doesn't it? The boys in the *chai* shops. In the country. One of their own striking a blow deep in the heart of the Raj.'

Parker shrugged, resigned to it.

'How did he get the letter out?' Davies said.

'No idea, I'm afraid.'

'He's out of the prison hospital now, isn't he?'

Parker nodded.

'Have Mukherji bring him over to the basement room. We'll have a word with our Mr Dinesh Gupta.'

2

Even from behind the two-way mirror, Davies could see that Gupta's lips were dry and cracked, his cheeks sunken and his eyes bright and large as if he was in a fever, but the prisoner kept his head up as if some mad guard dog inside him refused to relax its vigilance – though every muscle and bone in Gupta's body from his neck to his toes should be aching and cramping abominably by now.

In a few more minutes, he, Davies, would have to go in there and interrogate him. He had to remember that it was all a question of duty. He was in India serving his country. His country. It was his country, wasn't it? He was British. Had always felt British. Even if he spoke Welsh. Of course, he could understand the Fenians in a way. The Irish were Catholics. Hadn't ever accepted British rule. But the Welsh had been entangled with English government for seven hundred years. Families mixed up since the Norman invasion even. Most of the Welsh aristocracy had sided with the English monarchy anyway – so much so that a Welshman had founded the Tudor dynasty. Welshmen had flocked to join the army during the Great War, hadn't they? Would do again. There was a rebel Irish Republican Army and an Indian Republican Army but he could never imagine a Welsh Republican Army. Nothing had stopped Lloyd George becoming Prime Minister of the British Empire. And he, Owen Davies, had risen through the ranks of the British Army. Offered a post in intelligence after the war. He'd been flattered if anything. And then rapid promotion had followed under Colonel Devenish's patronage. India was a long way from the claustrophobia of the Welsh valleys. That distance gave him the freedom to be himself – that and his position in the army. In the army, he wasn't under the shadow of his father: the workers' champion in the pulpit. No doubt his father would be sympathetic to Gandhi, but his father could only be what he was, hold the views that he had, thanks to soldiers like Owen Davies protecting Britain from the likes of the Kaiser or Joe Stalin. As for the Indians wanting independence, he, Owen Davies, could understand that but he really didn't think they could handle it. Not on the defence front anyway. India had been part of the British Empire since Clive's day. That was the way the world was. And the Russians and Chinese were just on the other side of the mountains. He, Davies, had a clear-cut job to do. It was a straightforward military matter. He didn't begrudge Gandhi and Congress wanting more say in running the country, but they were completely incapable of defending the borders. And in Bengal, he had no time for Congress. The terrorists and the Calcutta Congress Party were hand in glove with each other. It was down to methods. This bombing and killing was clear-cut. He didn't have to agonise about a response to that. Just do his job.

Simpson was dead. Davies just wanted to get something out of Gupta that might lead the Department to others in his group. Gupta was a murderer. He, Davies, had to keep that in mind . . . Elizabeth Simpson's reaction when he told her the news of her husband's death. He thought about the kids. Thought about Simpson lying on his office floor with the hole in his cheek and half his brains on the carpet. He was ready now. Ready to do his job. Straightforward.

Captain Mukherji of the CID had brought Gupta from the prison hospital to the basement of the Writers' Building. Davies had left him waiting down there for three and a half hours: a few hours' wait with his arms twisted behind him and his wrists chafing under the irons to soften him up. Dinesh Gupta's wrists and ankles were raw and swollen from the shackles and his shifting around on the straight-backed, wooden chair. Wide iron rings were fastened by two links of rusty iron chain to an eighteen-inch bar so that the prisoner's legs were forced to remain open. He was wearing the white shirt and brown trousers in which he had been arrested. The shirt was now collarless, grubby and sweat-soaked, the trousers likewise stained beneath his buttocks and on the tops of his thighs. Above Gupta's head, the stained canvas wing of a hanging *punkah* batted uselessly at the sluggish air like the spread hand of an exhausted swimmer digging into a muddy pond. The fan's absurd electric motor creaked interminably as the pinion upon its flywheel reached its zenith and made its downward stroke.

We are Hindus. We know that death is not the end; it is the body that dies. The soul is indestructible. I am that soul and that soul is God.

'I don't see much sign of him weakening,' Davies said.

'A question of pressure,' said Captain Mukherji. 'If we put the right amount of pressure on him . . .'

'I'm not sure that I agree with you,' Davies said.

'What do we have to lose?' Mukherji said. 'He has no other home now but Deoli jail. We can speak to him any time we choose.'

Mukherji was a high-ranking Indian officer in the Calcutta CID. He spoke with an accent like that of an upper-class Englishman. He was an elegant man who wore a dark linen suit over his white shirt and a regimental tie. He kept his greying hair cut short at the sides and swept back; and his moustache had been waxed and teased into two tight points. His face was free of wrinkles. Captain Mukherji was around six feet two inches tall and kept himself in superb physical condition by a fanatical devotion to polo.

'Shall we start then?' Davies said.

Mukherji gave a curt nod. One of the three Sikh policemen opened the door to the interrogation room and Davies led the way through followed by Mukherji and two of his brawniest constables. This was the man who had killed Simpson. Would kill others given half a chance. He had to keep that in mind.

'Oh dear, oh dear,' Davies said. 'What on earth have they done to you, Mr Gupta?'

The tendons on the prisoner's neck stuck out like a set of push rods under his pale brown skin. He had big dark eyes made a lot bigger by his rage.

'Constable,' Davies said, 'unshackle this man. This is awful. Look at his poor ankles and his wrists.'

'I want some water,' Gupta said.

One of the two Sikh constables went behind the prisoner to unlock the manacles.

'I'll send a constable right away,' Davies said.

Gupta rubbed his scraped wrists as the constable knelt to unlock the ankle irons.

'I'm glad to see you out of hospital,' Davies said.

'We would really appreciate your full cooperation,' Mukherji said.

Mukherji circled around Gupta. Manacles rattled behind Davies as the constable set them down on a low table against one wall.

'My God, it's hot in here, isn't it?' Davies said.

He looked up at the useless fan above Gupta's head. Gupta leaned forward as if to come to his feet. Mukherji slammed a fist into his chest and sat him back down.

Gupta shot a glance at Davies.

'Mr Mukherji, please. Not so hasty,' Davies said. 'I'm so sorry, Mr Gupta. We can take the manacles off but prison regulations require you to remain seated while we conduct our interview. It won't take a moment, I'm sure.'

'I have nothing to say,' Gupta said.

'Bear with me,' Davies said, 'while I explain. You've committed a very grave crime. I think we can agree on that. I'm sure you understand the consequences in the courts if we can't come to some arrangement. Some sort of agreement here.'

Gupta's eyes were bulging but he kept his mouth tight shut.

'This is a sort of game, isn't it?' Davies said. 'That we're all involved in. You're on one side. We're on the other. This is not a personal matter, is it? Simply politics, isn't it? I have my job, my beliefs. You have your job, your beliefs. I respect that. I do.'

Gupta's eyes shifted from Davies to Mukherji and back.

'As far as your part in the struggle is concerned,' Davies said, 'from our point of view, it's all over. One way or the other, it's all over. But if we go to court without our coming to an agreement here, you will – and I think I can say this definitively – you will be sentenced to hang.'

Davies walked towards the table with the empty manacles. Mukherji lit a cigarette and the smell of tobacco smoke filled the stuffy room. He stood at Gupta's shoulder. Gupta glanced at him once and then back at Davies.

'Now,' Davies said, 'I won't pretend that I don't want you out of the game. I do. But it makes no odds to me how. If we can negotiate a prison sentence for you with the judge, you're still out of the game for me. Do you understand?'

Mukherji moved a step closer to Gupta. He dragged on his cigarette and blew smoke at the swinging fan that swirled the cloud around the room.

Gupta was not going to open his mouth.

'I'm sure you know that I want this to be an exchange,' Davies said. 'Of course. It's simple. A little information, isn't it?'

Gupta stared at him. Not a word.

'Please, Mr Gupta, let's be reasonable. I am only making a mutually beneficial suggestion.'

Gupta shook his head. Foolish. Captain Mukherji's backhand blow caught Gupta just below the cheekbone. His head snapped back. He didn't fall off the chair and Mukherji gripped him by the throat, fingers clawed around his windpipe. The other hand held the cigarette away. Instinctively, Gupta gripped Mukherji's wrist to try to twist the hand free. The butts of the constables' lathis slammed into Gupta's kidneys. He twisted on the chair and Mukherji wrenched away his arm from the prisoner's grip and the two constables flailed at Gupta from each side, all arms and fists and bamboo clubs. Gupta roared in his seat as they beat him, unable to come to his feet or even to fall to the ground to protect himself, while above his head the absurd and useless *punkah* batted the air and creaked incessantly.

'Stop!' yelled Davies.

The sweating Sikh constables stepped back. The boy's hands

were raised just off his knees as if he wished to touch his wounds or check himself but didn't want to show weakness. A large swelling had risen on his cheek and blood trickled from a slight cut above his puffy left eye. Davies leaned over in front of Gupta. He spoke quietly. Gupta stared back at him. Plain hatred.

'Can't we be sensible here?' Davies said. 'This is all up to you, Mr Gupta. I've no wish to see you hurt. All I want is one name, let's say. And an address. Then, we can go and check on your information and we have a mutually beneficial agreement. No one knows how we got the name or address. No one suspects you. We'll have one more player on your side out of the game. And you'll go to prison for a while. Who knows if there might not be some sort of amnesty later on. You see what I mean? We all have so much to gain here, Mr Gupta. You and I both.'

Gupta shook his head. Davies stood up.

'Has his water come yet?' he asked. 'Have a look, Constable Singh, please.'

Singh opened the door.

'Where's Surindar?' he asked.

'Not back.'

A disembodied voice outside the room, off set, off the little stage that they were all on while they waited for God to whip away Mr Gupta.

Singh closed the door again.

'I'm sorry,' Davies said. 'I'm sure he'll be here in a moment. I could do with a drop of water myself. It's so hot in here, isn't it?'

'Let me speak to him,' Mukherji said.

'Mr Mukherji wants a word,' Davies said. 'But I think that we might come to an understanding, you and I. I mean, just give me some indication that you are at least considering my proposal. I don't want anything else. No names. No addresses. Just a word that we might be trying to find some common ground. Then I promise. I'll give you another day to consider my proposal.'

55

Gupta shook his head.

'Listen to me,' Davies said. 'No names. No addresses. All you have to do today is to say that you will consider our offer and all this will stop. It's up to you, isn't it? You have complete control of your own fate.'

Mukherji took a lathi from the second constable.

'I have no patience with bloody terrorists,' Mukherji said.

He circled the chair. Davies crossed to the table where the manacles were and he sat on the edge of it. On Mukherji's third unholy circumambulation, he stepped close in behind the chair and brought the lathi across Gupta's throat. Mukherji braced his knee against the chair back and Gupta's face turned purple. His eyes bulged. The dry tongue protruded and the second constable slammed the butt of his lathi between Gupta's legs. The prisoner made a distressing mewling sound.

Davies slid off the table and quickly came up close to Gupta's swollen face. He was rasping and gasping for air, still pinned to the chair.

'Please, Mr Mukherji, let him go. Stand away, constable. Stand away. Please.'

Mukherji slackened his grip.

'There,' Davies said. 'Thank you. There you are, Mr Gupta. You are sitting on your chair, now. No one near you. Everything is in your hands once again. You are in complete control of the situation and my offer still stands.'

The door opened. Davies stepped away from Gupta. Constable Surindar held a glass of water on his left palm, steadied by the fingertips of his right hand. The glass was full. In the heat of the interrogation room the sides of it misted up immediately and droplets of condensation ran down it. The room was silent but for the creak, creak, creak of the useless fan.

'Mr Gupta is very thirsty,' Davies said. 'We'll both have something to drink in a minute.'

Surindar put the water glass down on the table next to the

manacles. Gupta turned for a second to look at it and then looked at the floor again.

'All I would like to hear today is one small concession,' Davies said. 'As I said. No names. No addresses. Just that you are considering my offer. That's all. Then these gentlemen, who have less patience than I have, will go home happy. Everything is in your hands, now. Give me the nod. You can go back to your cell and we'll all walk out happy for today.'

'Go to hell,' Gupta croaked.

Davies shook his head.

'I'm sorry it's like this. I was hoping that we might find some common ground between us.'

Davies crossed to the door and turned around once more.

'I'm sure that you'll help Mr Gupta back to his cell, Mr Mukherji.'

Mukherji shrugged. Davies left the room and closed the door behind him. The screams started almost immediately. He didn't look back through the two-way mirror.

It wasn't conventional, was it? But they had to do it, didn't they? That's why Gupta had tried the cyanide. He knew what he had been getting himself into. He accepted the rules of the game, didn't he? And he didn't want to give anything away under pressure. He knew the pressure would come. It was people like Gupta who helped set the rules, too, wasn't it? He had overstepped the mark. Guns and bombs. That was the reason why Davies could do this job. And do it well. What was horrifying was the realisation that he really enjoyed it. Davies left the anteroom. He felt sick. He walked along the cellar corridor and took the stairs that led back to the ground floor of the Writers' Building. All this bustling activity, with all these protocols and uniforms, and he was here to protect it all. Parker had invited him to his house for Christmas. And everyone in the Department would expect him to turn up at the New Year's Ball in the Grand Hotel. It was only going to make him more aware of that aching loneliness of being without Emma. He hadn't been able to protect her, had he? The Guptas of this world were easy to handle. Something physical you could get your hands on. Malaria was another matter: part of that insidious, silent India that was trying to poison the British and slough them off the back of the subcontinent. Davies welcomed the nausea. It made him feel part of the real world. If he could stay half-cut for another twelve days, it wouldn't be so bad. What he needed now was a good stiff gin.

CHAPTER SIX

I

GENERAL ALEXANDER MCKEOWAN WALKED INTO THE OFFICE WITH Parker at his elbow. McKeowan was clutching a green Department file in his thick fingers. He looked uncomfortable.

The sight of the file made Davies uneasy. There was no need to be anxious, he knew, but his nerves had been picked raw by all that gin over the infernal holiday period. All those parties. He had to dry out now. Once he'd started drinking it had proved almost impossible to stop. But it had already been a week since he'd drunk himself into oblivion from New Year's Eve until the second of January. He kept trying to convince himself that he'd done nothing wrong, had not said something embarrassing that he might regret; but the constant pick of anxiety kept digging at his insides like an incipient cancer. There were black gaps in his memory. Now, he could smell, or imagine the smell of, the poisons still seeping out of him through his pores. He had been glad to get back to the routine of the office, to get his hands on something tangible, to distract him from his constant worry. The trouble was that he still hadn't got a word out of Gupta.

'You look awful, Davies,' McKeowan said.

'I'll get over it,' Davies said.

McKeowan shrugged his massive shoulders. He was a big man. He had once played second row forward for Hawick rugby club before coming to India. It showed in his gnarled face: the heavy eyebrows with a narrow white scar knotting up over his left eye, the kink in his nose where it had been broken, the puffy lumps that curved over the top of his right ear. Davies often talked about the game with him. It gave them something in common. That was important in the Department for promotion, the plum jobs, and protection from getting a knife in the back.

'How're you getting on with Gupta?' McKeowan asked.

Davies shrugged, shook his head.

'We'll get nothing out of him, I'm sure. Up against a bit of wall, really.'

'Surveillance, then?' McKeowan said. 'The family and all that. Routine stuff.'

'I suppose so.'

'Well then, Parker can take care of it. He's up to date on Gupta and it's time he took a bit more responsibility anyway.'

Davies nodded. Interrogation. Rigorous interrogation. He did want to get away from it. He was aware of that. One hand was trembling, a sense of relief, too. Perhaps he was having a bit of trouble with his nerves.

'The trial won't be for a few months, you know that.'

Gupta had to heal up before they put him in the dock, that was certain.

'And I *still* want you to get Colonel Devenish out of Bhutan,' McKeowan said.

'Devenish?'

That affair seemed an age away.

'Devenish, yes,' McKeowan said. 'You'll be back in time for Gupta's trial, of course. Key witness. You know that.'

'Key witness, yes.'

Jesus Christ. He was the arresting officer. Of course he was going to be there.

'It might be better if you're out of the way for a bit, that's all,' McKeowan said. 'You know. They got Simpson pretty bloody easily. You'll be out of harm's way, won't you? Do whatever you need to organise the expedition. Manpower, equipment, and as soon as you can. But Parker's got a bit of news for you.'

'News?' Davies said.

Parker nodded.

'I just received a letter from Colonel Devenish's daughter in Bombay. She's asked me to organise equipment and coolies for her to get to the border of Bhutan. She's going up to Talo to meet her father.'

'His daughter?' Davies said. 'Going to Bhutan as well? Now?'

'Christina Devenish,' Parker said. 'She's wants me to put her up for a few days. She intends to stay long enough to get travel arrangements sorted out and then she'll leave.'

'She's a relative of yours, isn't she?' Davies said.

'Cousin of sorts,' Parker said. 'On her mother's side . . . Not blood exactly, but still . . . related.'

'I thought she was running some clinic in Bombay.'

'Bloody thing burned down, didn't it?' McKeowan said.

'Christina was always a bit of a crusader,' Parker said. 'Independence-wallahs got the wrong end of the stick, really.'

'They bloody destroyed everything she built up over there,' McKeowan said. 'So she's left Bombay and she's on her way to Bhutan to see her father.'

What was this? Now they wanted him to be nursemaid to a bloody do-gooder bluestocking while he was trying get her stubborn father out of Bhutan? Jesus Christ.

'How did she get permission from the Bhutanese?'

'According to her letter,' Parker said, 'her father will arrange it with the Shabdrung as soon as I've got the equipment and the coolies arranged.'

'What the hell is Devenish playing at?' Davies said. 'This whole bloody business arose out of the Shabdrung handing out bogus documents to foreigners. Is he using his daughter to make some kind of political point to the Maharaja? Or to us?'

'We have to pre-empt the permission business,' McKeowan said. 'Whatever he's up to we can avoid that little crisis by tying her in to your expedition to get the Colonel out.'

'To my expedition?'

'Yes. Apart from sending you to sort Devenish out, we also have another perfectly valid reason for you going to Bhutan, so you won't have to tell her you're going there to arrest her father. The Government of India will be awarding the Maharaja of Bhutan the honour of becoming a Knight Commander of the Indian Empire. He's delighted. And it ties us in closer with him. Sends the message we're one hundred per cent behind him in his dealings with the Shabdrung, no matter what Devenish is up to. The investiture will be in the middle of February. We have to send a contingent up there for the ceremony and you'll be the officer in charge. Christina Devenish can be absorbed into the expedition without any need for special permission from the Shabdrung. She'll accompany you into Bhutan and you can take her to the ceremony. That way, the Colonel's daughter pays her respects to the Maharaja first and then she gives us a handy excuse for you to be going on to Talo, where you, Major Davies, can see to it that Devenish gets out. Short of an arrest if possible, but whatever it takes.'

'Why don't we just stop her going?' Davies said.

'I'd rather the Colonel think that we're being very reasonable, very tractable,' McKeowan said, 'bringing his daughter to him. And I don't want another bloody loose cannon gadding about the Himalayas either.'

'When does she arrive?' Davies asked.

'She wants me to pick her up at Howrah station,' Parker said. 'Day after tomorrow. Train's arriving at five in the morning.'

'All right,' Davies said. 'All right. We'll pick her up in the Rover.'

Devenish's daughter? If she were anything like her father, she'd be a stubborn bitch. A little bloody holiday in the Himalayas with a bluestocking. Something about it made him jittery. A sudden obscene picture in his mind. The Colonel's head impaled on a pike and Davies rogering his daughter in front of it. Christ, what the hell was he thinking? He was losing his grip. This bloody interrogation business was getting to him. And the fact that he hadn't had a woman in a very long time. Perhaps he should pay a visit to Karaya Lane. Ease the pressure with a prostitute before meeting the Colonel's daughter. His nerves were squirming under his skin like an eruption of maggots. Thank God McKeowan and Parker couldn't see the images in his head.

'Yes,' Davies said. 'Good idea. Kill two birds with one stone, isn't it?'

2

He was in the Raja Bazaar, close to the Sealdah railway station but off among the maze of alleyways that made up the meat market. Their day almost over, the butchers stood in their bloody aprons and poured sheets of silvery water from rusty pails to wash down the sanguinary slats of their counters. Pariah dogs, skinny and mange-ridden, slunk close to the wheels of the carts, waiting for their chance to snap up clotted offal and to lap at the bloody rivers that washed into the gutters. Davies was aware of the risk he was taking, a Political Department man walking alone through the nightmare alleys of the city. But it was as if he couldn't stop himself – despite the fact that he could easily imagine Parker fishing his, Davies's, shit-covered corpse out of a sewage ditch one morning. Davies turned into a foetid alley between two dilapidated red-brick hotels and he picked his way through the detritus and street sewage while ragged urchins called and clutched at him as he passed. The brothel was off a small courtyard at the end of the lane.

Before he reached it, a leper stepped in front of him and held out a misshapen hand. One glaucous eye drooped under a sagging lid, the other bright and intelligent in its supplication, the leper's smile almost an affront to his ruined flesh. The open hand was all lesions, lumps and stumps. Davies scooped a handful of annas from his jacket pocket and let them fall into the pool of pus in the centre of the leper's palm.

Make a wish, Davies thought.

The leper looked down as if puzzled.

Emma's silver ring was nestled among the near weightless coins. The pus came over the scalloped edge of the ring that was now contaminated by that hideous disease-ridden bodily fluid.

'Wait,' Davies said. 'Not this.'

He plucked up the ring in his fingertips, all the while the leper's eyes upon his face. Davies hid his disgust at taking back the ring from that pestilent mess at the centre of the stumpy hand.

You couldn't get leprosy, could you, by such minimal contact? What did he know about leprosy? It was contagious over time. It took a long time, he was sure. Davies pushed past the beggar. He held the ring between the pads of his thumb and his index finger. Quickly, he dropped it back into his pocket and left the leper behind him. Hurried away. He had to wash his hands. He had come into contact with the pus. The horrible creeping disease might at this very moment be penetrating the pores of his fingertips, implanting the seeds of pestilence that would corrupt his entire body.

The ring was in his jacket pocket. He would disinfect it with a flame. Did he have to burn his jacket to keep himself free of the disease? Each time he put his hand in there, he would be coming into contact with the disease. Could some creeping colony of germs breed in the darkness and spread over the cloth and come into contact with his skin, corrupting him, eat him away slowly like that rotten beggar? He would have to burn the jacket. Or just throw it away. At this moment, on the crowded street, he could not pull it off and expose the Webley to sight.

He shouldn't panic. It took long contact before you could catch it, didn't it? What could he do with the ring? It was contaminating his pocket as he walked towards the brothel. The brothel. He couldn't go into the brothel now. Not like this. He would be touching the women. Touching himself as he put his cock in there . . . Impossible. He couldn't go through with it now, could he? He lifted the latch of the battered door and pushed it inwards. He entered a courtyard where a young Indian man, long-limbed and with a sparse moustache, raised himself from a charpoy on the veranda, looked him over and then disappeared into the shadows of the building.

'Come in, *babu*.'

She was plump and dressed in a skimpy parody of a sari, her breasts spilling out of green silk. She rolled her kohled eyes at him. Made an obscene display with her tongue.

Davies desperately wanted a woman but he couldn't do it, now. Not now. Not like this. Rotten and corrupted. He turned back into the alley and hurried towards Karaya Lane. He needed rest. Get out of Calcutta with this Christina Devenish. It would be all right. Not like this. This was all just getting completely out of hand.

CHAPTER SEVEN

THE TRAIN ROCKED OVER THE POINTS, CLATTERED AND screeched and thrust her out of the night's paradise of thought-less oblivion, close to another aching dawn. In the corner of her berth, Christina lay foetal, legs drawn up to her small breasts and her hands clasped beneath her chin. Her unseen thumb tips traced patterns on her red and glossy palms. The nerves beneath the unnatural smoothness still felt dead. The skin would soon dry more and split like a cocoon to reveal another layer of soft epidermis beneath. Leave her with wrinkled new hands. The rocking of the carriage and the clatter of bogie upon steel rail slowed its frenetic rhythm to a loud and steady metallic click and bump and, like the warning cry of some infernal bird, the screech of the train's brakes pierced her eardrums above the blasts of the steam whistle. She lifted herself up off the bed, her Kashmiri shawl about her shoulders, the soft wool holding sleep's night-heat and the stink of sweat that rose from her blue cotton dress.

Every joint was stiff from the thirty-six-hour train journey, and her tightly braided hair was itchy and greasy. Through the slatted windows, Calcutta's smoke-enshrouded, low-roofed slums took shadowy shape in the chill and pre-dawn dregs of the night. She knew the city. Her father had been based there when he had been in the Political Department, even if his area of oper-ation had always been to the north: in Sikkim, Bhutan and Tibet. The Political Department would help her to let him know that she would be arriving in Talo some time in mid-February, as soon as she had organised the expedition. Richard would help her with that.

The train clattered past the dark silhouette of the gasworks and under the Chanumari Bridge. It rocked its way between two high walls and pulled in under the riveted iron arches of Howrah station where it slowed and screeched to a halt. The platform beside her carriage was crowded with coolies already yelling for the attention of the passengers. Christina took her wide-brimmed straw hat off the luggage rack, stuffed her hair into it and jammed it down over her forehead. She opened her compartment door and made her way down the crowded corridor of the ladies' carriage. Servants in saris clutched carpetbags and Gladstones. They were mixed in with all forms of English woman-hood: the buxom, the dumpy, the big-boned, the willowy; like a mixed flock of unruly birds, wrapped and plumed ladies spilled out onto the platform, the servants in the primary brilliance of their silks and cottons, the memsahibs in whites and fawns, topped by wide-brimmed straws, the uniform of privilege. From the top of the steps Christina searched for a sign of her cousin Richard upon the dark and crowded platform that was only sparsely lit by a string of bare electric lightbulbs.

'There she is. Dr Devenish! Christina! Over here!'

It was Richard's voice. He was lean and his rumpled suit hung on him loosely. Perhaps he hadn't had time to shave since it was so early. At his shoulder stood a tall dark-haired Briton in a sharp white suit. The milling coolies seemed to keep a respectful distance from them both. Richard's companion had that quiet but unmis-takable aura of someone used to telling others what to do, but he seemed agitated, shifting from foot to foot, darting glances at the crowd as if searching for some imminent danger. He was definitely a Department man.

She raised a hand in greeting and six Indian policemen armed with lathis pushed their way into the crowd to make way for

Richard. He reached for her hand, a firm grip, and helped her down the steps to the platform.

The reek of coal and steam wafted beneath the arched metal roof of the station.

'Richard,' she said. 'I haven't seen you in years.'

'Yes. I wish the circumstances were better,' he said. 'I'm so sorry about the clinic.'

He didn't know about Lakshmi.

'Thank you for meeting me,' she said.

'Your baggage?'

'In the goods van.'

'I'll have it brought to the house.'

He turned to his colleague in the linen suit. The tanned face was slightly drawn. Oiled dark hair receding a little from the temples. A handsome man, but troubled, she thought, something eating at him.

'This is Major Davies of the Political Department. He knows your father very well.'

A few wrinkles appeared around Davies's eyes as he smiled but the tension in his face remained. She was about an inch shorter than he was. She could see that he had a gun under his suit jacket. There had been a shooting in Calcutta. She had read about it in the newspaper. Davies and Richard would both be potential targets, wouldn't they?

'Delighted to meet you,' she said.

'Dr Devenish,' Davies said. 'Your father was something of a mentor to me. I'm honoured to meet his daughter.'

That accent, Welsh wasn't it? She hadn't expected that from him. He had a very warm baritone, that strange stress and lilt, a bit like the way Indians spoke English. A major – then he outranked Richard. She offered him her hand to shake. He hesitated. He'd noticed how damaged it was, the red and wrinkled skin. She was surprised by the lightness of his touch. He held her hand for a moment and he raised his eyes to hers again, slightly shifty, a little too intimate, disconcerting, as if he was trying to read her mind with some kind of rough detective's clairvoyance. He let go of her hand. She wished that she had worn gloves.

'We'll do everything possible to help you,' he said.

He seemed sincere in that. He hadn't said it just to charm her.

'Thank you,' she said. 'I do hope to see my father soon. That's the main thing.'

'The guest room is all prepared,' Richard said. 'And the car's just outside.'

Major Davies said something in Hindi to the escort of Sikh policemen and they cleared a path along the thronged platform. Richard was at her left shoulder and Davies just ahead to her right. They cleared the station buildings. Rickshaw-wallahs by the dozen made a yelling cacophony and made it impossible to speak. A barrier of Sikh policemen separated her and Richard and Davies from the rest of chaotic India. Lakshmi had been her living link to that other India but Lakshmi was here no more, other than in scarred memories. With Richard and Davies at her shoulders, she crossed the Howrah station bazaar. It was packed with barrows and canopied carts with hanging lanterns upon their stanchions that shed a harsh light on the brightly coloured mangoes and pawpaws and peppers. Richard pointed out the car at the edge of the square: a big, open-topped, black Rover. Two Sikh soldiers, armed with rifles, bayonets fixed, stood on guard beside it. Richard hurried forward and opened the door of the Rover for her and she climbed into the spacious leather seat. To her surprise, it was Davies who joined her, not Richard. She was confused by his closeness. He winced as he settled down beside her.

'A touch of sciatica,' he said.

He smiled warmly enough.

'Oh, I'm sorry,' she said.

'Nothing really. Old rugby injury.'

Richard slammed the car door. She, being the guest, had to travel in the back with the man of the highest rank. She leaned back in the seat. Davies was pukka enough to keep a decent space between them. He ran his hands over his face, a nervous gesture, as if he was trying to compose himself, his expression. Richard climbed in beside the driver, and the car eased forward into the crowded square. The driver sounded the horn incessantly as if sound itself could clear a path for them. The car clattered onto the floating bridge over the Hooghly and it shifted and creaked beneath the wheels. The river below them was yellow, its eddies heavy with silt. The top mast-lights of tramp steamers anchored at the jute jetties on the ghats waved on either side of the bridge. Upriver, fires flickered upon Calcutta's own Burning Ghat and she could visualise Lakshmi's corpse, once more, consumed on the funeral pyre.

Richard turned around from the front seat.

'When I got your letter about Bhutan, we set about arranging for your expedition right away. That's why Major Davies is here. He's already been arranging things for you.'

'Major Davies? Really?' she said.

'Yes,' Davies said. 'You came at a rather for*tuit*ous time, really. Doesn't give you much time to catch your breath in Calcutta, I suppose, but the Political Department has an expedition that is just about to leave for Bhutan. We plan to set off in just a few days' time.'

'A few days?'

'Just as soon as everything's ready, yes.'

She couldn't read the look in his face. His eyes were flat, the mouth a straight line, all that strain just under the skin, ruthlessly suppressed.

'What's this expedition all about?' she asked.

'The Government of India is investing the Maharaja of Bhutan with the order of Knight Commander of the Indian Empire,'

Davies said. 'Formal ceremony, you see. I'm leading the Calcutta contingent. You'll be able to join us.'

'Join you?'

'Yes.'

'Forgive my curiosity,' she said to Richard, 'but this expedition – I expected to arrange something for myself.'

'But your letter . . .' he said.

Yes, she had, she had asked him to help her.

'This is all a bit overwhelming, really.'

'Your letter . . . I had to discuss it at the Department,' Richard said. 'Permits. Equipment. That sort of thing. And the countryside is absolutely unsafe at the moment. We've had cars and trains ambushed. From Calcutta all the way north to the Duars Plain. Major Davies is going to Bhutan anyway. We thought it would be ideal if you joined his party.'

'Killing two birds with one stone, if you see what I mean,' Davies said.

'Yes, I do,' she said. 'I understand.'

'We've already wired your father to let him know,' Richard said.

'Has he replied?' she asked.

'Not yet,' Richard said.

'He was going to send an escort to the border,' she said.

'No need for that now,' Richard said.

'If you don't mind my saying,' Davies said, 'we could always use another doctor on the expedition.'

Was he saying that to flatter her?

'Why on earth would you want another doctor?' she said. 'I mean, don't you have your own medical staff on expedition?'

'Yes, yes, of course,' Davies said, 'but you know, there's always . . . we're always sort of under siege. People turn up at every little village when we're on the march . . . every ailment you can possibly imagine. They know we've got doctors with us. And medicines. Richard thought that perhaps, you know . . .

you might prefer that. Having a position, something to do. And you won't have to waste any time here in Calcutta.'

'Yes, yes, of course,' she said.

Perhaps it wasn't such a bad idea. Do something useful. It might be a good opportunity. Perhaps it was 'for*tuit*ous' then, as Davies had said.

'Have you seen my father recently?' she asked.

Davies glanced away for a second and she couldn't see his expression.

'Not for some time,' he said. 'He came to the funeral when my wife passed away.'

The hands ran over his knees, his head dropped a little over the wide shoulders. His face turned to look at her again, slightly askew, tightness around the eyes and mouth again.

'Oh, I'm sorry,' she said.

'Oh. Oh no,' he said. 'I'm afraid, well . . . it was some time ago. Malaria. Couldn't bring the fever down.'

Christina blushed.

He straightened up in the seat beside her.

'Life goes on, doesn't it?' he said.

'Yes, yes of course,' she said.

'I'll see if we can have all the equipment ready by tomorrow,' Davies said.

'Tomorrow? Will you have medical supplies there, too?' she asked.

'Medical supplies. Yes, of course. And we can leave in just a few days. As soon as you're ready.'

She nodded.

'Yes, a few days.'

'We have to be in Bumthang by February the thirteenth,' Davies said. 'For the investiture.'

'The knighthood, yes . . . Will my father be there?'

'For the ceremony, no. But we'll see you get to Talo a few days after. Don't worry.'

72

This wasn't how she'd imagined that she'd be going to Bhutan at all – straightaway like this. Perhaps it was all for the better. Everything arranged. She would hardly have to think about anything logistically: tents, coolies, food, all provided by the Department. And running a small field clinic would keep her occupied on the long march.

She leaned back in her seat as the Rover inched through the early morning streets. Shawl-wrapped bodies raised themselves from low-slung charpoys close to the shop-front buildings to gaze at their passing. The morning chorus of hacking coughs, retching and spitting, mingled with the cries of fruitmongers and the barking of dogs and the rattle of barrows being wheeled onto their roadside pitches. Desultory cows swung up spittle-strung muzzles as the car passed, the horned heads tilting to focus big brown eyes on the passage of the Rover. The smoke of night fires still hung in the early morning air, the brown haze filtering the early sun's light into a diffuse pearlescence. From above the buildings, duelling muezzins wailed from unseen minarets. Garish shop signs angled over the muddy boulevard of Central Avenue, and the shopkeepers swung open wooden shutters ready for the day's trade. Ragged urchins stared out from littered alleys, the eyes of the children as big as those of the sacred cows, and just as curious of their passage.

'Dr Devenish?' Davies said.

'Yes?'

His hands were gripping his knees again.

'May I ask you a medical question?'

'Medical question?' she said. 'Do you want some help with the sciatica?'

He smiled.

'No, not that. It's about leprosy,' he said.

'Leprosy?'

Why on earth was he asking her about leprosy?

'Yes,' he said. 'How do you catch it?'

73

'Catch it?'

'If you touch them,' he said, 'just touch them, mind you, you can't get it, can you?

Christina shook her head.

'Why do you ask?' she said.

He pressed his fingertips to his temples for a moment, dropped his hands and then smiled again.

'I picked up an object that had been in contact with one of them,' he said.

She stiffened in the seat. She knew the medical facts, of course, but she suddenly felt a sense of revulsion. She had shaken hands with him. Her damaged hands on his. But it didn't matter. That's what the books said. You couldn't catch it like that.

'What kind of object?' she asked.

'It was a ring,' he said.

'A leper with a ring?'

'It wasn't the leper's,' he said. 'It was mine. I dropped it into his palm by mistake, with a coin.'

'When was this?' she said.

'The day before yesterday,' he said.

That recent! She couldn't catch it from him and he couldn't have possibly caught it from the leper. She knew that it was impossible.

She shook her head.

'There's no possibility at all,' she said. 'It would take years of contact . . . People work among lepers without ever becoming infected.'

He nodded.

'I suppose I knew that,' he said. 'But I just wanted to . . . It's a relief to hear it from a doctor.'

He must have known. Still, it was shocking. Even after all these years in India, seeing a leprosy-ravaged body gave her the shivers. Davies ravaged by lesions. That would be terrible: a man like that, so good-looking. Why had he brought it up? And on their first meeting? Well, she supposed it was understandable. For all his smiles and that hint of toying with her, he would have been disturbed by it, too, wouldn't he? Perhaps that was what had been playing on his mind, making him so nervous, that tight expression. But no, she thought, there's something else that's worrying him, something deeper. Was it about his wife? Or something else? Her father had cared enough about him to go to Mrs Davies's funeral, and now Davies would be accompanying Christina to see her father on this long expedition into Bhutan. Perhaps they'd be happy to see each other.

The Rover pulled through a wrought-iron gate just off Cotton Street, not far from the Presidency College, and up a narrow driveway overhung by the leaves of giant ferns and hanging palm fronds that clicked as the car passed beneath them. It stopped in front of the square-quoined portico of the wide, stone house, a bizarre Gothic edifice in the heart of India. With the whistles of the unseen birds in the trees and the high walls shutting out any noise of the world outside, the garden had a brooding elegance. Richard opened the car door for her and she got out. Hari, Richard's Tamil *chaprassi*, opened the front door of the house to them.

'Welcome back to Calcutta, madam,' he said.

'Thank you, Hari.'

'I'll have your luggage brought up to your room,' Richard said.

Hari led them into the lounge. The room was furnished with a white cotton three-piece suite and mosquito netting hung from the frames of the open windows. It was light and airy inside despite the heavy stone exterior. Persian carpets covered the floor, natural pigments pale in the early morning light, and through the high windows the heavy leaves of the plants filtered the rays of the warm winter sun.

'I've told Hari to prepare hot water for a bath,' Richard said.

'You've been too kind, Richard,' she said. 'And Major Davies, too.'

'I should leave you to your rest, Dr Devenish,' Davies said. 'You must be exhausted.'

She *was* tired from the journey and she couldn't quite think straight. This tying her into the expedition was a *fait accompli* and she didn't know whether to be angry or grateful. Davies led the way to the door and Richard followed him.

'When you've settled in,' Davies said, 'had a rest, I'll arrange for you to inspect the equipment, for the expedition.'

'Yes. Yes, of course,' she said. 'Thank you.'

'Anything you want . . . in Calcutta . . . don't hesitate to contact me,' Davies said.

'Yes, thank you,' she said.

He turned into the corridor and Richard followed him to the front door. She sat down on the sofa again. Well, she had asked Richard for his help and he had gone ahead and organised everything for her. She ought to be grateful.

She watched through the window netting as Davies got into the Rover. His driver started up and the leaves crackled under the tyres as the car set off down the driveway. Davies sat square in the rear seat and he didn't turn around for even the briefest farewell look at her or Richard as the Rover went out between the wrought-iron gates and took the road back towards the centre of Calcutta.

Hari arrived with a pot of tea and Richard came back in to join her.

'How do you like my OC?' Richard said.

He sat down in the armchair that Davies had vacated.

'It seems as if I'm going to get to know him very well.'

'Your father has a lot of respect for him. He's helped me no end in the Department.'

'Not an Oxbridge man?' she asked.

It was the accent. She suddenly felt herself to be a total prig but he didn't fit the usual image she had of a Department man.

'Rose through the ranks,' Richard said. 'Quite a character.

Distinguished Service Cross in the Great War. Wounded twice. Field commission. He won't talk about it himself, of course. General McKeowan told me.'

She nodded. Surprised, and for all her avowed pacifism, she had to admit to herself that she was impressed. Distinguished Service Cross. He was a brave man. Or had been. There was some damage in Davies that was not just to do with the loss of his wife. Left over from the war perhaps. Or was there some kind of class resentment in it?

She found him attractive. Physically, yes, how could she not? That was understandable. Biological even. The presence of the dominant male. Something about him disturbed her, though. She was conscious of how long she had kept her sexual passions locked up and buried under the mental and physical burden of her work. The loss of the clinic had freed her from that, and the loss of Lakshmi had freed her to let her emotions reach out for a different sort of companionship. How much she had relied on Lakshmi for warmth and friendship. She had used it as a substitute in some ways for her lack of a male companion. Every man she had met in India would have wanted her to act the memsahib. Now here was Major Davies inviting her to take part in his expedition as a doctor in charge of a field clinic. That was in his favour. But really, this way of thinking was beating about the bush. It wasn't the fact that he was offering her useful employment on a Department expedition that she found fascinating about him, it was that male physicality, which he had in abundance. There was a dark side to him. Something he kept hidden. She was attracted to that. Aware that there was something dangerous about it. And asking her about leprosy like that, that had been unnerving. And that strange vulnerability he had revealed when talking about his wife and her father. It was as though he were setting some kind of bait for her. Knowingly or unknowingly?

She was going to see her father, that was her main goal, that was what she intended to keep in mind. But whenever a man and a woman were placed in close proximity at least the thought of attraction and conjunction was bound to arise. That was a simple biological fact of which she was well aware. And if she wanted to explore those more secret aspects of Major Owen Davies's soul, then the opportunity was open to her: they were both about to leave behind the familiar and constricting confines of Raj society and set off on an expedition to the unknown kingdom of Bhutan. Some degree of intimacy there was certainly going to be.

'I say, Hari,' Richard said, 'would you mind pouring the tea?'

CHAPTER EIGHT

HE CAME OUT OF THE WRITERS' BUILDING. DOWN THE STEPS. HE
had to get away. That basement. They had taken Gupta back to
Deoli jail. Davies's mind was crawling. He wanted a woman.
After what he had done to Gupta . . . Every cell in his body
wanted that rushing, ecstatic release in the body of a woman.
And he had been to the brothel before. He knew where to go.
It would be so desperately embarrassing if they found out at the
office. He was losing his grip. The odds of his being seen going
into a brothel were minuscule. If he was seen, he could say that
he was investigating . . . No one would ever believe him. But
why should he deny it? Everyone went to brothels, didn't they?
On Dalhousie Square he crossed through the morning traffic
and onto the flat beggarlands around the Lal Dighi tank. A wall-
eyed dwarf plucked at his trousers and Davies flung his hand
back to slap the clinging beggar away. That bloody leper appeared
in front of him. The glaucous accusing eye, the leering rotten
grin over the *pan*-stained teeth. What was the filthy creature
thinking? Its look was accusing. Only reason that Davies had
been down there, wasn't it, the Raja Bazaar, for the brothel? And
now here was that bloody rotten leper again with his dirty smirk,
waiting for him. Davies had touched that rotten hand. Still had
the ring in his pocket. Emma's ring. He should throw it away.
Hurl it into the Lal Dighi tank for it to contaminate all who
bathed in its water.

'Baksheesh, sahib,' the leper said.

Davies rushed past him, but the leper followed him down through the crowds. A dirty, ash-covered yogi raised a painted face to him, three yellow lines on his forehead beneath his matted locks, a lifted trident, Shiva-*baba*.

'There's no escape from karma, *babu*.'

Did the filthy ash-covered bastard think he didn't know?

Davies pushed the yogi aside and the crowd around howled at his blasphemous assault. The leper clutched at his sleeve. And the wall-eyed dwarf was at his knee. A corpulent prostitute pulled back her cotton head shawl, rolled her kohl-rimmed eyes and flicked her tongue in and out at him. And then he saw her at the end of the alley – Christina Devenish. Her green eyes were glittering, her red hair like an electric halo around her freckled face, the wide red mouth curved in a predatory smile. She was in a white cotton-drill dress like a nurse at the hospital. But she was a doctor, wasn't she? What was she doing down here? She was standing by a butcher's stall, a pile of offal in front of her: lungs, heart, liver and kidneys, topped by a goat's head, the slit eye blind in death. He didn't want to face her. It would have been better if she hadn't seen him at all. He turned to run back in the direction he had come but a gaggle of urchins at his waist tugged at the hem of his linen jacket as if they would all drag him down and strip him. His legs felt as if they were moving through treacle, this tide of ragged infants, and their emaciated mothers with wrinkled dugs, pushing their empty fingers to their mouths in a gesture of starvation; and mad Brahmins, heads shaven, in dirty *khurtas*, exhorted him to purify himself: only three rupees for the ceremony. And they gripped him by his arms, while the leper raised his hands, and Davies pulled back as the suppurating palms closed upon his face and he woke sweating and feverish on the wrinkled pillow and damp sheets of his Sunday morning bed.

CHAPTER NINE

I

ON THE OTHER SIDE OF THE MOSQUITO NETTING, HARI SET THE tea tray down on the bedside table and left quietly. The sun slanted in through the window of her bedroom. She slipped out from under the sheet and the light cotton quilt and the net and pulled on her dressing gown over her white nightdress. Her bedroom looked out over the lush gardens and, beyond the wall, the Gothic spire of St Paul's pierced the sky above the rooftops and rose higher than any of Calcutta's minarets. Its bells pealed out the call to Sunday Eucharist. She had arranged with Major Davies an inspection of the expedition's equipment for eleven o'clock that morning. Then he was to bring her back to Richard's and they would all have lunch together.

She still felt disorientated. Her sleep cycle had been disrupted by both the train journey and the afternoon nap which she had taken the day before. And last night, despite the gin she'd drunk with Richard, she had lain wide awake for hours before falling asleep. She recalled the hypnogogic images of Richard and Lakshmi mixed up with her father and then there were some cavalry horses near Curzon Gardens. Major Davies came in his Rover and drove her to Howrah station, insisting that she dance to some kind of Strauss waltz on the platform and she was reluctant, afraid of the passage of time. Her last anxious dream images had been of trying to push through a crowd of coolies as she ran for a train and had no time to buy a ticket.

She poured a cup of tea for herself, the pale brown liquid swirling in the delicate white china. She let the thick condensed milk drop from the porcelain jug into the clear tea and stirred the blobs and strands patiently, before carrying her cup and sitting down in the wicker chair next to the window. She sipped at her tea, the hoped-for aroma of the Darjeeling overwhelmed by the sweetness of the condensed milk. Without the routine of the clinic to distract her she was aware of how long it had been since she had practised any kind of morning meditation exercise. Much as she had studied Theosophy and India's religions, she had lost the habit of daily breathing exercises to the day-to-day running of the clinic in Bombay. All the accounts to settle, the tickets to arrange, the medical records to keep, the ordering of condoms and douches and Dutch caps from England, not to speak of the endless queues of patients and the confrontations with the religious fanatics.

Lakshmi, on the other hand, had never neglected her daily devotions: her morning ablutions, lighting incense before a hand-painted image of Vishnu, reciting some dawn liturgy, while she, Christina, had always started the day in a frenetic rush. It was ironic that she was the one who was still alive while Lakshmi was dead. Christina stared at the vapour spiralling over the surface of the tea.

She had two hours before meeting Davies. She could have breakfast any time she wanted. She had time to do an exercise. It was simply a matter of overcoming inertia. And if she was to meet this Shabdrung, the man her father had called the 'real thing', shouldn't she at least prepare herself? She drained the tea and set down her empty cup.

The varnished floorboards were cool beneath her bare feet. She opened her trunk and rummaged along the edge of the folded clothes. From near the bottom she pulled out her pack of *tattwa* cards that were wrapped in a piece of black silk. She slipped back through the mosquito netting and hitched up her nightdress so that she could sit, tailor-fashion, on the bed. She folded the black cloth back from the hand-painted cards. Their symbols represented in colour and geometric form each of the elements: silver crescent for water; green circle for air; yellow square for earth; red triangle for fire; and dark blue egg for ether. The symbols could be made into twenty further combinations: fire of earth, water of air, fire of water, spirit of air, earth of water, water of earth and so on. These abstract forms seemed to hint at the meaning that was waiting to be read on the patterns of the dry brown soil of the Deccan, through the boiling clouds of the hot monsoon, the empty blue skies of the cool season, the icy peaks of the rocky Himalayas. She chose the *akasha* card. A simple blue egg. She straightened her back, stared hard at the image until the periphery of her vision blurred and all she could see was the blue egg on its golden background like a doorway through which she wanted to pass. She closed her eyes and the image remained there burned on her retina, reversed now, gold on blue, in the empty space inside her skull. Then the image faded. She waited as the darkness lightened to grey. But some voice, some reason, or reason itself, stopped her abandoning herself to her imagination. And even as blurry half-formed images of trees and mountains seemed to rise out of the fog, nagging doubt dispersed them; and she opened her eyes onto the space beneath the mosquito netting. She stared again at the blue egg, closed her eyes and tried to abandon all thought once more, but her muscles began to tense and her throat constricted with frustration and her eyes opened. She dropped the *akasha* card into her lap and leaned back against the headboard of the bed. Something was blocking her.

Back in London, when she had gone to the meetings of the Order, and had studied the *Clavicula Salomonis* and the *Goetia* and the *Book of the Sacred Magic of Abramelin the Mage*, the excitement – and the drugs – had fuelled light-filled fantasies; and had given her the impression that her spirit was on fire. She needed new inspiration. India and the clinic had loosened the grip of the Order upon her – just as the Order had once loosened the grip of her Catholic upbringing. But the clinic and its destruction had drained her. She was desperate for this journey to Bhutan to reignite that spark of spiritual passion and not to end in some bitter disappointment. She regrouped the *tattwa* cards and rewrapped them in their silk. It was time to get dressed for her meeting with Major Owen Davies.

2

He had sent the Rover for her to Richard's and as it turned left into the police barracks on Corporation Street she could see that Davies was waiting for her in the courtyard. He was dressed in his work clothes: white linen suit, which seemed slightly creased and soiled now, and a broad-striped, sky-blue and navy tie. Govinda, his sepoy driver, opened the door for her. Christina adjusted the brim of her straw hat to shade her eyes from the glare of the sun.

'It's getting hot,' she said.

'We're over here,' Davies said. 'In the armoury.'

They crossed the beaten-earth courtyard and went into a high-arched building with doors that were wide enough to admit a horse-drawn coach. One of those newfangled armoured cars which often patrolled the streets these days was parked just inside the doors. It was all rivets and steel plates and a vicious-looking machine gun poked out from the steel turret that topped it. They continued deeper into the inside of the building where it was cool and shady.

The equipment had been set up on tables close to the western wall. The tents were all in their heavy canvas tote bags. There were folding desks, camp beds and chairs.

'And here's the medical equipment,' he said.

Laid out on two trestle tables were dressings, drips, needles, suture, morphine, quinine, penicillin, plaster of Paris, Petrie dishes, test tubes and even a microscope. It had been taken from its wooden case and there was a slide in the clamp below the lens.

'Let me see this,' she said.

She pulled off her gloves and reached up to Davies's shoulder. She picked a dark hair off the weave of his jacket. He tilted his chin and looked down his nose.

'That's embarrassing,' he said.

'It's just a hair,' she said.

She leaned over the instrument, adjusted the mirror and clamped this tiny piece of Davies over the slide. She looked into the eyepiece, brought the slide into focus and examined the thick barrel of the hair, with its tiny flecks of skin clinging to its oily surface. Even the most well-groomed, if you looked closely enough, were made of dirt and scurf and secretions.

'What do you see?' he asked.

'Do you know that witches use a victim's hair to cast spells on them?' she said, to tease him.

There was a moment's silence as she stared into the eyepiece and played with the focus.

'Do you plan on bewitching me then?' he said.

She slid the hair off the slide.

'First class, that microscope,' she said.

'What have you done with that hair?' he said.

She rubbed her red thumb and index finger together and let it fall to the ground, happy that he was teasing her back a little. He seemed more relaxed today. They had a long journey ahead of them and at the very least she needed to get on with him.

'You've brought everything we could possibly want,' she said. 'And I haven't lifted a finger to help.'

'All in the stores,' he said.

She could diagnose and treat everything from cuts, breaks and contusions to pyorrhoea, diarrhoea, gonorrhoea, amoebas and malaria, all of which she might well expect to encounter on their expedition to Bhutan. Even leprosy. Perhaps he was over that worry now. She was.

'Everything to your satisfaction then?' Davies said.

'Yes, absolutely,' she said.

'We're ready to go. The day after tomorrow,' he said.

'My God, I've just about caught my breath,' she said.

'Six a.m.,' he said. 'I'll pick you up at Richard's.'

'First, I want to buy some presents,' she said. 'For my father and the Shabdrung.'

'I can help you with that, too,' he said.

'And I suppose I'll have to get a present for the Maharaja,' she said, 'if he's to be our host.'

Davies tucked his hands into his pockets.

'Yes, of course,' he said. 'Do you have something in mind?'

A pair of kings, she thought. And her father. Had to be something expensive.

'I know a little shop on Rotra Street,' she said. 'I went there with my father once.'

'A jeweller's then?'

'Yes,' she said.

'Let's go in the car, now,' Davies said. 'We still have an hour or two before Richard's.'

'You don't waste any time, do you?' she said.

'Well, they'll only try to cheat you if you go alone,' he said.

3

She picked up the small padded box off the glass-topped counter. The jeweller was a corpulent Bengali in a baggy, brown, European suit. He held his head forward in an effort to look at her through the top section of his bifocals, and the bare electric lightbulb above his head reflected on his high brown forehead.

'This is gorgeous,' she said.

She held up a gold pocket watch. Brazed upon the lid of the timepiece were intertwined letters of the Sanskrit alphabet forming a tree of words with trunk and branch and leaf and twig and even suggestions to her of the shapes of songbirds. Davies leaned closer to her. He placed his hand on her right shoulder. She enjoyed the weight of it. He was obviously pleased with himself as his face came closer to hers, scrutinising the craftsmanship, his big features calm and relaxed.

'It *is* stunning, isn't it?' he said.

Christina hung the watch at the height of her ribs, on the left, where a waistcoat pocket might be, and she stretched the chain across the flat of her green silk blouse just to imagine how it might look on her father.

'I'm going to buy it,' she said. 'I've never seen anything quite so beautiful.'

'Colonel Devenish will be delighted,' he said.

'I do hope so.'

She held up the exquisite watch by its gold chain to admire it one more time and then she put it back into its box.

'And I want that little gun for the Maharaja,' she said.

From among the bejewelled eggs, chintz clocks and Chinese jade carvings laid out on the counter, the jeweller picked up the red silk cloth and laid it on his palm. Resting in the centre of it was the small, single-shot American derringer, silver-plated and with a pearl handle.

'Do you think it too feminine?' she asked.

'Not at all. Sir Jigme will love it,' Davies said.

'And this,' she said, 'is for the Shabdrung.'

She picked out a small, heavily framed picture. It was about seven inches by seven and made of wrought silver. In the centre of it, a perfect-featured gold Buddha sat in front of a copper bodhi tree whose roots and branches filled up the picture with swirls and loops. The effect was like that of a Russian Orthodox icon. It was a perfect complement to the watch she had bought her father. She wondered if it had been made by the same craftsman.

'Very appropriate,' Davies said.

She wondered if he would disapprove of anything that she chose. Without waiting for her request or approval, Davies began to haggle in Bengali with the proprietor over the price of the three presents.

'All right, Major Davies,' the proprietor finally said. 'No less than two hundred and fifty rupees.' The jeweller pushed his bifocals back up to the bridge of his nose and turned to Christina. 'Madam,' he said. 'The gentleman wishes to steal from me and have my children starve.'

Davies smiled and nodded. Obviously he thought that he had done well. She thought so, too. Such exquisite craftsmanship. It was worth every anna. It would come out of her savings but she couldn't give something cheap to a king. Or her father.

'I'll write you a cheque,' she said.

'No doubt I can trust a lady who keeps the company of Major Davies.'

She took her chequebook from her handbag. The proprietor called his assistant to box up the three gifts. Davies drifted across to the door as she wrote the cheque. She wondered what Davies thought of her spending so much money. He seemed to be checking the streets. She took the boxes from the jeweller and dropped them into her canvas shopping bag. As they left the shop, Davies quietly scanned the length and breadth of the street. He *was* a soldier, wasn't he? They were a potential target. And the open-topped Rover didn't offer any protection at all, as if he was daring the terrorists to attack him.

Govinda, Davies's driver, held the back door open for her.

'God I could do with a cigarette,' she said.

Govinda's head moved back slightly in his surprise but he dipped a hand into the side pocket of his tunic and pulled out a packet of Player's Navy Cut.

'Have one of these, madam.'

'English cigarettes?' she said.

'From Major Davies, madam,' he said.

'I can't steal your gifts,' she said.

'Major Davies is very generous, madam,' he said. 'Endless supply.'

'Endless?'

'More or less.'

That smile and the Indian head waggle.

'Thank you,' she said.

She closed the cigarette in her gloved fist and got in the back of the car. Davies slid in beside her and dug into his jacket. He flicked a flame from his petrol lighter and held it for her as she leaned towards him. After so long, the first bite of the strong smoke into her lungs made her instantly giddy. She blew out a grey plume of smoke just as the Rover started.

'Richard's, then?' Davies said.

She picked a speck of tobacco from her tongue. After the first rush in her head she enjoyed the feel of the smoke slipping down her throat, the bite of it, blowing it out, and the tingle it gave her in her limbs. It made her cold, too, as the bloom of perspiration cooled on her face, despite the sun slanting down on her in the open back seat.

She nodded.

The Rover moved off north down Rotra Street. Davies twisted towards her. The sun was warm and pleasant on her skin and Davies's knee fell lightly against hers. Every follicle on her body prickled.

'Pardon my prying,' he said. 'But I heard that you suffered rather a tragedy in Bombay.'

She moved her knee away. Had the contact been deliberate? His arm rested on the back of the seat very casually. She looked down into her lap and adjusted her skirt.

'It was awful, really. Not so much the clinic, but I lost a very dear friend.'

'Oh, I'm sorry,' he said. 'I knew about the clinic but not about your friend.'

'Yes,' she said. 'In the fire . . . I just wanted to get away for a while. I couldn't face Bombay for another minute.'

'Of course not . . . If you don't mind,' he said. 'Well, my question is . . . well . . . the Muslim and the Hindu, they both pray for an abundance of children. Weren't they suspicious of you?'

'It's strange, isn't it?' she said. 'Some of them were worried that the clinic was a British plot to wipe out the population of India. As if we could. But the modern world isn't passing India by, is it? The more progressive thinkers understand. Gandhi does. But a lot of my patients were Englishwomen.'

He nodded.

'They required the utmost discretion, of course,' she said.

She expected him to ask more about her British patients but he avoided the subject. Had she been too forward? It was rather an intimate thing to say to him.

'To my way of thinking,' Davies said, 'Indians are taking the worst of what the modern world has to offer and now they're turning it against us.'

'Are you completely against the independence movement?' she asked.

'To be pragmatic,' he said, 'I can't see what anyone has to gain from independence. The country would simply disintegrate. Look at Congress. There are so many factions among them. They're ready to go at each other's throats at the drop of a hat. It's only Gandhi who keeps them from it, isn't it? I don't believe that Congress could ever keep a grip on law and order. Or on the country's defence. They need British officers. Indians don't have the experience. The Chinese or the Russians would be over the Himalayas and through here like a dose of salts, wouldn't they? Far worse for everyone.'

He looked at her hopefully. He obviously expected her to agree with him. She didn't want to disagree with him, to enter into an argument, but she had to be honest with him.

'I suppose it's true that we can't just pack up and leave,' she said. 'But I do think that we must hand over power to the Indians. And we'll have to work with Congress to make that transition, sooner or later.'

'Some people would say that we've gone a bit too far giving Congress any power at all,' Davies said. 'Churchill for one.'

'Churchill?' she said. 'I'm surprised that a Welshman would have any sympathy for him.'

He blushed. She was pleased that she had managed to embarrass him, make him uncomfortable.

'My father was outraged when he sent in troops against the miners in Tonypandy. Methodist minister, the people's preacher.'

'A minister on the side of the workers.'

'Valleys tradition. Radical methodism.'

'And you?'

'The whole Tonypandy business was tremendously exaggerated on both sides. Supposedly the troops opened fire and hundreds were killed. Rioters sacked the entire town. But that's just not true. There was a lot of bitterness, though; justifiably so, I suppose.'

'So you do sympathise with the miners.'

'Of course I do.'

'But you're still happy to be an officer of the Raj.'

'Four years after Tonypandy, I was fighting for His Majesty's armed forces against the Germans. And a lot of those miners were too. But the fact is, I feel so removed from it all out here: the war, the Welsh valleys. And I like it. In India I can be whatever I choose in a way. Gives me a sense of freedom.'

'From your father?'

'From the whole bloody parochial mess.'

'And what does your father think of you doing that?'

'I don't give a damn what he thinks. To be fair – the war – he was right behind me. I risk my life so that he can continue to think and say what he likes. So that everybody can. He still hates Churchill, of course. Probably sympathetic to Gandhi. But I think it's all rather more complicated than that. There'd be wider connotations if we lost India. With Russia and China, you see. The world stage. The Bolsheviks. The Bolsheviks would put my father against a wall and shoot him. It has its faults, but Britain has by far the best political system, don't you think? Especially nowadays. It might not be perfect but it's a guarantee that no one group can keep power. One man, one vote.'

'One woman, one vote since 1928,' she said. 'And no waiting until you're thirty years old like that ridiculous law of 1918.'

'There you are, you see. It gets fairer all the time.'

'Unless you're an Indian in India.'

His lower lip pressed upwards. Trying to convince himself of something.

'They're not ready yet. They're better off under the protection of the Empire. There'd be chaos here if we left and Congress took over. Some of them are decent enough. Mohammed Jinnah, I think, for one. But here in Calcutta, the bloody Corporation is hand in glove with the terrorists. You heard about Simpson?'

Christina nodded.

'Yes,' she said. 'In the newspaper. Did you know him?'

'I had lunch with him. Just before he was murdered in the afternoon. I had to take the news to his wife and children.'

Now it was her turn to flinch. It was funny how all these abstract arguments about politics and independence were transformed under the impact of personal violence.

'The Congress Party here,' he said. 'And the mayor, Bose, he's the worst of them. He's got no qualms about using violence to get us out. And then what, with people like him in power?'

'I trust in Gandhi's way,' she said.

The car turned into a narrower alleyway. Stalls, all these people around them now in the bazaar. Ordinary people from all over Bengal and Bihar and Madras come here to make a living, to sell their fruit and vegetables and ironmongery and weaving.

'You know Gandhi won't try to intervene when we go after terrorists?' he said. 'They're his enemies, too, aren't they?'

She smiled at that.

'You're awfully cynical, Major Davies, aren't you?'

'I'm just a realist,' he said. 'Gandhi and I happen to share the same position on terrorism.'

'Oh no, Major Davies, please!'

His tanned face relaxed into a broad smile. It was the first time she had seen him so calm. Davies and Gandhi sharing a position? She hardly thought so. But she enjoyed Davies's banter. She might even enjoy being with him on the long journey. She hoped she would.

The Rover pulled up once more outside the wrought-iron gates of Richard's house and she felt a sudden rush of doubt.

Richard was a Department man, too. This expedition was falling into place around her so quickly and efficiently. She was being wrapped up in some sort of Departmental cotton wool. As the car pulled into the garden, she experienced a sense of *déjà vu*, as if time and circumstance had been disjointed and had shifted like the earth's tectonic plates during an earthquake so that past and present, memory and moment, made a kaleido-scopic interface, poised on the point of disintegration. She glanced about her at the garden that now seemed both familiar and unfa-miliar. And this sense of *déjà vu* was not a momentary percep-tion. It continued – as if a gear kept slipping in her mind and her visual perception itself undermined her sense of the solidity of the house and garden and the city around her. She wanted to explain it to herself. Perhaps her suspicion of political duplicity was synchronous with some parallel shift in the workings of her unconscious mind.

Davies opened the door of the Rover for her. She was conscious of feeling equal dread and awe and she wondered if this was an inkling of what a psychotic might feel as he or she headed into a disintegrative episode. She breathed deeply, consciously, in order to regain her mental composure but she was glad to take the support of Davies's offered hand as she stepped down onto the gravel path. Davies was somehow solid. He had that working-class matter-of-factness, tempered by a sharp intelligence, and by the dreadful experiences which he must have endured, and within which he had excelled, during the war. And India was in a situation not far off a civil war. She could count on Davies to take care of all the logistics of the expedition while she concentrated on preparing herself to meet her father who, she was glaringly conscious at this moment, was a man she hardly knew.

Chapter Ten

HARI LED THEM TO THE STUDY. THE ROOM WAS IN SEMI-darkness and the narrow body of her cousin Richard rose out of the shadows of a heavy armchair. Bookshelves took up all four walls. Built into the one behind Richard was a glass-fronted cabinet. On the right-hand side of the chair was a well-stocked drinks table with a bottle of whisky, one of brandy, another of gin, a tall soda siphon, an ice bucket and, close to Richard's elbow, a crystal decanter of a tawny sherry. Her cousin's tie was loose and he had no jacket on. Perhaps he was a little drunk already.

'Have a seat, you two,' he said. 'Hari, pour Major Davies and Dr Devenish a glass of sherry.'

She sat down on the sofa – nowhere else to sit really – and Davies sat down beside her but he was careful not to crowd her. He was the consummate gentleman. The only light in the study came from a low-watt standing lamp with a red, paisley-pattern shade. It brought out the shadows in the angles of Davies's face.

Hari handed her, then Davies, a schooner of sherry.

Richard leaned forward on the edge of his armchair, his hands between his knees, the glass dangling from his fingers.

'Major Davies must have been up early this morning. He's prepared everything we need for the expedition,' Christina said.

'He had it all prepared by six o'clock last night,' Richard said.

'That left him free this morning so that he had enough time to go to early morning Eucharist.'

'Eucharist?' she said.

'Major Davies put in an appearance,' Richard said.

Davies flushed to the roots of his hair. Perhaps Richard had gone too far by revealing his OC's visit to church. Davies leaned towards him, his head thrust forward.

'How the hell do you know that, Parker?' Davies said.

'Little bird,' Richard said.

He had pulled back a little but he was obviously enjoying his commanding officer's discomfort.

'Bloody Calcutta,' Davies said.

But he smiled now. He would have been used to dealing with Richard. And he would have all the advantage when they got back into the office.

'And it was the Reverend Appleby who gave the sermon,' Richard said.

'You're a mine of intelligence,' Davies said. 'Were you there, too?'

'Marjorie Commander,' Richard said. 'I saw her on the Maidan this morning when I was out for a stroll.'

'Ah,' Davies said.

'So what was the sermon?' Christina asked.

'Sermon?' Davies said.

'At Eucharist,' she said.

Davies waved a dismissive hand.

'Appleby did the usual,' he said. 'Lest we forget, the Saviour was born to us so we all might pass through the gates of heaven and live for ever. From what he was saying, I pictured it as a rather stiff sort of cocktail party all gathered around the throne of a white-bearded peer of the realm.'

'A comfortable sort of heaven, then,' Christina said. 'Like the right kind of club.'

'Well,' Davies said, 'I suppose that isn't any more absurd than the god realms of the Hindus, or the heavenly gardens of the Muslims. But you hope, you know . . . from a priest speaking to adults, for a little more, I suppose . . . something a little more profound, you know. My father was quite the pulpit philosopher: rational explanation for everything in the Bible. "Reason," he always said, "strengthens the faith – never undermines it.""

'Your father, yes,' she said. 'So you're still a practising Christian. I mean . . . if you went to church?'

His hand came up to the back of his head and he smoothed down some imaginary untidiness in his oiled hair.

'My father would probably say that I've been seduced by all the pomp of the High Church. But I *like* the ritual. It's cleansing somehow. I like the way it gives things a sense of order.'

'Order, yes,' she said. She couldn't keep the note of sarcasm out of her voice. 'We all want order, don't we?'

But trying to find some kind of order, of stability, *was* appealing. She was hardly likely to get it setting off for the Himalayas. Travel was all disruption: tents, diarrhoea, aching marches. Davies promised to provide a sense of order in the middle of all that. A Department man. A man used to commanding. He sat back. But he seemed embarrassed by the question about religion. He looked down, lips tighter, the skin around the eyes tighter, face a lot darker than a blush.

'And you find order by going to church?' she said.

'The church . . . All those statues and pictures and stained glass,' he said, 'and the light streaming in. The effect creates an ordered state of mind, doesn't it? A state of grace.'

'A state of grace?'

'I suppose you could say it's an approximation of grace, at least.'

'An approximation of grace?' she asked.

'The architecture is there to create a particular state of mind. An ordered state of mind.'

'And what did you mean by cleansing?' she asked.

'We're all human, aren't we?' he said. 'Imperfect.'

He was blushing again.

'Imperfect, yes,' she said.

'In a lot of ways,' Davies said.

'And that needs cleansing?'

'Yes.'

He looked away. Something was troubling him. Was it sexual? It usually was.

'We all do,' he said. 'We all need cleansing.'

She wondered. She had to wonder, but she didn't want to pry. Well, not too much anyway.

'So your father . . .' she said. 'You've never stopped being religious.'

Davies ran his hand over his head again. She was staring at him and Richard was on the periphery of her vision, and this interrogation by her of his commanding officer was keeping him quiet.

'My father hoped that I'd follow in his footsteps. He was very domineering, as I'm sure you can imagine: a preacher, a rationalist preacher. But I couldn't stand it. Life in a Welsh mining village . . . it was suffocating. Everybody knowing your business, expecting you to act in exactly the same way every day . . . I thought joining the army was the easiest way to get away from it. *And* my father really. So I could become my own man.'

He had become his own man. You could see that. No doubt about it. Christ, a Distinguished Service Cross.

'We could all see the war coming,' Davies said. 'I thought it would better to be in the trenches rather than in the valleys. Well. What a joke! Then I was in France.'

He shook his head and smiled.

'That can make you religious,' he said, 'the front line. The promises I made to God . . .'

He smiled at her, or perhaps at his memories.

'You wouldn't believe them,' he said.

'Did you keep them?' she asked.

He shrugged, sipped his sherry. Licked his lips.

'Four years,' he said. 'And when I came out of it I just wanted a return to order. I wanted to live in a civilised world. An ordered world. I could never have become a Catholic but there was something appealing ... High Church ... Anglican ... that approximation of grace I was talking about. Sometimes it feels like the real thing. Moments of faith, I suppose. My father's Methodism seemed all a bit austere. It never lacked passion but that bloody religion ... it took the life ... took the mystery out of it.'

'Mystery?'

'Yes. Mystery. My father wanted a rational explanation for everything in the Bible. For everything in the world.'

'Even the war?' she said.

The muscles of his face contracted.

'I suppose so. But that war defied reason. You are close to God, though. I'll say that. At death's door. One short step to heaven or hell. And the war. There's nothing rational about what people do, and no ultimate value in being reasonable. Reason only serves up to a certain point. It's not something to be enshrined as some kind of golden mean. That's just a myth perpetrated by a lot of snotty intellectuals who've never had to face any enduring physical danger – or perverted by the Bolsheviks to justify their own mass killings. And how did we even get into that war? We're not even conscious of why we do half the things we do.'

'Like Dr Freud says?'

'I don't know anything about what Dr Freud says.'

She loved his candor, his assurance.

'In the war,' she said, 'you *became* an officer?'

'Yes ... Commissioned in the field. Decorated. But it's a joke ... You just take care of what's in front of you. Do everything you can not to get killed. That's all. That's all I did ...'

His eyes fixed on the carpet again as if he were searching for something in the pattern of the kilim.

'My father would look for a rational and a religious explanation,' he said. 'The hand of God. Divine reason. Even for the bloody war. Destiny, God's purpose . . . I'm sick of people looking for an explanation of God or an experience of the Divine in extremes of depravity. Going to the depths because that's the only place you feel alive. But what's the use if you can't find the Divine in the everyday? The politicians had plenty of reasons for the war. And the priests. Praying for victory, it's just the same. Look at this Gupta, the man who killed Simpson. To claim you know the will of God and slaughter on the strength of it. Sheer bloody arrogance. Convinced that he'll be reborn in a better place when he's hanged. Gupta wrote that himself in a letter to his mother. Some Nationalist rag just published it. Bastards. Just bastards. You have to be ruthless with people like that.'

He looked up at her, looked away. She knew that he wanted her to agree with him. She suspected that his duty . . . it must have put him into some difficult spots. Forced him to make some extremely difficult decisions. She could understand that but she couldn't just let him get away with that argument.

'It's not just that though, is it?' she said. 'These young men . . . like Gupta – they're so desperate for their independence . . .'

Glitter of anger in his eyes.

'Yes,' he said. 'What he did . . . I'll say this for him . . . he had courage. He walked right into the heart of the bloody Raj and shot a leading officer. I respect that as a soldier. But killing someone in the name of God . . . Well . . . it has to make you question your own belief, doesn't it? Doesn't strengthen it. Because if Gupta is convinced he's bound for a better world after shooting Simpson, what exactly do *we* believe we'll find after death? You for example, Dr Devenish, what do you believe?'

She was a bit shocked to be put on the spot.

'I suppose,' she said, 'I suppose I believe that consciousness goes on – experiences worlds that we don't even have any concept of.'

'You're a Theosophist, aren't you?' he said.

'Yes, I suppose I am,' she said. 'Of a sort.'

He leaned forward, not so inward-looking, a little angry still.

'Quite a mix, isn't it, Theosophy?' he said.

'I suppose it's trying to be universal,' she said. 'Open to all religions.'

'Open to all religions,' Davies said. 'But what do Theosophists actually believe in? Brahman and Atman? Allah? Jesus in Heaven?'

She was on the back foot because she wasn't entirely a true believer; but she didn't want it to appear that she was backing down in front of his aggressive argument.

'Evolution,' she said. 'Spiritual evolution: that we can learn how to discover the truth.'

'The truth?' he said.

'The answer to that well-known question . . .' she began.

'As revealed by Koot Hoomi and the Hidden Masters to the pipe-smoking Madame Blavatsky?'

Simpson, she thought. His death would be stark and present in his mind just now. She wanted to be sympathetic to him.

'Only if you're literal-minded,' she said.

'Most Theosophists seem to be,' Davies said. 'They all want to believe in HPB and *The Secret Doctrine*. Including Mrs Besant. I can't really buy it.'

'Never could myself,' Richard joined in, a little slurred.

'I suppose I don't take it at all literally,' she said. 'Perhaps I'm a Theosophical heretic.'

The truth was that she was disillusioned by Theosophy and she enjoyed Davies's relatively down-to-earth approach to religion. An approximation of grace – she liked that.

'Pardon my frankness . . .' Davies said.

He put down his glass on the coffee table.

'But I think the Theosophical Society is run by charlatans, cranks and con artists,' he said.

She sat back on the sofa. He was attacking her beliefs quite openly and, rather than make her angry, it made her appreciate what he was trying to find in the Anglican Church. He wasn't conditioned by the Applebys of the world. He was looking for something far simpler and far more profound – that grace, that mystery, that he'd talked about, and that was something she found genuinely attractive about him. But she couldn't let him attack everybody in the Theosophical Society.

'You're being unfair,' she said. 'For all her faults, you can't deny that Mrs Besant is an extraordinary woman. She's pioneered birth control, been president of the Indian National Congress, leader of the Theosophical Society. She's made a gigantic impact all over the world. Especially in women's lives. But not only for women. I'd stand by her one hundred per cent.'

'She's made the most abysmal public blunders,' Davies said. 'Proved herself a complete bloody charlatan in the public eye. She made a right balls-up over her Krishnamurti, didn't she? I'm shocked that you could give her so much credit after even her own so-called avatar disavowed her.'

The look in his eye was earnest, intimate and disconcerting.

'That still doesn't diminish her achievements, does it?' she said.

'I suppose that for me it does.'

'All her mistakes might look appalling because she operates on a grand scale.'

'Like Ivan the Terrible,' Davies said.

'No comparison,' Christina said. 'Mrs Besant will go down in history as a great woman. I doubt that your Reverend Appleby will be remembered for anything at all.'

His head tilted for a moment. He smiled at her.

'All right, all right,' Davies said. 'Appleby is a bloody disaster. But all this Indian religion, all these gods and goddesses, makes absolutely no sense, does it, Hindu or Muslim? And there's a good dose of that in your Theosophy.'

'Your mystery,' she said. 'That's what I'm interested in. And how you experience it: your state of grace. I don't think any religion has a monopoly on that. Certainly not Christianity. And if we British want to understand what's going on in India, all over Asia, we'll have to respect the beliefs of Hindu and Muslim on an equal footing with rationalism. An exclusive belief in reason has its own disastrously myopic limitations.'

'I suppose every religion has its own absurdity,' Davies said.

'And none of them seems capable of seeing it either,' Richard interjected.

Davies turned to Richard.

'What about you, Richard?' Davies said. 'When you were at Cambridge, did you subscribe to religion being the opium of the masses?'

Richard set down his sherry. His eyes looked a little blood-shot.

'I've no objection to a bit of opium,' Richard said. 'In moderation, of course. But all this religion can get you into a terrible confusion, can't it?'

'Confusion?' Christina said.

'Take your father,' Richard said. 'He seems to have bought into some bloody strange business up there in Bhutan, if you ask me.'

Davies grabbed his glass and shot Richard a hard look over the rim of it as he sipped. Richard missed it. Christina didn't.

'What about my father?' she asked.

A crooked drunken smile on Richard's face.

'You know how your father is,' Richard said. 'Once he gets obsessed with something – hook, line and sinker or not at all. And with this Shabdrung, Himalayan business, well . . . it's one thing to study it but the Colonel seems completely besotted by it.'

'How's that?' she asked.

'He's taken to this Shabdrung completely,' Richard said. 'And he's got himself into a lot of hot water through it, too.'

'Hot water?' she said.

Davies intervened.

'Your father got involved in trying to resolve a dispute in Bhutan but isn't having any success.'

'But why the hot water?' she said.

'This dispute . . . political dispute . . . the Department believes that your father has done all he can; and wants him to return to Calcutta. He insists on resolving the conflict before he leaves, out of loyalty to the Shabdrung. That doesn't sit well with the more impatient members of the Department. Especially with all this trouble going on. This Shabdrung . . . your father's become quite close to him but he's giving the political king a good deal of grief. The Maharaja feels that the Shabdrung is threatening his sovereignty.'

Davies's hand drifted up close to his temple again.

'It would be better if your father just came back here as we've asked him to,' he said. 'That's all. And left Bhutan to the Bhutanese.'

'Is that why *you're* going to Bhutan?' she said. 'To bring him back.'

'I have to try and persuade him,' Davies said.

'So you . . . weren't being honest with me about the Maharaja's investiture ceremony?'

Davies sat bolt upright in the sofa.

'Good God. I would never . . . Absolutely not . . . never deceive you over that. The investiture is on. We'll have the ceremony in Bumthang and then we'll go on to Talo to see your father. Just as I said. Of course . . .'

Davies shot Richard a furious glance. Richard scratched the back of his head and looked away.

'Of course,' Davies said, 'the Department wants your father to leave Bhutan and it's not very wise of him to refuse. But I'm sure I can persuade him to see reason and come back to Calcutta. We're old friends.'

She smoothed down her dress over her knees. The skin on

her hands began to itch again beneath her white cotton gloves. She took another sip of her sherry.

Hari came back into the room.

'Time for lunch, sahib,' he said.

She was joining an expedition to get her father out of Bhutan. All that talk about the war and order . . . and religion . . . and the Church, she had hoped she might share something with Davies. But Davies was full of secrets. Just like any damned Department man. Just like her father?

All right. Nothing had changed. She was still going to Bhutan with Davies who was leading this expedition with who knows how many reasons for going up there into the Himalayas: for the investiture, for her father, to resolve this political dispute between the monarchs. God knows there might be a whole lot more reasons of which she would have no inkling. That was what the Department was like. She knew all about that. It was what her father did and was still trying to do. She couldn't help but think that, up to now, she had been very naive over Davies, but it didn't make her any the less fascinated by him. She still wanted to understand him. And perhaps if she understood Davies she might understand her father a little better, too. These men who came to India, they were full of drive, initiative, obsession, love of power. And one of the ways they kept their power was through this maintenance of secrecy. Her father had kept his secrets even from his own family: from his wife, from her. Should she expect Davies to be any different? She was a grown woman living in India, a country in political turmoil. There was no reason why Bhutan should be any different. One of the aims of the expedition was to bring her father out of Bhutan.

After the disaster of the clinic, and the loss of Lakshmi, the talk of order had seemed so appealing for a moment. But order was something that was imposed upon the natural chaos of the universe. It was imposed by power. The power of Almighty God was conspicuous by its mystery at best, by its absence at worst.

The power of the Raj was conspicuous by its armies and weapons and soldiers and Political Departments that kept order in the political chaos of India. And its power was inconspicuous and perhaps more effective where it worked unseen. Davies was part of that structure. And so was her father. If she was being moved by the workings of some Divine and Mysterious Power towards some hidden goal, she was equally in the grip of the earthly workings of the Department as it sought to control the forces loose on the subcontinent.

She took Davies's hand. His eyes widened and his mouth opened slightly.

'These are difficult times for all of us,' she said. 'I understand that.'

Why had she said that? Why had she done that? She let go of his hand. Hands connected to the heart, she thought. Her damaged hands. And so was Davies's heart damaged? She could smell the hurt in him like the reek of blood in a butcher's shop. The war . . . what else . . . ? Something had got to him. That hard mask with which he faced the world – of his being so down to earth – it really was fractured. She wanted to expose him like peeling the cracked shell off a dead crab to reveal the soft and rotten meat beneath. She knew enough about psychology to know that she might very well be putting herself on dangerous ground. If she got too close to his hurt, he might lash out at her for prying. She had her own sense of guilt over Lakshmi; and for being her father's daughter, too. A Department man. Perhaps she was looking for punishment, too. Another kind of cleansing. She wasn't afraid of what she might discover in Davies's dark and damaged heart. It seemed to be giving her a lot of insight into her own. Perhaps that was why she found him so curiously attractive. She was a Theosophist. She liked to uncover secrets.

PART THREE

DEWANGIRI TO BUMTHANG, FEBRUARY 1931

CHAPTER ELEVEN

AS EACH CRAMP SQUEEZED THE MEAT OF HER WOMB LIKE A VICE, so her fingers dug into the soft leather edge of the back seat of the Rover while the stuffy car jolted its way over the rutted roads towards Dewangiri. She rested her head against a strut of the black canvas top that was up to protect them against the hot sun and the dust of the dirt road over the last of the Duars Plain. Through the grubby window, the rice paddies were brown and empty, desolate in this season, so long after the rains. She was nauseous and thirsty and sweaty and the pad between her legs was soaked and she didn't want to ask the driver to stop so that she might change it; she just wanted to get to their evening's camp.

Davies, beside her, gazed through the dust on his window as the sun dipped below the far horizon and the car lurched on into the hills. She had fallen asleep beside him in the heat of the day and let her head fall against him. When she had awoken, his arm had been around her shoulder. He'd disentangled himself before she was fully awake and let her gather her wits without being at all forward. He was still being the gentleman, even rather slow, shy with her, stiff and hot in his khaki uniform. He was holding himself back. She could sense that he was interested in her and she was enjoying his attention.

On each side of the dirt road, more banyan and banana trees appeared on the slopes above them as the *terai* took over from the plain. Flocks of pink-bellied parakeets took to the air and swirled through the trees, scared into flight by the noise of the engine. With the car's rise into the hills, bamboo thickets increasingly closed in on either side of them, and Govinda slowed the car and turned on its headlights to light up the thickly knuckled green trunks. Through the half-canopy of leaves, the sky's arch darkened to purple at the zenith, but burning with reds and oranges in the west, glinting between the black tree trunks that rose in denser growths as the road rose steadily towards the north.

'Look,' Davies said.

One hand fell beside her thigh and his other hand pointed past the driver's shoulder and beyond the windscreen. She could feel the butterflies in her belly with his hand that close to her leg. She peered ahead to where he was pointing. The forest was suddenly thinner and fires glimmered in the distance where the hillside flattened out. Relief and nausea flowed equally through her body at the signs of making camp. Her bladder was full. The car surged ahead, gears grinding, Govinda anxious, it seemed, to be done with his driving. Christina used her cotton handkerchief to wipe the sweat off her forehead. Wisps of red hair had come loose from her hairpins. Her linen frock stuck to her back. There was nothing she could do about that. She reached behind her for the panama on the seat back and then fitted it onto her head, its inner leather band sticky against her skin.

'Look,' she said. 'Now we're in Bhutan, can't I call you by your Christian name?'

He straightened up in his seat. His jaw tightened a little. He nodded.

'Owen,' he said. 'It's Owen.'

'Christina,' she said.

'Christina, yes, of course. Thank you.'

The Rover and the rattling Crossley behind it with their escort and all their tents and supplies reached a flat clearing in the forest and slowed to a stop. Dominating the entrance to the camp, standing on a small knoll, was a massive pipal tree, its roots forming thick buttresses at the base of its trunk and spreading its branches, heavy with leaves and hung with ragged scarves of rotted white cotton, as if in offering.

A flock of green, pintailed pigeons fluttered and tumbled through the branches, or primped and preened among them as if in some kind of ornithological metropolis. The fires of the camp cast flickering light among the birds, each one surrounded as if by a glowing nimbus. And if this incendiary play gave the camp the appearance of a dreamscape, then the soldiers who awaited them beyond the dusty windows of the Rover redoubled it. They were like something out of *Ivanhoe*, firelight glinting on steel breastplates and on their brazen spiked helmets.

She stared through the window of the Rover. The armoured soldiers had high cheekbones, wide faces, narrow eyes, thin moustaches. Chain mail hung like metal hair from their helmets to their shoulders. More chain mail hung from shoulders to elbows. Short striped skirts fell from waist to knees and their calves and feet were bare. Each soldier held a small hide shield, round and studded, in his left hand, and a long curved sword in the right, resting at shoulder arms.

A second company of soldiers was formed up at right angles to the armoured platoon. These others were dressed in modern uniform like a troop of dishevelled Gurkhas, but were also barefoot, their uniform trousers rolled and bunched above the calves. They wore slouch hats, one side of the brim fastened up to the side of the crown, and each man held a vintage rifle diagonally across his chest.

Owen ran a comb through his oiled hair and put on his peaked military cap. Govinda opened the door of the car and Owen got out first. The swords and rifles of the bizarre soldiers shifted to present arms and Owen saluted them. This parade-ground welcome was like a Gilbert and Sullivan operetta come to life. It would be easy to forget that these outlandish soldiers had once defeated a British Expeditionary Force in battle. Perhaps the generals of the Raj had also assumed them to be a pantomime army.

Govinda came around to Christina's side of the car and opened the door for her. She lifted her canvas satchel from between her feet, slid her sweaty body along the seat and pushed herself out of the car. She set foot on the soil of Bhutan, Alice through the looking glass racked with menstrual cramps, the sweat cooling on her forehead and on her back under her sticky frock, and she was desperate to empty her bladder in the shadows of the luxuriant rainforest.

The British expedition's own sepoy escort jumped down from the back of the Crossley and hastily formed a line beside their lorry. Sergeant Thomas, the NCO, got out of the cab and took his place at the end of the ranks. Military manoeuvres reminded her of boys at play.

Owen ushered her forward towards a short, moustachioed Bhutanese in a colourful striped tunic. The Bhutanese official held a white silk scarf on his open palms. He had a wide face, and his hair was cut short in the English manner; it had thinned considerably above the temples. He was a little jowly and slightly overweight. He approached Owen who saluted him and then bent his head while the official hung the scarf over his neck.

'Welcome back to Bhutan, Major Davies.'

'A pleasure, Sri Tobgye,' Owen said.

He was beaming with diplomatic affability, his face slightly flushed under the peak of his cap.

A young boy, in clothes similar to the official's, approached with another white scarf. The Bhutanese took the scarf from the child and approached Christina.

'And this must be Dr Devenish,' he said.

'This is Sri Sonam Tobgye,' Owen said. 'Personal adviser to the Maharaja, Jigme Wangchuk.'

Christina half bobbed in kind of reluctant curtsy. It was easy to imagine the Bhutanese Maharaja as some kind of Nanky Poo, though she suspected that his Lord High Executioner would not have a wooden sword, or be singing comic songs. India might at times seem alien to a Briton but, judging from these bizarre costumes, Bhutan was closer to the world of Topsy-Turvy.

She bowed her head instinctively for Tobgye to lay the scarf over her neck.

'Come this way, please,' he said.

Temporary huts with stilt-like trunks for pillars, palm-thatched roofs and a weave of split bamboo for the walls surrounded the clearing. Great cascades of flowers, gathered from the jungle thickets, hung down over every lintel, the opulence of whites and reds and oranges and yellows intensified by the dying of the sun's light.

'Please have a seat,' Tobgye said.

He indicated a camp chair in front of one of the makeshift huts. Canvas creaked as she lowered herself into the chair. Her back ached from the long car journey, and her bladder too, painfully so. Owen sat beside her with Tobgye on his left. Mosquitoes floated and whined around her head and she fanned at the insects with her gloved palm in order to stop them landing. Always a chance of malaria.

A Bhutanese officer barked an order and the armoured soldiers and their uniformed cohorts made an about face and marched off from beside the dust-covered Rover towards a group of tents that had been set up down the slope near the riverbank. About twenty horses and mules stood tethered at a picket line. The air was still and heavy.

There'll be hundreds of mosquitoes down there, she thought.

She began a rapid mental calculation of the amount of quinine that she had brought. Sergeant Thomas called out to their own escort and the sepoys all marched down to the riverbank, presumably to set up field quarters for themselves.

Throughout the upper camp, men taller than the outlandish soldiers drifted among the pots and boxes of the camp.

Newaris, she thought, from Nepal.

They all wore small woven hats of coloured cotton. Beneath their homespun smocks, their brown legs and feet were bare. Some knelt, their machetes rising and falling. There the clack, clack, clack of firewood being chopped; others were at the pots, stirring; three more squatted and slapped chapatis between their palms; and over one of the fires a spitted wild pig was roasting.

The young Bhutanese boy brought a wooden jug with a large well-turned wooden bowl that was clad in silver beaten into flower shapes. Tobgye stood and took the bowl from the child.

I could do with a drink, she thought. It might ease the cramps.

From the jug the child filled the bowl with a greyish liquid and then Tobgye stood and, with both hands, held it out to Owen. Familiar with the ritual no doubt, Owen stood up too. He was at least a head taller than the Bhutanese host. The only discomfort that Owen showed from the journey was that his face was damp with sweat under his peaked cap, his khaki uniform a little wrinkled.

'Please, Major Davies,' Tobgye said. 'Accept our welcome to Druk Yul.'

Owen tipped up the bowl of liquor and downed it in one gulp. Tobgye took the jug from the servant boy and refilled the bowl. Davies didn't hesitate on the second either and Tobgye refilled the bowl once more. Davies obliged him on that one, too.

'Thank you, Major Davies,' Tobgye said.

The Bhutanese boy took the jug from Tobgye's hands, and Tobgye took the bowl from Davies, and had the boy refill it again. He approached Christina, holding the bowl in the same gesture of offering as he had made to Davies. Davies waved her to her feet. She felt as if her bones were still vibrating after the jolting car ride. She took the first bowl and drained it. It was not unpleasant, slightly sweet and watery with a bitter aftertaste. She assumed it was *chang*, made from fermented barley. She offered the bowl back to Tobgye but he simply took the jug from his servant and refilled it for her. Everything in threes, then. She bolted the liquor back. Tobgye nodded in appreciation, waved the jug and filled her bowl for the third time. This *chang* was really quite refreshing. She downed the third bowl.

'Thank you, thank you,' he said.

'Owen,' Christina said. 'I really must excuse myself.'

'Oh, of course,' he said.

Tobgye handed bowl and jug back to the young servant.

'Do forgive me,' Tobgye said. 'I should have thought that you might have been uncomfortable after such a long journey. There are no women with us, but if you don't mind, I'll show you the way.'

She wondered where he had gone to learn English. Calcutta? Maybe St Paul's in Kalimpong? He had almost no accent.

'Thank you,' she said.

He walked her towards a bamboo thicket behind the hut. A path had been cut through the tall stalks.

'Through here,' he said, and left her to make her own way into the brake.

There was still enough light to see by and she looked for a place to squat. Fifteen yards into the brake, the patterns of the stalks and leaves formed an intricate cross-hatched screen which would hide her from the rest of the camp. The night chirping of the cicadas made a steady pulse in the woods all around her and the mosquitoes whined and danced around her face. She pulled down her drawers. Her pad was saturated. She wiped herself as best she could with the edge of it and laid it aside. The rich and earthy scent immediately drew a buzzing squadron of fat black flies that circled and settled and circled again, around and upon it.

She squatted and peed, relaxed the muscles of her body with the flow. The alcohol in the *chang* had started to take effect and a deep warmth penetrated her bones. Around her head more mosquitoes whined but she cared less about them now.

She retrieved her handkerchief from the pocket of her frock and patted herself dry with it, staining it a little. She would need to wash before bed. One of the bearers could bring her water from the river. She took a fresh cloth pad from her canvas satchel, tucked it between her legs and tied up the string. She was ready to face Tobgye and Davies again, but especially another drink. She pulled up her drawers, adjusted her frock and followed the path out of the thicket. Tobgye had waited for her. He seemed to want to say something to her but he didn't. They walked in silence back to the hut, Tobgye at her shoulder. Owen stood when they got back to the canvas chairs.

'Please, sit down,' Tobgye said. 'You must be famished.'

She was. Owen must be, too. Govinda would be eating with the soldiers. Newari bearers arrived with platters piled with saffron rice and set them down on the low table in front of their seats. But before they could touch the food, Tobgye filled the *chang* bowl again. Owen drank the customary three, and then she too knocked back another three. She was beginning to feel numbed and drunk. Finally, the Newaris spooned the rice into bowls and Tobgye took one and handed it to Owen; the next he gave to Christina; and then he handed them both a pair of chopsticks. He offered each of them a wooden cup filled with hot butter tea. He was being a very gracious host but there was something about the way he glanced at her that made her uneasy.

'Please, have some tea,' Tobgye said. 'And something to eat.'

The tea was rich. It didn't sit well with the beery taste of the *chang*. She hoped that she wouldn't have to vomit.

'How is His Majesty the Maharaja?' Owen ventured.

'He's very well and looking forward to seeing you,' Tobgye said. 'Colonel Marshall is with him. We should arrive in plenty of time for the investiture ceremony.'

'I'm sure Dr Devenish would like news of her father,' Owen said.

Tobgye nodded.

'Colonel Devenish is still with the Shabdrung. I believe Dr Devenish's father is in good health. Your father is a great friend to the Bhutanese people. He's attempting to mediate in this unfortunate border dispute. We've still not managed to come to an agreement, I'm afraid. The Shabdrung's chamberlain is being particularly difficult: an arrogant man giving very bad advice.'

Before she could reply, more platters arrived piled with roasted meat. It made her nervous that they had mentioned her father and then let the subject drop. She leaned forward and pulled off her gloves. Tobgye obviously noticed the still-healing skin.

'Please, have some meat,' he said.

She wished that Tobgye wouldn't stare at her so. She took a knife, chose the leanest of a rack of ribs and cut one bone loose to gnaw on. The meat dripped fat and made her fingers slippery. Whatever Tobgye said about her father would only be a political nicety anyway. She would have to wait and see what the real situation was.

Tobgye picked up the wooden jug and filled the *chang* bowl again. He was trying to get them drunk. Christina didn't care about that. She would happily oblige him. It would help her sleep. She was completely exhausted and overstimulated and when she finally lay down she didn't want her mind to race, thinking about all the problems and possibilities that lay ahead. The bowl appeared in front of her and she easily downed the sweet liquid. Owen took the bowl and had the young Bhutanese boy fill it. Returning the gesture, he offered three bowls to Tobgye and then turned to Christina.

Owen's face had slackened a little; his eyes had softened. He offered her the bowl with his shoulder to Tobgye. She held his gaze as she drank and then handed the bowl back to him. Tobgye's complexion was already dark from alcohol. He leaned forward towards her.

'We in Bhutan have great respect for your father, Dr Devenish.'

'I can't wait to see him,' she said. 'He's in Talo, isn't he?'

Tobgye nodded.

'So Major Davies has told you about the Shabdrung, Dr Devenish?'

'Very little,' she said. 'He's the religious leader of the country, isn't he?'

Tobgye's dark eyes immediately became lucid as if the alcohol had had no effect on him whatsoever.

'We have to wonder about that, I'm afraid,' he said.

'Really?'

'He's broken his monastic vows,' Tobgye said.

'Broken his vows?'

'Chastity. He's . . . Some of the clergy wonder, now, whether they were mistaken in thinking him the true reincarnation of the previous Shabdrung. The Maharaja is very concerned.'

He sat back. She glanced at Owen. He was sitting upright in his chair and seemed to have no intention of joining in any discussion about the Shabdrung's merits or demerits or his metaphysical status as god-king.

'To you Bhutan might seem rather backward in its beliefs,' Tobgye said. 'But there are rumours going around the countryside that the Shabdrung is practising magical rites to destroy the Maharaja.'

'Magical rites?'

'Some of the clergy say that the Shabdrung seems to be out of control. Possessed by some spirit. Anyway, not very appropriate for the religious guide of the country.'

It was bizarre to listen to this cultured and obviously Machiavellian diplomat talking about magical rites and reincarnations, although plenty of politicians in London and Bombay had joined the Theosophical Society.

'And what does my father have to say about this?' she asked.

'He doesn't want to see Bhutan divided by this dispute,' Tobgye said. 'He understands how grave the situation is, but there have been some problems at the border. The Shabdrung is being rather stubborn: perhaps because of this overinfluential chamberlain.'

'I'm sure that this dispute can be brought to an amicable conclusion,' Owen said.

'My advice to the Maharaja was to take more drastic action,' Tobgye said.

Had he let that slip because he was drunk or for a more calculated effect?

Tobgye refilled the *chang* bowl.

'But His Majesty,' continued Tobgye, 'respects the person of the Shabdrung, as do all Bhutanese. He is loath to act forcibly against the spiritual leader of the people.'

'My father's still with him?' she said.

'Colonel Devenish hates to give up,' Tobgye said and he smiled knowingly at her.

Yes, of course, she knew her father's character. But what about this Shabdrung? Practising black magic. Breaking his vows. Out of control. This didn't sound like the Hidden Master that she had hoped to find.

All the muscles of Tobgye's fleshy face were relaxed, the skin glowing, the eyes clear and open. He was used to dealing with the Department, sure that Davies, at least, was on his side. And he was trying to mould *her* views of the Shabdrung to match his own. What had her father said in the letter? *No country is without its political tensions.* It seemed as if they were already involved in some sort of medieval court intrigue. It might have all been magical and romantic if her father hadn't been so deeply involved. Owen rested a reassuring hand on her forearm, and it was her turn to be surprised. He was a little drunk. She wanted him to be on her side. She laid her left hand on the back of Owen's and intertwined her fingers with his. He squeezed her fingers for a moment and drew his hand away.

Three of the bizarrely armoured soldiers, like revenants who had drifted through a rupture in time, came up from the river-bank and squatted at the edge of the bamboo thicket not fifteen feet away from the hut. Their hard-angled faces were framed by the spiked helmets and the hanging chain mail. They stared at her silently as if she, not they, belonged to some epoch that was utterly alien.

CHAPTER TWELVE

I

SNOW CLUNG TO THE ROCKY PEAKS HIGH ABOVE THE PINE-forested valley and in the hollows on the hills which the sun had failed to reach. Mid-afternoon, on this ninth day of their march, Davies checked his watch. They had been in the saddle for nearly six hours with only one stop for tea and rice. Christina seemed to be bearing up well. Truth to tell, the deeper they got into Bhutan, the more radiant she looked. Those bright green eyes of hers glittered. Every morning she was ready for their daily routine: breakfast before dawn, then she dealt with the villagers who besieged her field clinic for the hour that they allowed every day. After she'd closed the clinic, the expedition set off on the next leg of the journey. And he was also aware of another change in her. Last night, at supper, she had leaned in close to him near the fire, her breast pressing against his upper arm. And he hadn't moved away from her. She must have known. He had held off thinking about an affair with her as best he could on the long trek towards Bumthang, but the feel of her so close to him made it all but impossible to ignore the possibility. He had to be careful in front of Tobgye. She was the Colonel's daughter, after all, and the Colonel was about as endearing to Tobgye as a splinter under the fingernails.

Up here on the high plains, Calcutta seemed like a bad dream.

But it was a bad dream that wouldn't go away, in which he, Davies, had perpetrated as many horrors as he had witnessed. Away from it now, he could see how much his life down there in the Ganges delta had hollowed him out. His helplessness watching Emma die had numbed him; and all those vigorous interrogations that he had personally had a hand in. He couldn't escape just by riding away and deeper into Bhutan. Up here, his sleep was lighter and the world of dream closer; images of Dinesh Gupta's face, swollen like a bruised and rotten pumpkin, filled his nightmares. And Gupta wasn't the only one who haunted him. Eleven years in India fighting the terrorists. And then there was everything he had seen and done in the trenches with bayonet, bullet and trench knife. Without the routine of everyday life in Calcutta, his memory was rotten with the faces of the dead and broken. And the world around him seemed more sharply defined in the Himalayan brightness: the edges of the peaks, the reflection of the sun on the distant snow, white turning to pink at sunset, the feathery edges of the pines. And this absurd army of Tobgye's with their medieval swords and rhinoceros-hide shields might have arisen from a malarial delirium.

He rode beside Christina Devenish in the centre of a column of soldiers. The afternoon sun slanted under the brim of her hat and lit up her freckled face, her graceful body. She was his still-solid link to the reality of the world of clubs and offices and green cardboard files, and motor cars and Webley .455 revolvers: the stuff of Raj, of Empire. This bohemian, once of Bloomsbury, birth control doctor of Bombay, this free-lover and Theosophist, was as much a part of Britain as he was. And part of India too in some grafted-on sort of way. And she had started to flirt with him. He hadn't imagined that. He did want to reach out to her. He would, he had to . . . at the first chance he got. She was the right age, unmarried, and a woman's touch, that's what he needed: someone to hold in his arms, to hold him in her arms, to ease away the awful bloody memories of what he had done, justified or not, in the service of his country. Cleansing grace. Being with a woman could give you that. He wasn't being mawkish. It was what he wanted: as simple as spreading salve on a burn. He was sick of what he had done. He had made himself numb, cut himself off from feeling anything, especially since Emma's death. That's what had made it so easy to be there at Gupta's beating and all those other interrogations.

'Owen?' she said.

She had caught him staring at her.

'I'm sorry,' he said.

She looked puzzled.

'Sorry?'

'Oh, it's nothing,' he said.

'I want to know,' she said. 'All this trouble with the Shabdrung. I mean . . . a simple border dispute over grazing rights turns into a potential civil war, supposedly backed by magical spells . . . Do you believe all that? It seems so absurd.'

He reined in closer to her, glanced around. Tobgye was well up in front, his back to them and out of earshot. Davies fidgeted with the reins.

'Nothing unusual for Bhutan,' he said.

'Not unusual?'

She leaned forward in the saddle to stretch her back and legs, her profile, all tweed-clad and in a brimmed straw hat, sharp against the dark and feathery pine backdrop, and then she eased back to sit again. He was glad that he had something to offer to her, this knowledge that he had, a lot of it gleaned from her father.

'Not in Bhutan,' he said. 'The state of Bhutan was founded by some sort of religious charismatic: a certain Ngawang Namgyal, the first of the Shabdrungs. And when he died, the clergy went looking for his reincarnation. When they were supposed to have found him, this young child, a regent was elected from among the Bhutanese nobility while they waited for the boy to grow up. So you had this system continue for centuries where they would look for reincarnation after reincarnation and choose a new child based on some kind of divination.'

'Like Tibet,' she said. 'The Dalai Lamas.'

'Exactly,' he said. 'Then, as time went on, many of the young Shabdrungs were murdered before they came of age so that the regents could keep their hold on power.'

'They killed the children?' she asked.

He nodded.

'And the aristocrats fought among each other for the regency.'

'That's awful.'

'Forty years ago,' he said, 'the present Maharaja's grandfather – he was known as the Black Regent – prayed to his protector gods and made a kind of vow. The gist of it was that, if he, the Black Regent, was the rightful ruler of Bhutan then he prayed that he might rip out the hearts and lungs of his enemies and offer them to his gods. And if he wasn't the rightful ruler, he prayed that his enemies might rip out *his* heart and lungs and offer them to *their* protector gods. It appears that he was, in fact, the rightful ruler.'

Her mouth was slightly open. But she had lived among the anomalies of India for long enough, as a Theosophist, so that she couldn't have been too surprised.

'And did he keep his pact?' she asked.

'Piled his enemies' guts on specially built altars and burned them,' Davies said.

'Good God,' she said. 'And what happened to him?'

'He remained in power all his life. Before he died, he declared his son to be the new king of Bhutan and abolished the secular rule of the Shabdrungs. He said that the Shabdrungs would be in charge of the religious affairs of the new kingdom, which kept the religious faithful happy, while he, and his heirs, would take care of the politics. Jigme Wangchuk is only the second king of Bhutan and he's afraid that the present Shabdrung is already a threat to his hold on power. That's the real dispute your father's trying to sort out.'

She guided the mule around a deep trench in the track. Davies came up on her left side again.

'But why would the Shabdrung be a threat if he's only the religious king?' she asked.

'The present Shabdrung is in his twenties. He sees the present Maharaja as bit of a despot. And doesn't like the influence of the British Empire in the country. That doesn't sit well with the ruling Maharaja. Or with the Department, of course.'

She nodded.

'But why is the Maharaja pro-British? They fought us once, didn't they?'

'Fifty years ago the Maharaja's grandfather beat us in a major battle. So we organised an expeditionary force the next year. This time the Bhutanese surrendered without much of a fight, with all the firepower we brought up here. But we had nothing significant to show for it except a bit of scrubland that we annexed on the Bengal border. Over the years, it became obvious that we had no intention of annexing the whole of Bhutan. So the present king's father became a lot more worried about the Tibetans and the Chinese. If they got the Shabdrung's favour, either of them could use the Shabdrung as a figurehead to justify an invasion. So the Maharaja allied himself with the British. Perfect for us, of course. Bhutan is an ideal buffer against China. Himalayan border, terrible terrain for an army to cross.'

He turned in the saddle and nodded towards the mountains. The land through which they advanced had become flat and wide, but to the north the rocky snow-capped peaks of the Himalayas formed a massive natural wall between Bhutan and Tibet.

'Do you think that this Shabdrung really practises black magic?' she asked.

'I have absolutely no idea,' he said. 'The Bhutanese *are* famous for poisons. Maybe that's a sort of black art. Their religion is officially Buddhism, but they've absorbed enough of the old primitive folk beliefs that it wouldn't surprise me if they did practise some bloody bizarre rituals. Each district has its protectors and mountain gods. Fearsome-looking images. You see them painted on the walls of the village temples.'

She fell into silence as she rode beside him.

He hoped that he had impressed her with his knowledge of the history of the country and its customs. It had been her father who had taught him just about all he knew of it, too. Had not just taught him but had taken him to see some of the most bizarre rituals imaginable. Spirit possession, where ordinary farmers, men and women both, had become utterly crazed and had flayed a live pig, tearing off the skin with their bare hands. They performed impossible feats of strength to overpower the squealing, terrified animal that they'd imprisoned in a deep and wide pit. All that blood and terror by firelight. Like a vision of hell. The Colonel had revelled in it. And Davies had to admit to himself that he had too. He had taken part in rituals that very few Europeans could ever hope to see. He and the Colonel had become lost in it. Sought them out. Davies could understand where the Colonel's daughter had acquired her reputation as an occultist and free-lover. She could easily have inherited some bizarre passions from her father's bloodline. Perhaps he, Davies, could take her to see some special ritual on one of the festivals of the ferocious gods on the Hindu calendar. It would be very tempting should the chance arise.

In front of them, the head of the column halted on a spur of land upon which was a small thicket of rhododendron bushes and the syces and bearers were already unpacking the tents and stringing up a picket line between two alder trees for the mules. Davies pulled up the mule and slid from the saddle. Christina dismounted too. Davies ordered a syce to lead their animals away. If he was to make a move for her, it would have to be soon. Well before they came to her father. By then, she would be completely taken up by the reunion and he would fade into the background of her thoughts.

'Come on,' Davies said. 'Let's go for a walk. It's so bloody frustrating sitting in a saddle all day, don't you think?'

She looked a little surprised.

'A walk?' she said. 'Where could we possibly go?'

'Down along that stream bed,' he said.

He pointed down along the small watercourse lined with white poplars. The stream led between two small hills.

'All right then,' she said.

She touched his forearm and immediately began to walk away from him towards the stream. As they passed the sepoy cooks, he picked up a square wooden crate top that had been prised off a ration box. He swung it casually as he hurried to catch up with her. The path led down into a copse of poplars and she was soon out of sight. The only sound was that of the stream bubbling beside him. She slowed down when she reached the small wood and he enjoyed the swing of her hips, the slim body, the sun on her copper hair, the straightness of her back under her tweed jacket. He came up behind her, touched her arm and she turned to face him.

'Do you shoot?' he asked.

Her eyes widened.

'Shoot?'

'Yes, shoot. I imagine that the Colonel would have taught you.'

It was true, of course. The women and girls in the various cantonments had usually learned to shoot, especially in times of terrorist scares.

'I haven't fired a gun in years,' she said. 'And I don't like to shoot animals.'

'Then you do know how to use a gun,' he said.

He smiled at her and swung up the crate top like a square shield between them.

'We'll have some target practice,' he said. 'Fire off a few rounds with the Webley. I don't want to get too rusty. And it'll blow away the bloody cobwebs from sitting in the saddle all day.'

She reached out to touch his wrist again.

'All right,' she said. 'I'll try.'

And her hand fell away. They were both being coy with each other.

At a bend in the stream was a large open space where the trees had all been felled. Nothing but stumps remained from the stream side to the low scrubby hill about fifty yards away. The late afternoon sun slanted down and lit up the scrub and slash that littered the clearing.

'This'll do,' he said. 'Just watch out for snakes here. They like the slash.'

She shrugged and smiled at his tease. She was an old India hand. She was unlikely to be put out at the mention of snakes. He jogged over to the hillside and set up the square crate top in front of a tree stump about ten yards up the slope. He hadn't had a lot of target practice himself and he didn't want to make a fool of himself in front of her. He made his way back to her. She slipped off her tweed jacket and slid her shirt cuffs back a little. He folded his own jacket, laid it on the ground next to hers, then drew the Webley from his shiny brown leather shoulder holster. She folded her arms under her small breasts.

'You first,' she said.

He nodded, took a sideways stance and levelled the Webley. He closed his left eye and sighted. The bang was harsh and metallic. His right ear hissed. A small puff of dust drifted back to earth about six inches away from the crate top.

'Blast,' he said.

He'd missed badly when he'd shot at Gupta, too. Simpson was already dead by that point. Shooting was really a bloody clumsy business. He sighted again. She raised a hand to the ear closest to him, pressed against it. The pistol bucked and banged in his hand and the target jumped on the hillside, a great divot of wood spiking into the air.

'That's better,' he said.

He fired off four shots in rapid succession, the pistol tight in his grip, and each time the crate top bucked and splintered. It was still only slightly off-square on the hillside.

'Very good,' she said.

It would be embarrassing if she hit the target with her first shot.

'Your turn,' he said.

He ejected the spent casings and reloaded the chambers with the ammunition that he kept on his leather belt. She grasped the Webley and swung it up. It was rather heavy for her to hold steady but she took her stance, sideways to the target like an expert, bent elbow raised to shoulder height, and then swung the revolver down level. She sighted along the barrel and squeezed on the trigger; the bang and the buck were instantaneous. A thick puff of dust drifted on the hillside just above the target. Her arm wavered a little but she brought the gun down level with more confidence this time. The next shot sprayed splinters into the air from the edge of the crate top. She fired again, smack into the middle of the target; it fell over flat.

'Oh, Owen, set it up again, please,' she said. 'This is wonderful.'

'All right,' he said. 'But keep that bloody thing down now.'

She held the hot pistol down by her side and he trotted off through the slash and scrub to set up the battered target again. He jogged back to her and reached for the gun.

'Let's reload it,' he said.

She let him take the Webley and replace the three spent casings with live rounds. He handed the revolver back to her. She swung up the gun again, her high breasts pressing against the cotton of her blouse. She missed with her first shot, her breasts rising and falling with the gun's recoil. She hit dead centre with the next shot, holed it consistently with the next three and spun the target over with the last. He knelt beside his jacket and slipped a box of .455 ammunition from the pocket. She was thrilled. He reloaded and handed her the gun. She fired off another six rounds and the crate top was reduced to splinters. The clearing was in shade and it was chilly now that the sun had sunk behind the high mountains. She was flushed with the noise and excited by the destructive power of the Webley.

'Owen, that was such fun,' she said.

She handed him the reeking pistol and he slipped it back into his holster. Her face was mobile now: the wide mouth twisted, the eyes a little wild.

'Guns,' she said. 'I mean, I know what they can do, what they're for, but you know, it's exhilarating, shooting. You can't help it.'

'Come on, let's go back for some supper,' he said. 'I'm ravenous.'

She put a hand on his shoulder. He reached up for her hand and she let him take it. He ran his fingertips over her left cheek and she pressed her cheek into the backs of his fingers. He leaned over and pressed his lips against hers and her mouth opened under his. He pulled her body into his and her arms were around his back. She pressed into him and then their bodies and mouths and hands seemed to be out of control. He pulled back his head to take a breath and she seemed to recover and she stepped back but gripped him by his shirt front. He looked around them but there was nowhere that they could lie down among the rocks and twigs and broken branches and no guarantee that some sepoy or cook wouldn't come up here looking for firewood.

'We do have a bottle or two of champagne, don't we?' she said.

'We can make it a special occasion,' he said.

She broke away from him and picked up her jacket.

'You're a hell of a shot,' he said.

'It's like riding a bicycle,' she said.

Slow down, he thought.

He took her arm and they started down the path beside the stream and she leaned against him, pressing herself into his ribs until they were in sight of the camp.

2

She had changed into a cotton blouse and white skirt for dinner. She had her Kashmiri shawl to keep off the night's chill but now she was luxuriating in the heat of the campfire, flushed from the champagne. She looked wonderful and she had made that crucial move towards him, and now they were at the start of something and he didn't know where it was going to take them but wherever it was, he wanted it to be somewhere that was good and simple, where he wouldn't have to dirty his hands any more. God, he would have to be careful with her. But not tonight. He didn't want to be careful about anything. He just wanted her in his bed.

'My legs and arms feel as if they're going to float off my body,' she said.

'Champagne at altitude,' he said. 'Can't beat it.'

Truth was that he could feel a slight headache coming on that could well get worse if they carried on drinking. Davies leaned against her in the flickering light. She let the shawl slip from her shoulders. She turned her freckled face to him and pressed her breast against his upper arm and kept it there.

'Time to turn in,' he whispered.

She looked about the campsite. Discreetly, the others had left them alone. There was no sign of Tobgye.

'Come on,' she said.

He stood up and pulled her to her feet. He guided her away from the campfire and into the shadows and drew her – the champagne had worked wonders – towards her tent. It had to be her tent. He would have to slip away later back to his own so as not to arouse suspicion. He lifted the flap for her and she ducked beneath it and he followed her in, no lantern lit, but only the distant firelight on the canvas to light up the bed. His arms were tight around her; and her breath was wine-fresh in his nostrils as he bent his mouth to hers. She pressed back against his kisses and then pulled away as if to reject him, but he gripped her arm and twisted it ever so gently into the small of her back, bending her spine but holding her there, supported so that she knew he wouldn't let her fall backwards. She was light enough. His fingers pressed into her ribcage, and she let her head fall back. His lips were on her clavicle and then the edge of his teeth pressed against her jugular. She let him pull at the buttons of her blouse. He pushed her slip up above her breasts. The bed was right behind her.

'Lift the netting,' he said.

She slipped from his grip. The skin of her wrist was marked where his fingers had been tight around it and that made him harder. She was on the edge of control and abandon: playing victim and seductress. She was used to this kind of play. He found that both arousing and threatening. Other lovers — she'd certainly had them. He had a flush of anger at the unchangeable past. But he wanted her so badly now, he could push his jealousy aside. Push it down.

She lifted the mosquito net. Her back to him, he pulled her towards him and slid her skirt up along her thighs so that it rode up over her buttocks to her waist. Her arms were still above her head, the netting bunched in her fingers. His right hand closed on her small breast. She pushed her buttocks back at the hard press of him. He let her turn to face him and her mouth came up to kiss him. Her lips curled up in a half-drunk and hungry smile. He lowered her back onto the bed, the canvas creaking beneath her. The mosquito net dropped behind him like the drapes of a medieval bed. She lay on her back and let her thighs fall open so that he lay between them. She reached down and pulled at the leather of his belt. He was poised above her, holding up his weight, one hand beside each shoulder, and she unfastened the buttons of his trousers. His cock swung loose and she held the weight of it on her hand. She was so confident in her desire for him, not in the least shy or demure, but he didn't care who she had slept with before. He lowered himself onto one elbow, slid down her cotton drawers and rubbed her belly just above her curly hair. She kicked off her drawers, reached for him again and rubbed the head of his cock against her lower lips, already moist.

'Go on,' she said. 'It's safe.'

Her voice had a rasp to it.

'Safe?'

'Dutch cap,' she said. 'I put it in earlier.'

Strange how he could feel shocked by her – that she had planned all this. Her head dropped back against the pillow. He slid forward and entered her wet heat.

CHAPTER THIRTEEN

HE AWOKE JUST AS THE EARLY MORNING LIGHT LIT UP THE canvas roof of the tent and suffused the hanging folds of the mosquito netting. His shoulder and back ached from being cramped up in the camp bed with her. And he had a horrible headache, his mouth dry from the after-effects of the champagne at altitude. He was also pressed up against the warmth and smoothness of her skin, the curve of her legs, the undulations of her spine; immediately he wanted her again, his cock pressing hard and hot against her back. He slid his arm around her shoulder, laying the weight of his palm against her. She responded by turning to face him, eyes half open, still sleepy, but she lifted her chin as he pressed his lips against her throat, nipped at the skin, kissed along her jaw line and took her earlobe in his teeth. She made a sleepy moaning noise and he lifted his head, kissed the soft skin over her cheekbones, then each eyelid. He pulled back from her. Her eyes opened wider now, then rolled a little, and closed again.

On the pillowcase, damp from dewfall, her hair spread out, wiry and dishevelled. Her breath tasted morning stale, a unique taste of her that aroused him all the more. He slid his hand over her belly and she arched her hips to press against it, still aroused from their lovemaking in the night. He moved his slow palm, making circles on the flesh above her womb, his little finger brushing her curly hair with each rotation. She opened her mouth. Her lips were a little dry. He ran his tongue along them and the tip of her tongue flicked out to touch his. He moved slowly so that the pain behind his eyes didn't lance through his brain.

He lifted her with his palm behind her ribs, pulled her forward and her breasts pressed to his chest. She was light in his arms. He ran his fingertips along the bumps of her backbone, slipped his fingers into her crinkly red hair and her mouth came up to his again, her kiss more conscious now and her arms were around him, clining to him. Her palms pressed against his shoulder blades. And then she was caressing him. Massaging down his body, over his kidneys – a delicious warmth – and she pressed over the roundness of his buttocks, pulling his hips towards her. He lifted himself on his arms. The canvas of the camp bed creaked. Her head rolled on the pillow, still sleepy, but her desire obvious in the way she pulled back one thigh to invite him between her legs again. Her head lifted, eyelids closed, and her mouth opened to kiss him again, breath warm, mouth wet. The head of his cock brushed up against the softness of her sex and again her hips lifted to accommodate him. His breath caught. She was still wet and open, a little sticky. He reached down and guided himself into the warmth of her. Her muscles contracted around it. Deliberately. No innocent, was she? Her arms tightened around him, and she rolled her pelvis so that he slid all the way into her and her pubic bone pressed into the root of him. Her breathing was hungry in his ear. He began to move and she pushed forward in time with him, making slight sounds. The muscles around his eyes tightened against the pain in his skull. And as she picked up her rhythm, her green eyes were suddenly open, looking into him as if to search through his thoughts like some clairvoyant, as if she might see right inside his head, as impossible as that was. As if she was searching through all the whorls and convolutions and the chambers of memory where the bruised head of Dinesh Gupta and a hundred other terrorists were hidden. Thank God she couldn't see them. He squeezed his eyes closed and shut them out.

And then it was as if he were floating in some empty space with her. Each move they made caused more pleasure to well up inside him and he could sense hers from the roll of her body and this open-eyed telepathy and her little noises becoming louder. He didn't care who heard her, now. My God, she was already slipping over the edge. She rolled herself down harder on him and then her eyes widened and glazed, her mouth opened and deep sound came from her throat. His whole body melted at that sound and poured outwards – and a burst of heaven lit up his skull, melting the pain, and her fingertips pressed into his back. And the canvas creaked and groaned beneath them until the great wave of pleasure that had lifted them up just as quickly subsided and they clung to each other like victims of a shipwreck, flung up on the sagging camp bed. They had weeks of journey ahead of them, and in Calcutta there was no one who had any claim on him. No woman. Only the Department. And she had no one, had she? Only her father to claim her attention. It was dangerous what he was doing. He knew that. He would have to do the job he had come to do but he wasn't going to lose her. He had always got on with the Colonel. Somehow he would persuade him to go back with them.

'I want to know everything about you,' she said.

His muscles tightened involuntarily. Shut his mind. He felt himself slide out of her. He was a little nauseous. His breath was sour in his mouth.

'Oh,' she said. 'That's a pity.'

He kissed her lightly on the lips, lifted himself out of her embrace, and rolled onto his side, the frame of the bed digging into his back. He looked up at the drape of the mosquito net. Tried to shut out the images that arose in his head. Gupta. In that room. And Mukherji. The chains and the lathis. And the others, no more than children some of them, in the villages after that raid on the armoury at Chittagong. He'd done it to teach them a lesson. To warn off any others whom he thought might have similar ideas about an armed uprising. He saw it as his duty: burn out the cancer of violence. But the contortion and terror on those once defiant faces were unforgettable. No woman should know about that. She was supposed to help him forget all that.

My God, he thought. She has no idea.

There was no need for her to know.

'Yes. We've got so much to discover about each other,' he said. 'That's what's so wonderful really. We've only just begun, haven't we?'

Of course, she knew what Davies was; and what the Department did. Must know. Her father had been in the service all her life, hadn't he? She wasn't so bloody naive. She would never have ended up in this bed if she were.

Privilege, he thought. That's the key. She'd been born to privilege – and privilege was seductive. It had corrupted him, hadn't it? Rank, money, but above all power – the freedom to belong to the ruling race here in India. A few of those pukka Eton and Oxford bastards in the Department made snide remarks about his accent, or where he came from, but few of them could match what he did, or what he had done, in India or in France. She was one of *them* in a way. But saved in a sense by being a woman. No Eton or Oxford for her. And she was hardly the type to toe the British line. But, as eccentric as they were, Colonel Devenish and her mother were hardly part of the starving masses. Privilege was in Christina's flesh, blood and bones: the flesh, blood and bones that had all night been wrapped up in his flesh, blood and bones.

He slid his arm around her shoulders and drew her to him and her head was on his chest, her hand on his ribs. She'd been described to him as an occultist, a believer in free love. You could only be all these things if you had been born to privilege, couldn't you? Jesus Christ, what was he thinking? He was in love with this woman. She wasn't limited by anything. That was the best thing about her. Even this Theosophy business was entirely her own interpretation. You only had to hear her speak, see how her body moved as she sipped a drink, or pushed back her hair, or watch those wide lips relax in a smile, or feel her underneath you as you entered her body. The canvas of the tent was getting brighter. Christ, someone might well have heard her moans. The bearers might well be talking and joking about it even now.

'I have to go,' he said. 'We don't want to cause a scandal up here, do you see?'

'I do wish you could stay,' she said.

'Perhaps tonight,' he said.

'Yes, you'd better,' she said.

He ran his hand over her hair, lifted himself up, slid his feet over the edge of the bed and pulled back the mosquito netting. Again that spike of pain through his head. The groundsheet was cold and damp under his bare feet. He retrieved his underpants and trousers off the canvas chair. He was still half-hard even as he pulled them on. He got into his vest, shirt and waistcoat and then sat to pull on his socks and riding boots. He slung the leather holster and the Webley over one shoulder and draped his jacket over the other without putting his arms in the sleeves.

'See you at breakfast,' he whispered.

'Kiss me again,' she said, a silhouette behind the bed veil.

He lifted the net and kissed her full on her hungry mouth. She seemed to feel no ill effects from the champagne.

'That's better,' she said.

She pulled the covers around herself again, her pointed chin and halo of hair all that was visible of her. He dropped the net again and then he was at the flaps of the tent, loosening the ties. He slipped out and retied the flaps behind him.

Across the clearing, two of the Newari cooks drifted about

in the early morning fog, bringing wood to rekindle the smouldering fires. More Newaris were busy with the highland villagers who were already lining up to be seen by Christina at the field clinic. Davies felt light-headed, as if he was still a little drunk. He had hardly slept. Vague in the mists, the shadowy rhododendron bushes were humped above the tents. The early morning light was bright in his eyes. His mouth was dry. But what a wonderful night he had had. He had never felt so good with a woman as he had with Christina. And the way that she had planned it all out. Even taking the precautions. He had to admit to himself that her modernity frightened him a little – but more than anything else, it excited him. He had never known any woman like her in India – or in Britain for that matter. He could see himself with Christina on his arm at some glittering ball in Calcutta. Envy. He'd be the envy of Calcutta with a woman like her. But they had a long way to go before they got back to Calcutta. And that was wonderful, too. All this time together in Bhutan and if she had given herself to him once, she would do it again; and hadn't she just called him back for another kiss and made him promise to go to her tent again tonight? This was a journey into paradise. But his bladder was still uncomfortably full.

He chose a path among the wax-leafed plants and tight buds and stopped in a small clearing. He unbuttoned his trousers. His cock was still slick from her. Steam rose around the trunks and low branches as he pissed copiously, the sour stink of it rising with the steam. As if he might divine his future, he stared at the twisted roots of the tree and the foaming liquid like an ancient priest scrutinising the smoking entrails of a sacrificed beast. But try as he might he couldn't read the portents. He wanted them to be good. Was that too much to ask? Signs and portents? What on earth was he thinking? Djinns and bloody mountain gods? This benighted medieval country was starting to get to him, too.

CHAPTER FOURTEEN

ALL DAY IN THE SADDLE THE ANTICIPATION HAD BEEN EATING her up from the inside out and now it was evening again and she had eaten with him and was preparing for bed, alone in her tent. But he was going to come to her any minute now.

What a wonderful man he was. He was so capable. He was accustomed to command and that made her feel safe with him as the expedition moved deeper into Bhutan. Whatever he had said about her Theosophy at Richard's house, she sensed that he respected her. She could command that respect by her own competence, too, but so many men would discount her as a 'mere' woman. Owen didn't. She was sure that he had his secrets, and he was very reticent about his deepest thoughts on religion, but what he had said at Richard's house about grace and mystery had seemed somehow more attractive and sensible the more she thought about it. She had to admit that his reasoning had caused her a certain disillusionment with some of the more wishy-washy manifestations of Theosophy. He was also a bit of an outsider, just as she was – she for her radical beliefs, he for being rather lower class in the privileged environment of the Department. If she found any fault with him it was that he found it so difficult to be romantic, but he wasn't exactly a bohemian, was he? Despite her Theosophy, she wasn't very romantic herself, either. She was a doctor: clinical, practical. Increasingly so, recently. Owen had a somewhat clinical side, too.

She could see him being a wonderful companion. And then there was the physical side. She wasn't likely to underestimate that.

It had been so long since she had gone to bed with a man and he had woken her body up to want more, to want him. He had a strong body, had kept himself fit, only a little fat on him, but riding and shooting and his natural body type were hardly going to see him run to seed in the very near future. He was a lot like her father really.

She wished Owen would come to her immediately. But he was discussing something with Tobgye. She had nothing to do but wait for him. She couldn't read or write in her diary – she was too nervous with anticipation.

The sun had long gone down. She unhooked the lantern from the ridge pole and set it on the folding table next to the bottle of champagne. The bull's-eye lens reflected dully in the dark glass of the bottle that a bearer had brought from the precious store. The cold had caused little droplets to condense on it and the label was saturated where it had been chilled in the icy stream. It was an extravagance and she was anxious that they might run out before they had even reached her father. The cost of a bottle of champagne was not going to end all poverty on the subcontinent but she did feel mild pangs of guilt over the poverty of her patients. Those poor villagers showed up every morning to get medicines and treatment for awful goitres, infections and the odd broken bone. She was sorry to turn any of them away but time was so limited. And now here she was in the evening looking forward to another bottle of champagne, courtesy of His Majesty's Political Department.

She wrapped a shawl around herself as she sat in the camp chair to wait for him. She couldn't help but worry that this might turn out to be only a shipboard romance. Perhaps they would both come to their senses after leaving Bhutan and they were back in Calcutta. That was well over a month away or more. Whatever happened between them, she was going to enjoy it while it lasted. And she had yet to negotiate her way through her meeting with her father.

Her blouse was stale from the day's ride but it didn't matter that much. She opened the top buttons so that she showed some cleavage. The skin between her breasts was a little damaged from the sun but Owen wasn't so young either, was he? Her hands – look at her bloody hands – still red and shiny since the fire. Nothing she could do about that though.

All the fine hairs on her body prickled at the approach of his footsteps coming across the camp. She took a breath, let it out, smoothed down her long tweed riding skirt over the slight curve of her belly and then he slipped between the flaps of the tent, his face shadowed by the brim of his grey felt hat. He didn't look at her until he had fastened the ties. He smiled that wary smile of his. He seemed a little nervous.

'Come in,' she said.

She got up off the chair and then his arms were around her and his lips were on hers and she could smell and taste the musk of him, the slight scrape of his cheek against hers. His palms slid over her body, one over the smooth cotton of her blouse and into the small of her back and the other on the roundness of her buttocks. Her head went back and he was kissing her stretched neck.

Under his jacket, the starched cotton of his shirt was rough beneath her damaged fingertips and under the cotton she pressed the flesh and firmness of his chest and his back. She slipped the jacket off his shoulders with the backs of her hands and he helped it fall over the end of the bed. She plucked the knot of his tie, the silk sliding apart under her touch and then her red fingers fumbled at the buttons of his shirt to reveal the smooth light skin of his chest. He eased her back towards the bed. The mosquito net was up on the side closest to them and she let him lower her onto the light cotton quilt.

'I don't want to lose you,' he said.

'Why should you?' she asked, but she knew why he might and she suppressed all thought of it as he kissed her again and she opened her mouth, and imagined her breath passing into the dark red interiors of him, under skin and flesh and the cage of his bones, infiltrating the membranes and the spaces of his throat and lungs, his veins and heart, and would remain inside him, her own vital energy possessing him. And she could feel the warmth in her belly and the pleasure between her thighs, getting her moist already. He plucked at the buttons of her blouse and it fell open. She shrugged off the strap of her slip so that one breast was bare and his fingertip could brush over the edge of the nipple that rose under his touch and the cold air.

'Let me get out of these clothes,' she said.

He unbuckled her belt and she raised her hips so that he could unbutton her skirt and then she was lying back with her slip already half off. She slid off her cotton drawers, unclasped her suspender belt and rolled down her stockings.

He shed his clothes as quickly as she did hers, kneeling over her under the net canopy of the bed. Both naked now – how white her body was compared to his. He was already erect, a small clear drop of lubricant glistening at the tip of it. His arms came around her waist and squeezed her.

'The net,' she said.

He knelt over her, reached up and tugged at the strings that held up the mosquito net and the gauze curtain dropped to cocoon them on the canvas bed. She lay back and laid a hand on his fleshy stomach, touched the swaying head of his erection.

'Turn over,' he said. 'Go on, turn over on your front.'

She felt a little shy, wary, but she did as he asked. If he wanted her that way, she would let him. She'd done it before with Oliver Haddo. As long as Owen was careful and didn't hurt her, she would let him, too. He took her wrists and laid her arms down slightly away from each side of her body. A light draught drifted across her skin, cooling her in the evening warmth. He knelt over her body and then his fingers eased into the muscles of her shoulders, his thumbs and fingertips moving down on each side of her spine. It was exquisite; she felt her muscles relax under his fingers, making her ever more conscious of each part of the body that he touched. The inside of his thighs pressed against her hips, and the heaviness of his erection lay lightly on the crease of her buttocks. She almost hoped he would try her there. But now he kneaded the flesh of her buttocks and continued down to her thighs. Then his hand was on her hip and he eased her over onto her back. She opened her arms and her legs so she could hold onto all of him. She so wanted him inside her but he moved away again as he kissed her on the lips and then on the neck and between her breasts. His hands held her ribcage. He kissed her breasts. His mouth and tongue were on her navel, his palm on her belly. She lifted her hips. She could feel her own wetness run down between her buttocks as she waited for it to happen. His mouth pressed above her pubic bone and closed on her and she couldn't help the sound in her throat as his tongue searched between the folds and the press of his hand on her belly stretched her out and she closed her eyes. A delicious tension built throughout her body under his tongue and lips and she was rocking on the swell of her pleasure. There was a red glow behind her eyes and then little flashes of light and the ball of warmth in her belly expanded up to her navel and her heart and her breasts and throat and then she was moaning again and it was as if something melted behind her eyes and her whole body arched and her hands pressed into his hair, his head, his skull, her hips up and she was pressing herself against his mouth as she came in slow waves. She pulled at his shoulders to lift him up onto her body. She tasted herself on his lips and reached down to guide him inside her again.

CHAPTER FIFTEEN

BESIDE THEM, THE WATERY RUSH OF THE CHAMKA CHU MADE mellower counterpoint to the hoofbeats of the mules, the chankle of harnesses, the clank of weapons. The sun sparkled on the chain mail of Tobgye's strange army and lit up the far peaks of the Himalayas. A ball of warmth seemed to undulate, pleasant and soft, in her belly as she rolled with the motion of the mule and the press of the saddle between the thighs and knees of her tweed jodhpurs. Her whole body was supple with pleasure and the antic-ipation of more filled her with a sense of exhilaration. The expe-dition had climbed above the lush forests to the dry highlands and they seemed now to be in the hard physical heart of Bhutan. Bhutan claimed to be founded on the openness and compassion of its religion but was darkened by the occult ambitions of its polit-ical and military rulers and even – perhaps especially – by its clergy.

Some two hundred yards beyond the head of the column was a roofed, cantilever bridge, built over the churning stream. The bridge had a fortified gatehouse at each end. Not a quarter of a mile beyond the bridge stood a white-walled fortress, its formi-dable central tower dominating the pagoda roofs below. It was like nothing she had seen in India. If lands were like dreams then Bhutan was the massive threshold between the Vedic and the Central Asian civilisations.

'That's Bya-Gar Dzong,' Owen said. 'The main fortress of the Maharaja.'

She nodded and walked her mule closer to Owen's.

They reached the covered bridge and passed under the shadow of the gatehouse. The hooves of their mules rattled upon the boards and echoed along the bridge beneath the shadowy rafters. Then she was out from under the arch of the furthest gatehouse and back into the cold mountain air. Above her, the walls of the *dzong* rose white and featureless for a good eighteen feet and then there was a row of ornately carved, maroon-painted window frames. There was something military, religious and prison-like about it. She spurred the mule on and scattered a group of long-tailed magpies which had been picking at some featureless carrion by the roadside.

The massive double gate of the fortress was wide open, files of soldiers massed on either side of it, as a guard of honour. They presented arms as Tobgye passed through and then Christina and Owen rode into the dark courtyard. On three sides, the inner *dzong* was overhung by high galleries supported by thick wooden trunks that had been painted orange. Beneath the galleries were shadowed cloisters whose railings were as ornately carved and brightly painted as the window frames. Steep wooden stairways connected the lower cloisters to the galleries and catwalks.

Four young monks – no more than fourteen years old, she guessed – stared down at her from behind the upper railings of a precariously perched balcony on the western wall. The great gates of the *dzong* creaked shut behind them to enclose the yard that was now completely jammed with men and animals and scattered with fresh nuggets of straw-yellow dung and spattered with the rank and copious urine of horse and mule.

Christina slid down from her saddle and a syce took her mule's bridle. Sonam Tobgye ushered her and Owen through the doorway of the eastern building and down a low corridor that took them deep into the heart of the *dzong*. Tobgye slid past her and stopped before an inner doorway. He half bowed to her and Owen and urged them over the threshold of a low-ceilinged room that was grey-lit by square paper screens framed into deep insets in the thick, white-plastered wall.

'His Royal Highness, Jigme Wangchuk, Precious Master of Power, Maharaja of Druk Yul,' announced Sonam Tobgye.

Her eyes slowly adjusted to the gloom.

The Maharaja was seated — cross-legged, she thought, though it was difficult to see — upon the ornate throne that dominated the claustrophobic space. The lower half of his body was hidden behind an ornately carved table upon which was a teacup and a bowl heaped with untouched fruit, like a shadowy still life. Despite the darkness, his bright yellow brocade jerkin held a glow from the flat light. The Maharaja was about twenty-eight. His face was dark, and the clean-shaven jaw prominent. His intense and narrow eyes inspected first Owen, then herself.

'I am honoured to meet Your Highness, once again,' Owen said. 'As I was always honoured to meet your father.'

'Please accept our rather rude hospitality, Major Davies,' the young Maharaja said in slightly accented English.

Perhaps the Maharaja and his chamberlain Sonam Tobgye had both been educated at the same British school. She couldn't help but think that the language itself was cog and gear to fasten them to the political machinery of the Raj.

It was then that she noticed the two British officers in the blue uniform of the Political Department who were sitting at the table to the Maharaja's left.

Owen made a slight bow to the young Maharaja.

'In my experience,' he said, 'Your Majesty's hospitality is anything but rude.'

The dark face remained completely impassive. The Maharaja nodded once at Christina and turned back to Owen.

'You must be tired after your long journey,' the monarch said. 'Please sit down.'

He indicated the table to his left.

The two British officers stood up. One of them was even

taller than Owen, but much thinner, and his moustache was closely trimmed upon his upper lip which made him seem older than he probably was.

'Have you met Colonel Marshall?' Owen asked her, his head tilted, the smile affectionate, whether for her or for Colonel Marshall, she wasn't sure.

'I've never had the honour,' Christina said.

'Colonel Marshall, Dr Christina Devenish,' Owen said.

Marshall nodded. He had rather narrow eyes, wrinkled from squinting into the sun, and a straight-lipped mouth that smiled under the moustache. He seemed surprised when she held out her hand for him to shake, but he took it and shook it firmly enough.

'Delighted to meet you, Dr Devenish,' he said. 'I'm an old colleague of your father's.'

'And this is Lieutenant Sinclair, Indian Medical Service,' Owen said.

The dark-bearded officer nodded to her. He was a lot younger than Marshall.

'Then you and I have something in common,' she said.

'My experience in Asia is rather limited,' Sinclair said. 'I've heard yours is rather more profound.'

'You've heard?' she said.

'From Colonel Marshall,' he said.

'My reputation precedes me, then,' she said.

Sinclair smiled at her, that bland, diplomatic sort of smile that told you nothing, but there was something immediately masculine about the way he squared his shoulders and puffed his chest out. Perhaps she was the first white woman he had seen in months. She noticed the glint of gold on his left hand and wondered where his wife might be: down in India or back in England?

Marshall waved towards the bench, but just as she and Owen were about to sit, eight elderly monks came into the room and

148

took their places along the wall to the right of the king. Following the example of the British officers, she remained standing. Then, five Bhutanese generals – or so she assumed by the steel helmets with quilted neck guards and rich brocade tunics – came through the low doorway and occupied the benches to the right of it. They lifted off their helmets and set them down on the tables in front of them. Marshall and Sinclair now resumed their seats and Owen pulled at the creases of his grey trousers and seated himself next to Sinclair. Christina tugged at the knees of her jodhpurs and sat down on the carpeted bench next to Owen. Servants entered and laid platters of saffron rice and mangoes and jack fruit in front of them. Another bearer carried an enormous silver kettle under his right arm; yet another, a stack of wooden bowls. The kettle-bearer poured a pool of hot liquid into his palm and drank it: presumably to demonstrate that it was not poisoned. Next, the kettle-bearer took the Maharaja's silver bowl and filled it while the other servant distributed bowls to the assembly. A bowl arrived in front of her and she waited for the Maharaja to sip his tea first, then raised hers to her lips. It was thick and creamy and might easily disguise the taste of any foreign element. One of the armoured soldiers approached the throne and began to speak with the Maharaja in a low voice. Ignoring the exchange, Marshall leaned across Sinclair and spoke to Owen.

'You and Dr Devenish made it just in time for the investiture,' he said.

'I'm sure Dr Devenish will be delighted to witness the ceremony,' Owen said.

'Well, the king's astrologers have declared that tomorrow will be an auspicious day for it,' Marshall said.

'Do you have any news of my father?' she asked.

Marshall's eyes flitted towards the throne and then back to her.

'Your father, yes,' Marshall said. 'He's rather in the thick of it at the moment. You know he's with the Shabdrung, of course?'

She nodded.

'It appears that matters have taken rather a turn for the worse,' Marshall said. 'Bad news in dispatches, I'm afraid. As soon as Gandhi came out of prison, the Shabdrung had an emissary waiting to speak to him, looking to enlist Gandhi's support in the Shabdrung's claim to the throne.'

Her hand lifted to her mouth involuntarily and she lowered it into her lap. Gandhi? No wonder the Department was wary of the Shadbrung. The news tore at her dreadfully. Gandhi was an enemy of the Raj. Her father's position – if indeed he were supporting the Shabdrung – would be completely untenable in their eyes.

'And there's worse,' he said. 'The Maharaja received word yesterday that the Shabdrung has contacted the Panchen Lama of Tibet to ask for his support.'

'But what could he do?' she said. 'The Panchen's just a sort of bishop, isn't he?'

'The Shabdrung wants him to enlist the help of a Chinese warlord and bring an army to assist him.'

She felt stunned.

'Your father isn't involved,' Sinclair said.

'The Bhutanese New Year celebrations come three days after the investiture. The Maharaja will wait a day or so after the festivities and then he'll send Tobgye with a regiment of soldiers to occupy Talo,' Marshall said. 'Now it really is essential that Colonel Devenish leaves Talo. We don't want one of ours caught in the middle of a war. Major Davies can make sure that Colonel Devenish is evacuated with all due haste.'

'Perhaps it would be better if Christina stayed here,' Owen said.

'I can't stay here, Owen,' she snapped. 'I have to see my father.' She looked ferociously at Marshall.

'Don't worry,' Marshall said. 'The mountain passes from Tibet are difficult to cross at this time of year. Sonam Tobgye will lead the Bhutanese expeditionary force to secure Talo before the Chinese can get there. I'd think it would be better if you travelled with Major Davies, Dr Devenish. There's a route out of Bhutan directly south of Talo. You can pick up your father and go on from there down to India.'

'I'm sure Colonel Devenish will see that he's done all that he can, now that the Chinese are involved,' Sinclair said.

'As long as he's safe,' she said.

'It's this wretched Shabdrung,' Marshall said. 'Once he's out of the way, I'm sure the country'll be stable again. Awfully bad luck for you to be caught in the middle of all this. Bhutan is such a wonderful country really. And it does rather put a pall on the New Year celebrations, I'm afraid. I thought you might enjoy them.'

He said that with obvious sincerity. He was one of these British men who had come to India sincerely believing that he was on the side of moral right; and – because of that – he would happily impose his will on as much of an entire subcontinent as he was able to, playing off one king against another, wary of China and Russia and any movement that might undermine British influence. How could so few people from such a small island in the cold and grey North Atlantic control so much of the earth's territory?

And she did have a certain sympathy for Marshall's position here in Bhutan: Gandhi and the Chinese as a joint threat would be one the Department's worse nightmares.

She couldn't imagine her father underestimating such an obviously dangerous alliance on the border of Bengal.

'I just want to see my father safe,' she said.

'I'm sure you do,' said Marshall.

She glanced up towards Tobgye and the Maharaja, two powerful pieces that were set firmly on the Empire's chessboard. By coming to Bhutan she had become a player herself in these forces that controlled the acts of nations. She was already embroiled. There was something quite thrilling about it. Perhaps that was why a significant number of British officers, including her father and Owen, had become obsessed by the Himalayas, the kingdoms of India and the wilds of Central Asia. It would be so easy to become addicted to the exercise of power. She knew that she had influence over Owen. That influence could even be the lever that would move the Maharaja and Tobgye and Marshall and the British Political Department, if she were careful and skilful enough to use it. She couldn't help but think of herself as an isolated piece deep in the hostile half of the board, and that her father was playing knight to the Maharaja's opposing king.

CHAPTER SIXTEEN

SHE SAT ON THE EDGE OF THE BED, FULLY DRESSED IN HER TWEED riding skirt and long boots, waiting for his knock. It was hardly the most attractive outfit she had ever worn but February in Bhutan was freezing cold. She kept looking up at the door every time she heard a noise outside, wanting it to be Owen, just like the other times she had been in love, so many years ago. For the first time in days, Owen hadn't come to her bed. She had enjoyed a deep and undisturbed sleep but she'd missed having his body beside her when she woke. And immediately she'd started to fret about her father. The news of the Shabdrung's involvement with the Chinese had shocked her. It must have shocked Owen, too. Her father surely couldn't have had anything to do with that. She knew him well enough that he would never side with the Chinese against imperial interests. And neither did she want Marshall and the Department sabotaging what she had with Owen.

Horses outside. She picked up her riding crop, slung her canvas bag on her shoulder and opened the door of the hut. Flowers still hung from the lintel, their white petals browned at the edges from the cold of the night. A thick ground mist obscured the slopes of the hillsides. Owen, Marshall and Sinclair, uniformed and absurd, sat on their horses in front of the hut. The brisk wind lifted the plumes of their bicorn dress hats. The style of their dress uniforms was completely at odds with the medieval armour of the Bhutanese, as if these British officers had stepped out of a separate storybook, one by Kipling or Wilkie Collins rather than Sir Walter Scott.

'Bright and early,' Owen said.

'The investiture, then,' she said.

A Bhutanese syce held a black mule by its bridle ready for her. She swung up onto the saddle, arranged the heavy folds of her skirt and eased the mule forward. Owen walked his mount up on the black mule's flank. Of course, they would have to be discreet around Marshall and Sinclair to avoid scandal. Tobgye she didn't care about. Once they had left Bhutan she would probably never see Tobgye again.

Sergeant Thomas and the squad of sepoys formed the escort and marched behind them towards the temple of La-Me Monastery. Four sepoys led mules loaded with long boxes.

'We'll be gone from Bumthang in a few days,' Owen said.

'They're desperate to get rid of this Shabdrung, aren't they?' she said.

'They'll work out a way to bring him under control,' he said. 'The Shabdrung is still the country's religious leader.'

'Has anyone talked to my father since this news of Gandhi and the Chinese?'

'That's our job,' Owen said. 'I'm sure he'll come round now.'

She nodded. She was in the middle of a potential civil war. At the time of his letter to her, her father couldn't have known what was about to develop, otherwise he would never have invited her. But he hadn't tried to warn her off since, either. The fact was she wouldn't have wanted to be warned off. She would have wanted to come anyway.

The river beside them tinkled like broken glass, and choughs fluttered on the juniper bushes, their curved beaks and legs a bright and shiny red as if they had feasted and waded in blood. On the windy hillside above, prayer flags cracked around a small temple. A great Himalayan griffon soared above the cliff, its body all white and its white wings tipped with black, lazily riding the mountain thermals beyond all the turmoil in the valleys below.

'You see that temple perched on the cliff,' Marshall said. 'There's a small cave behind it. They call it Tu-je. According to the local legend, ten centuries ago their tantric saint, Padmasambhava, meditated there. Practised magical rituals to subdue the local demons. Place was rife with demons once upon a time if you listen to the Bhutanese.'

'It seems that one or two might be acting up again,' she said.

Marshall laughed. He seemed comfortable with her and that put her at her ease over her father. Perhaps his manner was meant to do that. But Owen was relaxed with him too and hadn't warned her that Marshall might be at all hostile to her father.

Up ahead, a huge crowd of horses and soldiers had gathered among the monks at the entrance of La-Me temple. The Bhutanese, all men, stared at her as she dismounted from her mule and another young syce took it by the bridle. The Maharaja had obtained special dispensation for her from the abbot to allow her to enter the monastery walls to witness his investiture. Marshall and Sinclair entered the temple first.

Owen escorted her down the low dark corridor to the great hall where the ceremony was to take place. Back by her side again. She was reassured by that. Marshall and Sinclair seated themselves on a bench below the throne and Christina stepped back to allow Owen to sit next to the young medical officer. They were seated below a huge statue draped with white silk scarves, some soot-stained, others pristine. Marshall leaned across Owen.

'That's their saint, Padmasambhava,' he said.

'The magician in the cave?' she said.

'Exactly.'

Marshall leaned back in his seat again.

Christina found the image of the saint rather bizarre. He was not depicted in monk's robes. The eyes were wide open and glared down ferociously over the assembly. He cradled a trident in his left arm, decorated with the bronze-cast ornaments of three severed heads. He held a vase on one palm and with the other hand pointed a thunderbolt of Indra in a menacing gesture. More magician than monk, then. Himalayan Buddhism was very different from that of Ceylon or Burma.

Seven long shelves of butter lamps were set up in front of the statue and Christina was close enough to feel their heat. For Marshall, Sinclair and Owen in their uniforms it must have been unbearable. The greasy smoke caught in her throat and stung her eyes. She unslung her canvas shoulder bag just as the Maharaja and his entourage of monks and generals entered the hall. She stood up along with everyone else until the Maharaja took his place on the throne.

The hall was loud with scraping benches and hacking coughs. Immediately the monks began their droning chants. Yet others flooded into the hall carrying kettles full of tea and trays of jasmine rice and oranges, serving the king first and then Marshall and the other British guests as the monks chanted on. When everyone's bowl was full, they fell silent.

Now a line of nobles from the surrounding *dzongs* came into the hall and approached the throne. They were followed by their retainers all dressed in striped gowns. In front of Jigme Wangchuk's throne, they laid down their gifts and white scarves. The scarves formed a white cotton mound similar to the one in front of the statue. Marshall stood up as Sergeant Thomas and the sepoys brought in long wooden crates and green metal boxes. Thomas levered open one of the crates. The greased gunmetal of six new Lee Enfield .303 rifles glinted with the light of the butter lamps. The three Department officers stood to attention facing the throne. She could see the sharp profile of Owen's tanned face, lips tight, eyes fixed. She hadn't known about these guns. She had seen them load the mules with boxes which had tarps tied over them. With gifts like these, there was no doubt but that they were backing the Maharaja's government. If the Chinese were on the march, they would be used very soon.

The sepoys carried in more boxes and Sergeant Thomas levered up the lids with his crowbar to reveal more peaceful offerings: bolts of bright brocades and silks. How incongruous the colours looked beside the brutal metallic reality of the rifles. She had been part of the expedition that had brought all this to Bumthang. The Department was in the business of defence, overt or covert, and her father had been part of that all his life. He had been crossing and recrossing the Himalayas for decades, probably carrying gifts just such as these.

Owen turned slightly towards her and indicated the throne by widening his eyes.

Time to present my own gift, she thought.

She slipped from behind her table and dipped into her canvas bag for a white silk scarf. She took out the padded gift box, placed it on the scarf and approached the throne. She handed scarf and box up to the dark-faced young Maharaja who looked at her with surprise. He took the box from her and lifted the lid. His face was all pleasure when he saw the silver-plated, pearl-handled derringer. And that smile left her with the cold sensation that she had presented him with some kind of magical means to eliminate his enemies, as if all he needed to do was aim it and a psychic bullet would destroy his target where a lead bullet might not. She suddenly wished that she could take the present back. There was something horribly ill-omened about it. She stepped back from the throne and returned to her place beside Owen. His hand squeezed hers under the table and she squeezed back.

Now Marshall rose and approached the throne with the medical officer, Sinclair. The two British officers snapped to attention and saluted the Maharaja.

Marshall addressed the Maharaja in the Dzongkha language for some minutes. Presumably it was the investiture speech. Then Sinclair opened a long flat box, and from it Marshall lifted up a pure white ribbon with a silver star-burst medal. Then he ceremoniously hung the glittering pendant around the neck of the Bhutanese monarch. Knight Commander of the Indian Empire. That ribbon and the bright silver star would yoke the Maharaja yet more inextricably to the British cause. As Marshall and Sinclair returned to their seats, the monks began another rumbling chant accompanied by the pounding of drums and the clash of cymbals.

The flames of the butter lamps seemed to have sucked all the air out of the room and it was becoming unbearably hot. She watched a trickle of sweat run down Owen's cheek, just in front of his ear. With a final crash of cymbals, the monastic choir fell silent.

Beaming, the Maharaja rose from the throne and lifted the star on his chest for a moment to display it to his monks, ministers and generals who all came to their feet. Owen's hand brushed hers as they stood up. She raised her eyes to acknowledge him but now she felt a sickening, disconcerting feeling of being unconnected with reality, as if she were stuck in a bizarre dream. Tobgye helped the Maharaja down from the high throne. The monks, the ministers and the generals began to file out of the room behind him. Marshall led the British contingent into the corridor, and Christina was crushed among the Bhutanese guests as they filed out along the dark and narrow corridor of La-Me temple. Losing sight of Owen, she let herself be carried along by the press of bodies until she was pushed out through the gates of the temple and into the icy winds of the Bya-Gar valley.

Grey clouds had descended to make a vaporous lid over the dark hills. Wind flicked the stinging rain at her. The soldiers roared salutations to their king. Retainers carried trays of *arakh* to them.

Suddenly Tobgye appeared and took her by the arm.

'Please come with me,' he said.

'What?'

She was shocked at his physicality.

'Come with me,' he said.

He half dragged her towards a group of women who stood at a distance from the main congregation. Their rich brocade jackets and long brown dresses made them all seem rather short and stout. Their hair was cropped to their ears and revealed massive hooped gold earrings on each side of their broad faces. Heavy strings of coral and turquoise hung around their necks and silver bracelets on their thick wrists. Their whole appearance was made doubly bizarre by the incongruity of the white canvas tennis shoes on their feet.

Tobgye waved in the direction of the women.

'The Maharani, her sisters and her daughters warmly welcome you to Bumthang,' Tobgye said. 'They would like to invite Dr Devenish to join them for the women's celebration.'

She was disarmed by the guileless smiles of the Maharani and her entourage of women. Since Lakshmi had died, she thought, she had been almost exclusively in the domain of men, so it might be a relief to be with them.

'Here is your mule,' Tobgye said.

'Just one minute,' she said. 'Just wait. Please.'

Owen, Marshall and Sinclair were surrounded by a crowd of Bhutanese generals.

'Owen,' she called.

He raised a shot of *arakh* in her direction and downed it. She wished he would take off the bicorn hat. His dark hair was far more attractive than that ridiculous headgear. Owen shouldered his way through the celebrants. He was beaming, perhaps glad to be among a military fraternity again, in his element. Here, the Raj seemed to be winning the battle for the subcontinent, as opposed to the unceasing daily erosion of British power all over India – and especially in Calcutta. He wouldn't have been able to enjoy such a situation for years, stuck, as he had been, in the Writers' Building on Dalhousie Square.

Tobgye stood away from her as Owen reached them, his face flushed under his tan.

'They want me to go with the Maharani,' she said.

'Oh, of course,' Owen said. 'You know how they are. Customs and all that. I'm sure you'll be all right. There'll be a long party today. I'll come down to the Maharani's for you as soon as the formalities are over.'

Owen took the black mule's bridle from the syce and she pulled herself into the saddle. He laid a hand on the top of her leather riding boot.

'Don't worry,' he said. 'We'll be in Talo in a few days. No more delay. And I spoke with Marshall last night. He promised me that we'll do everything we possibly can for your father with the Department, once we get back to Calcutta.'

Owen touched his lips with two fingers, waved them up at her where she sat on the mule. She was chilled to think that Owen and Marshall had been discussing her father out of her presence. What had they been saying? She could no more control him than he could control her. She nodded to him and then Owen turned back towards Marshall, Sinclair and the hard-drinking generals. She allowed the syce to lead the mule onto the path back down the valley where the seven women called to her and waved their arms, urging her to hurry on and join them.

A thin-faced young woman, with her hair cropped in a pageboy cut, stepped out from among them as the mule caught up with them on the path.

'I can translate for you,' the woman said. 'My name is Yongchen Gyamtso.'

Christina was shocked that a Bhutanese woman could speak English.

'Oh yes, thank you,' Christina said.

'My father is Sonam Tobgye,' she said.

Perhaps she had been in Calcutta or Sikkim, too. Christina couldn't decide if Tobgye had provided his daughter's services out of kindness, or merely to keep an eye on her. But whatever the reason, Christina was buoyed by the prospect that she wouldn't be lost for hours, confused and dumbly polite, in the closeted world of the Bhutanese women. She had a means of entry.

CHAPTER SEVENTEEN

A MUD-BUILT STOVE FILLED THE AIR WITH THE SMOKE OF DRIED animal dung but did little to heat the low-roofed room. The window screens rattled as they were battered by the chill mountain blasts. Christina's eyes began to smart and the smoke picked at her throat.

'Please sit next to the Maharani,' Yongchen said.

Christina nodded and bowed to the Maharani. She seemed to wear a permanent smile. Perhaps she had a lot less to worry about than her husband. Christina settled on a bench seat on her right, and Yongchen slid in beside her. Christina lowered her head to breathe the air where the atmosphere was slightly less dense.

The Maharani said something to her in Dzongkha.

'Are you hungry?' Yongchen asked.

'Oh no, I've already had breakfast.'

But the question wasn't meant to address her needs, and a great plate of puffy fried dough appeared on the red lacquer table in front of her. A female servant filled her bowl with butter tea. She didn't go through the whole ceremonial paraphernalia of pouring it into her palm. Perhaps that was only done for the Maharaja.

The Maharani spoke to her again.

'Would you like to have your fortune told?' Yongchen asked.

This time the question seemed genuine and Christina didn't know what to answer.

'Are you a fortune teller?' Christina asked.

The young woman shook her head.

'Oh no,' she said, 'not me. Padma Khadro is a medium. She'll go into a trance. The Maharani wants to ask one of the mountain goddesses a question.'

Christina had been at a number of seances in Bloomsbury and Bombay, but, in truth, she didn't want to have any idea of what was supposed to be in her future. If the prediction was negative, she didn't want to be responsible for any self-fulfilling prophecy. And the spirits that came from the other side never seemed to be entirely trustworthy, much like some of the mediums who contacted them.

'That is Padma Khadro,' Yongchen said.

She waved towards the north side of the room.

Seated on a stool on a raised dais was a rather ordinary-looking old woman, her face a nut-brown colour, with a deep tracery of wrinkles. Her eyes were cloudy and her mouth was slack and down-turned. She wore a woven tunic, its geometrical bands of colours striking and bright, but the old woman seemed to be shrivelled up within this heavy *khira*.

Again the Maharani spoke.

'The Maharani has asked that the mountain goddess speak to you.'

It was no use to object, she supposed. She hardly thought of the practices of a medium as entertainment. Some of the seances she had been to in the past had been quite nerve-shattering at times. She tried to convince herself that to be spoken to by a Bhutanese mountain goddess via this medium was an experience not to be missed, but the tightness in her muscles and the rawness of her nerves belied her attempt at being rational.

Now incense smoke mingled with the thick smoke of the animal dung and some of the women began to chant a low prayer below the altar where there was a scroll painting of a dark blue, naked, emaciated goddess, mounted on a black ass.

The three eyes of the divinity stared balefully out of a dimension of flame and smoke.

Two of the Maharani's attendants began to load the old medium with a huge brass breastplate upon which were inscribed letters of a native alphabet that Christina suspected were the syllabic formulae to invoke that very goddess whose scroll painting hung above the assembly. The women set a five-plated crown on the medium's head. The weight was such that the old woman's neck bent still more.

From a small side room, the two attendants brought in a red lacquer table carved with dragons and jewels and set it in front of the medium. Upon the table they laid a broadsword and a double-bladed axe and a long arrow with coloured streamers attached to it. It had a small mirror fixed below the flights. Next, they brought in a large polished silver mirror as wide as a warrior's buckler and set that on the table; and then a cup that had obviously been fashioned from a human skull. They filled it with some kind of liquor. Lastly, they placed a bell on the table, and the nine-pointed thunderbolt of Indra, those ubiquitous symbols of Buddhist tantrism. Already with the heavy crown and breastplate it seemed as if the old woman was being weighed down upon the earth, her frail bones breaking under the burden of the metal. Was she expected to lift up all this hardware lying in front of her, too?

The old woman began to chant in time with the other women, a chant that gained in volume and rhythm as she swayed beneath the awesome weight attached to her body. Her face was still hidden from Christina below the five plates of the brass crown because her head was inclined forward. Her voice began to get lower and Christina sensed, rather than saw, the air in the room get darker. She glanced towards the rattling, rice-paper window screens which were obscured by thickening smoke. The hairs on the back of her neck began to prickle and her skin chilled as if lightly touched by a feather. The very air in the room seemed to have filled up with the sounds of invisible animals, strange twitters and squeaks on the threshold of hearing like a bizarre ventriloquism. Was this some kind of trick of the medium? This was not like any seance she had been to with the Theosophical Society. She began to laugh to herself but the sound in her head echoed horribly, as if the laughter were not really part of her but had come bubbling up from some unknown region deep inside her, as if her rational mind was succumbing to some dark and psychotic impulse orchestrated by what was happening in front of her.

The old woman swayed, her brown hands stretched out over the table. The medium's narrow shoulders had opened and broadened. Her neck stretched out straight and her head swivelled beneath the crown and now she was standing but Christina had not seen any transition from her crouch to the body's impossibly full extension. No longer was the medium's face creased and sunken, or the eyes rheumy, but the skin was smooth and brown and the eyes wide and glaring. Her lips pulled back from the white teeth in a tight smile, enough to show the pink gums, as if some interior entity had stretched taut the frail envelope of the old woman's body and made the withered muscles swell within the desiccated skin. Words came out of the medium's throat, like barks and growls, but neither teeth nor lips moved. In one hand, she held the broadsword upright and in the other the ribboned arrow. She began to spin upon the dais, very slowly, as if she was being controlled by some unnatural puppeteer, and her fingers and thumbs suddenly splayed open, but the heavy weapons did not fall to the ground but seemed fastened to her palms without needing to be gripped. Christina suspected some shaman's trick, but this suspension of the laws of gravity made her stomach turn over as if her intestines were being pulled around in her abdomen by an invisible hand. The smoke in the room was choking her and she found Yongchen Gyamtso's arm around her shoulder, a hand supporting her under the chin as she leaned with her forehead almost to the surface of the table, though the medium still seemed to be right in front of her eyes, as if the laws of optics had likewise been disrupted along with those of gravity; or was it that the medium's mirror had been somehow placed under her face? She wished that Yongchen would translate the words of the medium for they seemed directed at her, Christina, but she just couldn't understand. She stared at the ferocious divinity's face, stunned by the guttural language coming out of that transformed body, and suddenly she was awfully drowsy. This reminded her of opium. Lights popped at the periphery of her vision. She tried to be rational: these symptoms in a patient she would have diagnosed as the onset of a migraine attack, or an epileptic fit. She was terrified that she might suddenly lose control of herself. She felt as if some horrifically powerful and intangible entity was intent on pushing her consciousness out of her body and into oblivion, or into some uncontrollable dream. She wanted to resist the pressure but there was nothing with which she could get to grips, or push away; just this awful sense of violation, this terror, this presence which could only be malignant. Voices shouted strange syllables in her left ear and she spun her head to face them but there was nothing there. The medium's distorted face was again directly in front of her own as if in a hideous mirror.

This is all my imagination, she thought. Nothing can push my consciousness from my body. It's an aberration.

She leaned back against the wall behind her and closed her eyes to shut out the distorted face of the medium. She felt sickeningly as if she was falling into a pit of swirling, coloured light. This was all like a drug experience, induced somehow by the medium, and it was slipping out of her conscious control; but now she didn't want to stop it. There was a roar in her ears as if the building was crumbling. She risked letting her senses slip into that visionary glow, letting the images rise behind her eyelids, and this eased the sense of violation as if her struggle and fear had been the cause of it. Still, no gentle visions appeared but sudden vivid scenes of barbarous and bloody murder, all of it unreal, she knew, but as clear as a reflection appearing in a mirror, or the vivid images of a dream. She was running through the corridors of a Bhutanese *dzong*. Those armoured soldiers who had formed her escort from Dewangiri to Bumthang were hunting its corridors for her or for someone else. She hid under a wooden staircase and the soldiers came upon a monk in the corridor. Her stomach turned as four of the soldiers hacked at him with their swords. She could hear the screams of panic, see the blades cut into flesh, the spatter of blood. More monks fled screaming down the corridors pursued by the invading soldiers. Now she lost all bodily sensation and she was just a witness to the vision, helpless to stop the soldiers, or to change the vision by will. The soldiers were hunting someone in particular. But, as if something within her had judged her incapable of supporting more scenes of brutality, the vision in her head paled and became smoky. Now she saw steam rising from the black metallic valves of a gigantic railway engine. She was staring at a scene on the platform of Victoria station in Bombay. Her father, as she had last seen him, was leaning out of the window of a moving carriage. He was reaching out for her desperately as the train picked up speed. She couldn't catch up with him because she was trapped in a panicked crowd of Indian men and women. Then Owen and Richard, at the head of a squad of soldiers, attacked the crowd with lathis, and she was swept backwards and away from her father and the departing train in a wave of terrified bodies. As she was pushed down the platform, Lakshmi appeared among the crowd and frantically pointed for her to look skywards. A tower – from the *dzong* – flew through the air and disappeared over the horizon and someone shouted in her left ear. Her head jerked back and behind her eyes was only darkness, the visions just as suddenly gone and she stared again into the room in Bumthang. She was left with a terrific sense of loss, of grief. Her head rested against the hard stone wall behind her. Yongchen's arm was still around her shoulder. Whatever force or entity had tried to invade her mind had now ebbed away and she was fully herself again, even if a little stunned, but the images of her visions were vivid in her memory. The wizened old woman was lying on the floor unconscious as if she and Christina had collided violently in a scene from a slapstick film. The medium's two attendants were stripping her of the ceremonial metal crown and breastplate. Another waited with a bowl of water for the old woman to regain her senses. Her wrinkled face was drained and pallid, all sign of her raging possession gone.

Then the Maharani's face, smiling somewhat inanely, appeared directly in front of Christina's as the possessed medium's had done earlier. The Maharani asked her something in Dzongkha.

'Are you all right?' Yongchen asked. 'You almost passed out when the goddess was speaking to you.'

Christina leaned forward.

'I'd like some water,' she said.

Then, on the other side of the room, Owen was standing in the doorway, one hand against the jamb as if to keep his precarious balance. He was drunk, still in his dark blue dress uniform with its ribbons and medals, and his cockaded bicorn hat was clamped beneath his elbow. His broad face was deeply flushed with alcohol.

'Are you enjoying the festivities, dear?' he said. 'We've set up the projector. The Charlie Chaplin film is about to begin.'

CHAPTER EIGHTEEN

THE STRAIGHT SHAFT OF SHIFTING WHITE LIGHT FROM THE projector separated him from Christina in the shadowy room. Davies was mightily drunk from the afternoon's celebration with Marshall, Sinclair, the king and his generals. He concentrated on the screen, a sheet nailed onto a beam, which was almost totally light with the odd dark patch that sketched the hat and moustache of the Little Tramp. The tramp was lost in a white Alaskan landscape and a whirl of snow as if he was fighting to emerge from a world of pure light into one of definition, like a half-memory trying to form itself in the imagination's eye.

Davies half turned towards Christina to refocus his eyesight. Her face flickered beyond the beam in sharp profile, her frizzy hair a halo, electric; her skin pale and patchy like leprosy, the scattered freckles shifting like fishes on the white skin as the image on the screen changed and cast its shadows back. Christina's eyes were fixed, looking towards the screen but hardly seeing, as if she was gazing on some other world even than that projected; and unseen by everyone else in the room. Something had affected her in the afternoon. She didn't seem drunk but rather shocked or dazed.

He was this close to her and unable to touch her. The beam of light cut him off. He wanted to ask her if she was all right but he was afraid of slurring and making a fool of himself in front of her. Marshall and Sinclair were seated next to him, and away from her, laughing heartily at the antics on the screen. At the front of the room, Tobgye translated the screen's captions for the assembled court and kept a wary eye on all of them. The Maharaja, the Maharani and the generals all roared with laughter. Not just at the screen either. The moving images, and the projector that produced them, had the court in a state of delight, as well as Sergeant Thomas with his comic accompaniment on the piano-accordion, swaying the bellows from side to side in time with the tramp's waddle down a narrow and snowy cliff-side path. A howl of fear and merriment brought Davies's full attention to the screen again where a large black bear had appeared behind the unsuspecting tramp, a frightening animal familiar enough to a Himalayan audience. He congratulated himself every time the royal court erupted into laughter. The Little Tramp arrived in a mining town and, as the drink flowed in the film's dance hall, Davies became aware that his mouth had dried out, and a sharp, tight pain was building behind his right eye and across the top of his head. Dancing girls filled the screen. He glanced across the light at Christina. She shifted in her seat, looking around, he guessed, for a means of escape. She didn't seem to be enjoying the show. Something had happened to her with the Maharani and it had left her utterly distracted. She was obsessed by something. Her whole body seemed charged, as if anyone who might dare to touch her would receive a massive jolt of electricity. He turned back to the screen to get his mind off the tightening headache, off the dryness in his mouth and the pressure on his bladder. Not far to the end of the first reel now.

On screen, Handsome Jack, the ladies' man, was in competition with the Little Tramp to impress Georgia, the dancing girl. The Bhutanese were embarrassed by the overt coquetry of the women on the screen, but they still laughed as the Little Tramp fought and got the better of Handsome Jack through all those lucky, slapstick accidents. Then the wall clock dropped on Jack's head and he was out for the count.

For some reason, the tramp reminded Davies of Gandhi, and Handsome Jack of himself. Gandhi was going to win, wasn't he? Just like that little tramp in the moving picture. Signs and bloody portents. The *arakh* and the superstitions of this benighted bloody country were seeping like poison through his bloodstream. He had to see to it that Gandhi did not get a foothold in this kingdom. Did Christina understand the political reality? Could he count on her for that? She might sympathise with Gandhi, but surely she could see – when it was a matter of international defence – that Gandhi's politics were positively dangerous for every Himalayan country. Better the British than the Chinese, surely?

The first reel ran out and the tail of the film flap–flap–flapped against the hard, grey body of the projector, and from the lens a harsh white light, unflickering, lit up the screen. He pressed his palms to his eyes against the glare.

'Owen,' she whispered.

He sat bolt upright and shook off the blurry incoherence. She gripped his forearm.

'I must go to my room,' she said. 'Please take me out of here.'

He nodded to her. Her bright green eyes stared into his.

Sergeant Thomas laid down his accordion in order to change the reel. He switched off the bulb and opened the second can.

Damn that bloody *arakh*, Davies thought, it's tilted me completely off-kilter.

His skin chilled as he stood up. The sweat on his body turned icy.

'You look ill, Owen,' she said. 'You're so pale.'

'I'm fine,' he said. 'It's nothing.'

He breathed deep to get his balance under control. This ridiculous drunkenness had been unavoidable after the investiture ceremony. Toast after bloody toast. He stumbled against a bench.

'I'm sorry,' he said. '*Arakh*. Come on. Let's get you to your room.'

She ducked under the low lintel and he followed her. He took her arm in the dark corridor.

'Owen, are you all right?' she said. 'Can you manage?'

He was fighting against the *arakh* in his blood and brain; it was causing his eyes to lose focus. He didn't want to be as far gone as this with her.

'Just have to shake it off,' he said. 'Bloody *arakh*. But look, the Maharani. How did it all go?'

Her eyes flitted this way and that, her mouth slightly open.

'Something strange,' she said. 'There was a medium there. Quite shocking.'

'Shocking?'

'Yes. I felt quite overwhelmed. I don't know if . . . I can't explain.'

He put his arm around her and she leaned into him with the weight and warmth of her body. He didn't care what anyone might think, neither Tobgye nor Marshall. He wished his head were clearer.

'It's going to be all right,' he said.

'I'll be fine,' she said. 'I just need to rest a moment. Gather my thoughts.'

They picked their way among the manure piles in the court-yard and crossed to the massive gate. The armour-clad guards stared at them from under their helmets as they passed, arm in arm, out of the *dzong* and down the slope to the east where the guest huts had been built. Much as he didn't want to, he closed in on himself like a crab, avoided eye contact with them.

Smoke rose from the campfires of the sepoys. Wrapped in greatcoats, six British-Indian soldiers patrolled the perimeter of camp. Davies breathed in the cold air. It would sober him up. They reached the door of her hut. She turned to face him, laid a hand on his cheek.

'I'll stay with you,' he said.

'No,' she said. 'You can't. Marshall, Sinclair. It wouldn't do.'

She kissed him on the mouth.

'I love you, Christina,' he said.

'Yes, I know,' she said.

She smiled at him but her eyes seemed to be looking at something beyond him. He wanted to go into her hut with her and get her into bed and curl up with her.

'Let me come inside,' he said.

She glanced towards the sentries, and back up the slope to the *dzong,* then pulled him as she stepped backwards through the door. Her mouth was on his again. His head was spinning. Had she said that she loved him? He couldn't remember clearly. Her hands were under his jacket. She didn't need to say it with her mouth on his like this. Holding onto each other, they squatted down awkwardly and rolled sideways onto the canvas camp bed.

'Just hold me,' she said. 'Just hold me for now.'

Yes. He just wanted to hold her, too. That was enough. He kept his eyes open and breathed deeply through his mouth. He didn't want his head to spin, the nausea to rise. He wouldn't drink like this again. This bloody investiture. From here on in, he would need all the clarity he could muster to deal with her, with Marshall and the Department, and then there was Devenish, her bloody father. Investiture over, now. These bloody pagan New Year ceremonies to come. Then her father would be waiting for them in Talo.

PART FOUR

TALO, LATE FEBRUARY 1931

CHAPTER NINETEEN

THE SWIRL OF COLOUR OF THE LAMA DANCES TO DRIVE OUT the demons of the old year, and the pageantry of the Maharaja's archery competitions to celebrate the dawn of the new, had all blurred together with the visions induced by the medium so that each day she'd remained at Bumthang had been like a dream arising from anxiety. She'd felt a sense of relief when they'd set off for Talo and taken to the mountain passes – despite the presence of the Maharaja's army and the ugly equipment of war, and then the hardness of the freezing march. Now, they were within half a day of Talo. And even on this day, when she knew she was going to meet her father, those mediumistic visions came flooding back into her memory to mix with the nervous anticipation of reunion, a rawness of perception as if the world had turned into a canto by Dante that conjured the coldness of the outer dark. The streams beside the rocky path bubbled unseen beneath plates of ice, and low scrubby bushes rattled in the relentless wind. The boiling clouds above the column were a dense grey. Behind her came the tramp of the sepoy company, tight puttees over polished black boots and all in khaki turbans and immaculate uniforms. And on their pack mules were yet more of the ugly accoutrements of war: the fat barrel of a Vickers machine gun and its folded tripod and heavy green boxes of ammunition. All this weaponry brought to bear against a religious leader who had invoked the aid of Gandhi and a foreign warlord, all linked in her mind with the medium's revelation which had bared a parallel conflict going on in some unseen shadow realm. She was a doctor and she was aware of how mental pathologies could reveal themselves through dreams and fantasy or even visions but, not surprisingly, she hadn't discussed this psychic suspicion with Owen. He might have some notion of the spiritual but it stopped well short of pantheons of gods and demons. Even if she wanted to be rational and scientific about it, the weather itself seemed to have turned against them so that the spirit guardians of the mountains – in which these Bhutanese people so fervently believed – were conspiring in that battle between kings. Brutal February storms had assaulted the expedition upon every pass: Gye Sa, and Tongsa, and Tsong Ka, and Chand Bi, and Ri Da, and Sam Ten Gang. On each pass, they had waded for hours through thigh-high snow and had to cling to the tails of mule and yak to pull them through the stinging blizzards. It had left all of them exhausted. But for all the ire of the mountain gods, the expedition had not been fated to be stopped; the storms had finally abated their wrath as they came down into the wide and fertile Wangdi Phodrak valley.

If there *was* some kind of war going on among the psychic forces of Bhutan, the Maharaja's protectors, not those of the Shabdrung, had won this round of the campaign. She imagined those steaming piles of guts burned by the Maharaja's grand-father. Perhaps the Maharaja had his own magicians at work in the cellars of Bya-Gar Dzong, performing some arcane medieval rite. Or was this all a morbid fantasy on her part, seeking to objectify the forces at war within her own psyche, unleashed by the destruction of the clinic and the loss of Lakshmi, by the medium-induced visions and the unease she felt about meeting her father? It was as if the cold winds of the Himalayas were blowing through the cavities of her skull.

A hundred yards ahead of her, Sonam Tobgye led his armoured cavalrymen up the rough track towards Talo. His mounted escort was followed by two companies of Bhutanese infantry all armed with the modern Lee Enfield rifles that Owen, and she in some way, had brought as gifts for the Maharaja, now ready to be used against the rebellious Shabdrung and the invading Chinese army. Behind the infantry marched the artillery. Four mules bore upon their backs the dismantled parts of an ancient smooth-bore cannon: two wooden wheels, rimmed and studded with brass, a curved carriage of wood and a brass-mouthed barrel cast in the form of a dragon. Yet more mules carried powder and shot, while the artillerymen marched alongside with ramrod and swab-pole and pikes slanted on the shoulders of their quilted blue jerkins. It was a vision which carried along with it a promise of some infernal hybrid of Agincourt and Ypres.

She leaned forward on her stirrups, lifting her hips to stretch out her long legs and shifting her aching shoulders. She ran a palm over the mule's neck to reassure her. The column followed a path westwards and upwards beside a feeder stream to the main valley that ran north–south. It began to narrow as the expedition continued into the mountains. Tall blue pines and hemlocks darkened the valley sides and the path passed upwards through scattered houses on the mountainsides whose occupants had barred their gates and remained hidden from the visitors. She could only imagine that they feared the passage of the allied army. Her mule plodded steadily on the muddy path until up ahead, rising above the dark green points of the pines, appeared the curved beams and slate roofs of a split-level building with a central pagoda tower, its slit windows commanding a view of the valley below. The *dzong*'s damp-stained and whitewashed walls were built onto the steep slope, and the grounds around it terraced to form a kind of windswept meadow.

A squad of soldiers stood to the right of the heavy wooden gate, all of them armoured, some with ancient muskets and others with swords and pikes. Their commander was short and broad, a dark-skinned man with a huge curved sword hanging from his belt. They certainly did not seem capable of putting up any resistance to the Maharaja's army, backed by the British sepoys. To the left of the soldiers stood a crowd of frightened-looking, maroon-robed monks, incongruously bearing white scarves of welcome. The two groups parted to make way for a Bhutanese man in a heavy brocade jacket over his *gho* robe – obviously a figure of some authority – who stood between the two groups, soldiers and monks.

Then her father appeared from between the gates. He was far taller than any of the others, and a good deal broader, made more so by a heavy, green sheepskin jacket which he wore over an Indian-style homespun *khurta*, his trousers tucked into Bhutanese felt boots. His great walrus moustache and long grey hair framed his deeply tanned face. Something caught in the pit of her stomach.

'There he is, Owen,' she said.

Owen nodded.

'Finally,' he said.

Owen seemed more nervous than happy, his shoulders hunched somewhat like an animal taking wary cover. She supposed that was normal for a man facing the father of the woman he was sleeping with.

Tobgye halted his bay at the edge of the flat terrace, waved one hand and called out orders to his army corps. Each contingent of his force – cavalry, infantry and artillery – flowed towards a separate part of the clearing below Talo Dzong.

'We can ride up to the gate,' Tobgye said.

He reached behind into one of his saddlebags and brought out a white silk scarf. A peace offering?

The tall Bhutanese in the brocade jacket came forward to meet Tobgye as Christina and Owen guided their mounts up the path towards her father and the monks. The monks let their white scarves flutter down over their open palms to welcome them. Tobgye and the *dzong*'s minister exchanged formal greetings but Christina had eyes only for her father. His grey hair was longer and more unruly than the last time she had seen him in India and the nut-brown grooves of the wrinkles around his eyes were deeper and more exaggerated by the broadness of his smile. His long years in the sun and wind at high altitude had wrinkled his face into a tracery like a mountain contour map. Within that lined face, his grey eyes shone, glacial and lucent. But behind that scalpel-sharp gaze of his, she sensed that the hardness and distance with which she had always associated her father had been transformed into something that was somehow softer and more expansive than what she was used to. She read in his face a pleasure in seeing her, but not without the unease he must feel at confronting Tobgye's expeditionary force.

'Welcome to Talo,' he called, the familiar voice deep and resonant.

She slid from the mule.

'Oh, it's so good to see you,' she said.

She took his hands in hers and they held each other at a distance. Then his hands squeezed hers and he leaned towards her. She embraced him, her face buried in the greasy lanolin of his sheepskin, his arms around her. She lifted her head and kissed him on the cheek.

'I'm glad to see you in one piece after what happened in Bombay,' he said.

'Just the hands,' she said.

He let go of her suddenly as if afraid that he might have hurt her.

'It's all right,' she said, 'they're almost completely healed now.'

'I'm so sorry about Lakshmi,' he said.

'Yes, of course,' she said.

'How was your journey?'

'Eventful,' she said. 'To say the least. I met Marshall in Bumthang. And the Maharaja.'

'You must tell me all about it by and by,' he said.

'Of course,' she said.

'You've brought Major Davies, too.'

She smiled towards Owen and then glanced behind her.

'And half the bloody Bhutanese army, I think,' she said.

'Don't worry,' he said.

As he stepped back from her, the monks swarmed around her suddenly and a flurry of white scarves fluttered in front of her eyes. Soon they festooned her neck and shoulders.

'Delighted to see you again, Colonel Devenish,' Owen said.

Owen too was garlanded in white silk over the shoulders of his tweed jacket. He reached out and shook the Colonel's hand.

'You've looked after my daughter,' her father said. 'Thank you.'

'She looks after herself very well,' Owen said.

Then her father turned to Tobgye and shook hands with him.

'I see you've brought company,' he said to him.

'The Maharaja sends his compliments,' Tobgye said.

Her father nodded curtly and turned back to Christina.

'The Shabdrung's chamberlain has had a room prepared for you in the *dzong*, close to the gatehouse,' he said.

He indicated the man in the brocade jacket.

Tobgye spoke rapidly to the chamberlain. She couldn't understand what was going on, but the *dzong*'s soldiers now looked both agitated and powerless. Something was going on between Tobgye and the chamberlain and it didn't seem at all friendly. Her father and Owen exchanged glances.

'I'm sorry, Colonel,' Owen said.

Her father shook his head.

'Been expecting him,' he said.

This seemed such an inauspicious way to meet her father, and an equally inauspicious start to this Bhutanese year of the Iron Sheep. But he was here in Talo because he was deeply involved in Bhutanese politics for the Raj. This had always been a part of his life, the part that had always distanced him from her. Owen stood rather rigidly, not quite at attention, his slightly wrinkled face reddened by the chill winds. He seemed genuinely pleased to see her father but maintained his diplomatic poker-faced expression. Was that for the benefit of Tobgye or her father?

'Tobgye is demanding an immediate audience with the Shabdrung,' her father said. 'But the Shabdrung's already waiting for us.'

The Shabdrung's chamberlain bowed and stood back from the gates and ushered the small party forward. Tobgye went into the courtyard first. Owen nodded to her, and to her father, and followed Tobgye's lead.

Her father took her by the upper arm.

'We have to go in with them,' he said.

Her legs were a little shaky from the riding and the exhaustion, and the anxiety that this meeting with her father was going to swirl them both into the middle of some danger which was about to reveal itself.

'Is everything all right?' she asked.

'I'm all right,' he said. 'Don't worry.'

Which made her all the more anxious. She slipped her arm through her father's for comfort as they entered the *dzong*. The atmosphere of the fortress was like that of an ancient medieval cathedral, like Chartres or Rouen or the cathedral fortress of Le Puy. She suddenly felt like a bride being escorted to the altar, even as Tobgye's soldiers occupied cloisters and buildings and the monks scattered about the courtyard. An elderly monk with about an inch of grey hair and spidery whiskers at the corner of his mouth slipped quickly by her and her father to guide Tobgye and Owen into a narrow doorway. The Shabdrung's chamberlain seemed to have disappeared. Her father looked back towards the gate but Tobgye's soldiers had already blocked it completely.

'What the hell . . . ?'

He called back something in Dzongkha but none of the

soldiers answered him. A monk said something to him and he nodded. The ground was beginning to feel very unsteady beneath her feet and Christina didn't know whether to look to her father or to Owen to help her regain her balance. It was her father's arm that was linked with hers.

'What's the matter?' she asked him. 'What's going on?'

'Sonam Tsering,' he said, 'the chamberlain. They've taken him somewhere. And the commander of the Shabdrung's bodyguard.'

Then he shook his head as if to tell her not to involve herself in it, and he indicated the narrow doorway with a movement of his chin. Christina ducked under the lintel where Owen and Tobgye had gone. She was in a dark passage with steep wooden stairs to climb.

'My God, what's happening?' she asked.

'Tobgye's not wasting any time,' he said. 'He's taking control of the *dzong*. I'm sorry, Chrissie. I had no idea that you'd arrive in the middle of all this. It's all getting so out of hand.'

He pulled her closer to him

'We'll go up to see the Shabdrung,' he said. 'Then we can talk a little. I'll have to talk with Tobgye soon. And with Davies.'

Owen, Tobgye and the monk with the spidery whiskers waited for them on the landing above. Then the monk set off down another long and narrow corridor. If there had been any New Year celebrations going on in Talo, the arrival of this invading army must have instantly snuffed them out. Through the swaying bodies of the three men in front of her she could see down the passage to another low and narrow door. Owen, Tobgye and the monk passed through it and into a room. Framed by the door jambs and lintel, and at the far end of the small room, she could see a low throne that was lit from the right as if there was a rice-paper window screen just out of sight. Seated on the throne was a young man, his broad, smooth face framed by scores of long braids that fell from under a gold brocade crown.

She couldn't take her eyes off him as the old monk ushered

her forward. She was sure that this was the Shabdrung, the man the Bhutanese claimed as their god-king. The young man's eyebrows made high arches on his wide forehead, giving him a rather feminine look. His nose, too, was wide and the lips full and delicately curved above the strong square chin. He seemed completely relaxed and alert, with a deep and powerful presence. She'd heard so much praise and condemnation of this young Bhutanese aristocrat whom her father was trying to protect. She struggled awkwardly with her canvas bag, searching for her white scarf and for the gift that she had brought for him.

'His Majesty, Jigme Dorje, the Shabdrung Rimpoche, Dharmaraja of Bhutan.'

It was her father who made the introduction.

Tobgye was the first to approach the god-king, and they exchanged a number of words in Dzongkha which no one translated for her. Tobgye, still bowed, shuffled back from the throne, still facing the Shabdrung in an obviously insincere show of religious devotion. Owen was next to offer the Shabdrung a white scarf. He too spoke Dzongkha. She felt quite excluded. Then the Shabdrung looked directly at her. She held her white scarf out to him on her open palms, her gift gripped in her fingertips. The Shabdrung reached down. He pulled the silk away from the small, silver-framed picture of the perfectly featured gold Buddha. Without comment or thanks or even any change of expression, he handed the framed picture to one of his robed attendants. To her surprise, he flipped the white scarf over her neck. He touched his fingertips to her temples and tapped his forehead to hers and even with that light impact she felt as if an electric bulb had flooded her brain with light. A deep swell of pleasure warmed and expanded in her belly, but she panicked at the physical effect that he had on her. It was too like her experience of the medium. Her head was pressed between his hands and his forehead and she couldn't pull away. With his fingertips still on her temples, his head came back and she stared into the blackness of his eyes. His smile was outrageously sensual. She relaxed. What had he done to her? Then his fingertips fell from her head and his face was open to the room again.

'Welcome to my home,' he said. 'You will have to forgive my poor English.'

The rest of the room was like a shifting kaleidoscope of motion on the periphery of her vision.

'I've waited such a long time to meet you,' she said. 'Since my father's letter described you, I've been thinking about you so much.'

She refocused on the room as she heard her father translate for her. The Shabdrung looked genuinely surprised. He said something in Dzongkha and her father provided the English.

'He asks if there's much to think about?' her father said.

She nodded.

'Oh yes,' she said. 'I've been studying . . . not here but in London . . . and India . . . with the Theosophical Society.'

Her father translated again.

'Oh, Mrs Besant,' the Shabdrung said.

Those words she understood for herself. Her father provided the rest.

'Many Western people study religion in the Theosophical Society, don't they?'

The young Shabdrung seemed pleased about that. And if he knew and approved of Mrs Besant, then perhaps he would know about Madame Blavatsky.

'Perhaps I might ask some questions of you,' Christina said.

Her father translated for her. The Shabdrung nodded and spoke again.

'If we have time,' her father said.

She glanced at Owen. He seemed puzzled and upset by this exchange. Not surprising. It was the pure biological instinct of one male seeing the effect of another over a claimed female.

She was certain that Owen understood the effect that the Shabdrung had had on her. 'The real thing.'

One real thing – it was no marvel to her that the Shabdrung was rumoured to have slept with women. She had studied yoga with Oliver Haddo so she knew something of the aims of sexual sublimation. Perhaps years of training in such a physical discipline and in meditation had given the Shabdrung this intensely sensual air of spirituality. Or had he been born that way? Much as she wanted to remain cold and scientific, it seemed as if her whole body was now charged with light and warmth under his touch. This was why her father had brought her here. It was as if she had been waiting for a meeting like this all her life. 'The real thing.'

And she suddenly felt a deep and loving gratitude to Owen for having made it possible for her to come here to Talo to meet her father and to meet the Shabdrung under this best and worst juxtaposition of circumstances. Her skin prickled and chilled as her mind's eye refocused on the violent and vivid visions conjured up by the medium in Bumthang.

CHAPTER TWENTY

HER FATHER SAT ON THE EDGE OF A BIER-LIKE BED THAT HAD been built out from the wood-panelled walls. There was little enough room in her father's living quarters and the tiny room had been shrunk yet more by the ornate, red-painted cabinetry that crowded around three of the walls. She and Owen were cramped together on a low bench opposite him. Since her meeting with the Shabdrung, she had hardly had time to say two words to Owen. Perhaps that was better. She was in turmoil: stunned by the effect that the Shabdrung had had on her; something electric was still prickling her nerves, some visceral melting still going on right under her navel. And here she was, in her father's room, desperate to speak to him but more than a little over-whelmed, not just by the Shabdrung's effect on her but also by the swift and hostile occupation of Talo Dzong by Tobgye's soldiers. She was sure Owen could feel her agitation, seated, as he was, thigh by thigh with her.

'You haven't arrived under the happiest of circumstances,' her father said. 'I'm sorry about that. But I'm so glad you're here, Christina.'

'Owen and Colonel Marshall explained to me what was going on with the Shabdrung,' she said. 'It's so awful.'

'Marshall, yes.' Her father nodded, poker-faced. 'Thank you for that, Davies.'

She had hoped that her father and Owen were going to get

on. She felt rather like a young debutante presenting her father with a suitor. One she had already slept with. But this introduction had all become confused by her reaction to the Shabdrung.

'I'd been hoping for a less fraught reunion,' she said.

Her father reached out, squeezed her hand, nodded and smiled.

'We haven't seen enough of each other at all, have we? I'm getting on now. And I've been a terrible father to you, I know that.'

She didn't want to agree with him but in a sense it was true.

'Don't say that,' she said.

Owen shifted next to her. She wanted to do or say something to reassure him, knowing that if she did, she would be deceiving him. After this whirl of sudden emotion, she wanted to catch her breath for a moment. Relax. Take stock of what was going on. This was no time to be falling in love – she couldn't be falling in love – not with someone who was so impossible to possess as this young god-king. She needed to get a grip on herself. In the month that she had known him, she had already built something steady with Owen. Was it love or just that shipboard romance falling apart under the impact of the meeting with her father? She had to be aware of what was going on in her mind without being overwhelmed. She was a doctor. She wasn't going to forget that. Was she subject to some kind of Electra complex that was causing her to reject Owen in order to cling to her father? She didn't want to throw away what she had with Owen. Of course, this was difficult. Whatever subconscious currents were swaying her, right this second, she had to concentrate on her father. She had come to Bhutan to be reconciled with him. She had to give that a chance.

On his palm, her father cradled the heavy silver fob watch that she'd given to him. He turned it over in his fingers as if he were trying to decipher the hidden combinations of those intertwined letters of the Sanskrit alphabet: all those curled forms, which made a tree of words with trunk and branch and leaf and the shapes of songbirds.

Owen was silent, as if he didn't want to intrude on their reunion but didn't want to be absent from it either.

'I feel like I've brought all this trouble here,' she said.

'You can't blame yourself for that,' her father said. 'This has all been slowly getting worse over the past few months. I never thought the rivalry between the two kings would reach this stage.'

'You've done everything you can to avert it, I'm sure,' Owen said.

Her father stared straight at Owen.

'I'm sure you've read the dispatches, Davies,' he said.

'Yes, of course,' Owen said.

'And the Department sent you up here to negotiate with me.'

'No,' Owen said. 'They sent me up here to bring you back.'

She turned to look at Owen. His eyes were candid, his face relaxed. She was relieved that he hadn't tried to hide anything from her father.

'Of course,' her father said. 'I expected it. Do you know what happened to the Shabdrung's chamberlain, Sonam Tsering?'

'He's been arrested,' Owen said.

'Arrested?' her father said.

He glanced up at her from under his thick shock of grey hair.

'They say he's been poisoning the ear of the Shabdrung against the Maharaja,' Owen said.

Her father nodded.

'True in a way,' he said.

She was surprised he'd said that. She could sense Owen's relief beside her that her father had agreed with him. It was a relief to her that they were talking about the political situation and not about her and Owen's love life. But, as usual, all this discussion about politics was keeping her away from any meaningful talk with her father. Nothing had changed. Her father was now as distant from her as ever. Even sitting here in this room.

The Colonel continued to stare at the watch in silence. Above his head, there was a bronze Buddha image of Padmasambhava – the tantric saint. It was in a small wall niche. Scroll paintings hung off picture rails on either side of the statue and acted as curtains for yet more shelves. She couldn't fail to recognise the fierce image of that mule-riding mountain goddess holding a sword. Her father was completely immersed in this Himalayan world. During all these years in the mountains, he must have been a participant in even stranger psychic phenomena than the seance in Bumthang. She wanted to know about that. She wondered if she ever would.

'The Shabdrung's chamberlain is a bloody fool,' her father said. 'Of that, there's no doubt. He drove out one of his rivals at court so that he could have the man's wife. The woman, of course, wanted nothing to do with him. The courtier blamed the Shabdrung for doing nothing to stop his chamberlain disgracing him and then allied himself with the Paro Ponlop, one of the Maharaja's generals. He told the Ponlop that the Shabdrung was practising black magic to harm both him and the Maharaja. And both of *them* saw an ideal opportunity to cut down the Shabdrung. Yes, the chamberlain is a bloody fool.'

'Tobgye has him in custody now,' Owen said.

Her father tightened up opposite her.

'Tobgye'll go for the Shabdrung next,' her father said.

She tightened on her seat.

'He hasn't yet,' Owen said.

'He's waiting for you to get me out of the way.'

Owen nodded.

'Why?' Christina said.

'Well,' her father said. 'Tobgye can threaten and intimidate anybody in Talo to keep quiet about what he does, but not the representative of a foreign power. He needs me out of the way.

They can't do anything too vicious to the Shabdrung while I'm here because they know that I'll broadcast it to the world whether the Department likes it or not. My word is respected up here. I'm well known. I could sour their relations with Tibet and the Chinese, not to mention the Bhutanese faithful, if I were witness to some sort of foul play.'

She suddenly realised how terribly vulnerable her father was. And that the Shabdrung was terribly vulnerable, too.

'If he's not careful,' her father continued, 'the Maharaja could spark a border war, or another civil war. He *is* treading carefully. If the Shabdrung disappears quietly, without any witnesses, then there may be suspicion, but no proof. Then the Maharaja can reign virtually unopposed – with our support against the Tibetans or the Chinese.'

She glanced from one to the other. Disappear quietly? Even the thought of it . . . But she couldn't say anything without it coming out like a protestation to Owen, and Owen remained silent. Her father closed the lid of his new watch and tucked it into the breast pocket of his homespun *khurta*.

'How long have we got, Davies?' her father asked.

Owen clasped his hands together and brought them up under his chin.

'A week at the most,' he said. 'Then the Paro Ponlop will arrive. We have to be gone by then.'

'The Paro Ponlop,' her father said.

She was suddenly uncomfortable sitting this close to Owen, as if the space she occupied were making her Owen's ally against her father, but she didn't want her father to fight him either. She wanted them to find a solution. They were Department men. Strange how she had confidence in both of them – in the power of the Raj to tip over the policies of these tiny kingdoms.

Owen leaned forward, his hands now clasped between his knees.

'The Maharaja is sending the general to take over from Tobgye,' Owen said.

'You can see what's coming, can't you?' her father said.

Owen leaned back. The tendons in his neck stood out tight.

'House arrest, I imagine,' Owen said, 'with Tobgye's army outside.'

'House arrest?' her father said. 'He's already under house arrest.'

'I understand,' Owen said.

'I asked Marshall, you know,' her father said, 'if we could get permission for the Shabdrung to enter India. Absolutely refused, of course.'

'It's that Gandhi business, isn't it?' Owen said. 'That was a big mistake. The Shabdrung shouldn't have contacted Gandhi. Makes him *persona non grata* for the Department. If he came to India, the Shabdrung would be arrested on sight and turned back at the border.'

They were locked in Department business now and Christina felt sidelined.

'He wanted to go to Tibet, you know,' her father said.

'Marshall told me,' Owen said. 'It seems the Shabdrung asked the Panchen Lama for help in recruiting some Chinese warlord.'

'Come on, Davies. You aren't that bloody naive. First the border dispute. Over bloody grazing rights, for God's sake. And that becomes a threat to the Maharaja's sovereignty. Then broken vows of chastity. That was to provoke the monastic hierarchy and our bloody British moral outrage. And it's a ridiculous charge. Anyone who knows Bhutanese culture would know that the Shabdrung's expected to have a consort. It's normal. Then they claim there are all these black magic rituals to kill the king, which no one can corroborate. Now our dear Maharaja raises the spectre of a Chinese army about to invade Bhutan. We'd have to react to that, wouldn't we? But I can't believe that even Marshall would ever buy it. Unless he wants to use it as the diplomatic way out for the Department to cover up in Calcutta whatever's coming next.'

'Are you saying that the Shabdrung made no appeal to the Panchen Lama?' Owen said.

'Oh, he appealed all right,' her father said. 'He asked if he could enter Tibet when we refused to let him into India. He thought he could find safe exile close to the Panchen Lama's seat, at Shigatse.'

'But wouldn't that be ideal for the Maharaja?' Christina said. 'The Shabdrung would be out of his hair if he was in Tibet.'

Her father gave her a wry smile.

'He doesn't want him out of his hair,' he said. 'He wants him out of the way. Completely.'

'How can you be so sure?' Owen interrupted.

'Because the Panchen Lama did offer the Shabdrung asylum,' her father said. 'And when he sent his baggage ahead to the border, your friend the general, the Paro Ponlop, took an army corps and tracked down the caravan. He stopped it at the border and ransacked the encampment, announcing that he was personally going to kill the treasonous Shabdrung the moment he found him. But the Shabdrung wasn't there. He was still with his family here in Talo. If he *had* got away to Tibet, I would have come back to Calcutta in a trice.'

'But why kill him? Why wouldn't the Maharaja just let him get out of Bhutan?' Christina asked.

'While the Shabrung's alive,' her father said, 'he's still a potential threat to the throne. For the Bhutanese, he's the living reincarnation of the founder of Bhutan. A rival political faction might adopt him as a figurehead, whether the Shabdrung consents to it or not. Whether he's inside Bhutan or not. The Wangchuk family has always been completely ruthless when it comes to rivals to their claim to the throne. They like to string their enemies' guts over the branches of trees. I'm sure Owen could provide you with the details.'

'He already has,' she said.

The Colonel glanced over at Owen.

'But the Shabdrung is some kind of god-king to them,' Christina said. 'They couldn't kill their own god.'

'Hence the defamation,' her father said. '"The god-king has degraded himself by sex and black magic." Claiming they were mistaken in choosing the reincarnation. But any country is run by politicians.'

'Bhutan and Tibet are no exceptions,' Owen said.

He seemed anxious to find a point of agreement with her father.

'Yes,' the Colonel said. 'And if the Paro Ponlop is coming here, I'm not leaving. You know that, don't you, Owen? That bastard has already threatened to kill the Shabdrung. I won't leave him unprotected. Marshall and the Department can go to hell.'

Owen's eyes widened. He breathed out. Her father had just overstepped the mark. She knew that.

'There's nothing we can do, Colonel Devenish,' Owen said.

'I won't stand by and let them butcher him.'

'I can't see them doing that,' Owen said. 'He's still the religious king. It might ignite the country if they killed him. He'll be under house arrest, but nothing worse than that.'

Owen's hand went up to his hair. He dropped it again onto his thigh.

'We have to leave in a few days,' Owen said. 'I'll do everything I can for the Shabdrung but we have to leave, Colonel. That's a direct order from the Department.'

'I won't leave,' her father said.

Owen stood up and her father did, too. Eye to eye.

'Let's talk in the morning,' Owen said.

She put her arm on Owen's wrist but he ignored it. He was looking straight ahead at her father. She had that awful sense of anguish one felt when two once-close friends took up irrevocable positions of absolute opposition.

'I'll have to have a word with Tobgye,' Owen said.

She felt her heart slump at Tobgye's name.

'Yes, Tobgye,' her father said.

Owen nodded to her father.

'Good night, Christina,' Owen said to her.

'Good night, Owen,' she said.

He ducked under the low lintel of the room. The metal on the heels of his boots clacked against the flagstones of the corridor outside and then there was silence.

Her father smoothed the sides of his thick moustache.

'You've made it impossible for him,' Christina said.

You bull-headed bastard, she thought.

'We might as well have it out in the open,' he said.

'Couldn't you look for some compromise?'

'No room. They won't let the Shabdrung out of the country. They don't want me to stay.'

'They won't kill him, will they?'

Her father looked at her as if she was mad.

'What's going to happen, now?' she asked.

'I don't know,' he said.

His answer was simple enough. She only hoped that her father had a clear idea of what it was that he was doing. His stand against the Department would be political suicide. It might even have criminal consequences, defying such an order. And what would he say if he knew – he must know – that she had been sleeping with Owen? He would have sensed it.

'I'm sorry,' he said. 'I never expected . . . When I wrote to you, all this intrigue was just a stupid little dispute over cattle. And I did just want to see you. I wanted to have you safe. Even as the situation started to get worse, I still wanted you to come. I wanted you to meet the Shabdrung. I wanted you to have this opportunity before it was too late. Something you would never forget . . . You're a Theosophist. I've studied here . . . And the Shabdrung . . . I thought this was something worthwhile that we could do together.'

Her father was protecting this young man. If her father had indeed become a student of the Shabdrung, she knew that he would almost certainly have that peculiarly Eastern type of relationship that she had seen often enough in India among Hindus and Sufis. A student of Tantra, young or old, would be prepared to lay down his life to protect his spiritual teacher. If her father was no exception, he was not going to make it easy for Owen, no matter how much he may have liked and respected him in the past. And when she thought of the meeting she had had with the Shabdrung that afternoon, the thought of any harm coming to him was abhorrent. She wanted her father to bring this business to a peaceful and happy conclusion. She didn't want to deal with even more fire and bloodshed.

CHAPTER TWENTY-ONE

I

THAT STUBBORN BASTARD DEVENISH WAS DETERMINED TO WRECK any possibility of a solution to the two kings' conflict and now, Davies could sense it, Christina was ready to get dragged into this Shabdrung nonsense too, and really muddy the waters. He'd seen other Theosophists in Calcutta getting misty-eyed about so-called sacred masters. He'd seen Annie Besant at the top of the pole, and Marjorie Commander, Richard's little bird who had reported on Davies going to matins, who could get all shivery over their Jiddu Krishnamurti, no matter how hare-brained their idea of a new world saviour. Even their new world saviour had thought them hare-brained. Christina was attracted to this 'Great Master' as if to a new lover. The best approach was probably to stand aside and let this blind infatuation run its course. It was infuriating to see her drawn to another man like that but he couldn't interfere. He'd always known about her Theosophy. He could only hope that her attraction to the Shabdrung would be sublimated onto the spiritual plane and that she would not end up in his bed. Davies didn't want her to end up in the Shabdrung's bed. The image of her lying under the young Bhutanese monarch loomed in his mind and he shut it off. It wasn't too far-fetched, was it? Tobgye had said that the clergy had been objecting to the Shabdrung sleeping with women.

He could just imagine it, her throwing herself at some so-called Master. She was fragile and vulnerable, too. But it would be harder for Christina to do it in secret than a Bhutanese woman. As an Englishwoman, all eyes would be on her. The real problem was that she would ally herself with her father, and that would complicate further Davies's search for a solution to the diplomatic mess that the Colonel was determined to exacerbate. It had to be thought of as a logistical problem. But all the muscles of his back and shoulders tightened when once again he imagined Christina and the Shabdrung together.

Butter lamps flickered dimly in the small, sooty wall alcoves of the corridor. His boots clacked on the flagstones. The door out to the courtyard rattled as it attempted to keep out the wind. The Colonel was living a fantasy. He had lost touch. All these old Orientalist gentleman-adventurers in the Great Game, like Younghusband, Burton or Devenish, were like dinosaurs: about to become extinct. Times were changing rapidly: the Bolsheviks were in power in Russia. Mao Tse-tung and the Chinese Communists could easily give Chiang Kai-shek a run for his money. This was the age of pragmatism. Raw political power was all that had ruled the earth since the Great War.

Since the Great War? Since the beginning of human beings on earth.

Marshall wanted Davies to arrest the Colonel, but quite simply, he, Davies, couldn't do it. If Christina saw her father in handcuffs, or marched away by Sergeant Thomas and a squad of sepoys, that would be the end of it. He might be able to convince her that he had had no choice. He might even convince her of the logic of an arrest. But seeing her own flesh and blood, her father, whom she had come so far to see . . . If she saw him arrested, he risked killing everything between them. He didn't want that.

Davies slid back the flat wooden latch and a gust of wind flung the door open and the butter lamps fluttered crazily, flinging shadows around the walls and ceiling, the air damp already against his face. He pulled the door shut, his back to the buffeting wind. He turned and passed under the cloisters as stinging hail slashed across the inner courtyard of Talo Dzong. He waited under the sheltering roof while a brawny monk, hooded and shadowed under a heavy fold of his wine-dark robe, rushed out into the icy fury to lift the thick oak crossbar out of the brackets on the gates.

What the hell am I doing here? he thought. I was born in that narrow valley in Wales to a narrow-minded Methodist minister and his long-suffering wife, where small dark men dig coal and smelt iron into steel and keep their noses in their beer and their wives' bellies full of kids. How the hell did I find myself in this bloody country, time-locked in the Middle Ages?

He laughed to himself.

I joined the army. That's how, I got away. That was it. No going back.

The monk by the gate called to him, gruff and irate under the slashing hail. Davies pulled his felt hat down on his head, holding the brim as he ran. Hailstones stung his fingers and the back of his right hand. With his left, he clutched the lapels of his tweed jacket tightly closed below his chin. The wind drove, wet and stinging, into the back of his trousers so that the cloth clung to his thighs and calves even before he was out of the *dzong* and into the flickering light of the huge fire that defied the rain. It blazed up in front of the gate and cast its jittery brightness upon a desultory group of Tobgye's soldiers huddled under oilskins beneath the slashing storm. Davies skirted the blaze and ran across the terraced meadow down towards the tents, his wet boots slithering over the slick path, then sucked down into thick muck pools. Water seeped cold into his socks.

All around him, the tents of the encamped army rattled and rippled in the wind, a canvas sea lashed by the stinging hail. The flames of the soldiers' campfires in the troughs between the tents flickered and wavered westwards, whipped up by the wind. And within the battered canvas, swinging lanterns cast crazy shadows of hunched bodies huddled against the chilling damp of the mountain air.

'Sonam Tobgye,' Davies called.

A squall of hail stung the side of his face, and an icy trickle ran down his cheek and under his collar. An armoured body-guard fidgeted at the entrance to Tobgye's tent and then lifted the flap to usher Davies inside. The lanterns hanging from the ridge poles at about head height swayed with the tent as the wind squalled again. Tobgye sat behind a campaign table, his moustachioed face peering out from under the hood of a woollen shawl. The table was scattered with ink and pens and parchment. One heavy sheet had been marked with a wax seal.

'Sit down,' Tobgye said,

His face was black with drink. He said something to the soldier in a dialect that Davies didn't understand and the soldier left the tent. Davies lowered himself into the damp canvas camp chair in front of Tobgye's table. Water dripped from the brim of his hat.

'You'll catch your death in those wet clothes,' Tobgye said.

No slurring but the eyes had all the meanness of a spirit-poisoned liver.

'I'll survive,' Davies said.

From a dark green bottle on the table, Tobgye poured out two large glasses of amber liquid and handed one to Davies. Davies raised the glass, swallowed deeply and let the sweet liquid warm him from the inside out. This was good French brandy. There wasn't much left in the bottle. Tobgye peered out from under his blanket hood, his brandy glass under his nose, his palms warming the golden liquid in the glass balloon. Trickles of cold water picked their way down Davies's legs.

'Colonel Devenish isn't going to make this easy for us,' Davies said.

Tobgye's head tilted back and the muscles in his face tightened in concentration.

'What does that mean?'

'He says he won't leave.'

'Will you arrest him?'

'I'd rather not.'

'Do you want to take more drastic action?'

Drastic action – the Department's code word for elimination.

'Good God, absolutely not,' Davies said.

Tobgye took large swallow of brandy.

'It's the woman, isn't it?' Tobgye said.

Davies's stomach fluttered. He couldn't deny it. Tobgye was sharp enough to divine it.

'I need some time to ease him aside,' Davies said.

'Ease him aside?'

Davies nodded, kept a hard face to Tobgye, gave away nothing.

'I can help you,' Tobgye said. 'To ease him aside.'

Davies raised his chin.

'Something from the pharmacy,' Tobgye said. 'Every monastery has a very good pharmacy.'

'The pharmacy?'

'Some medicines can make you ill. Might last for a few weeks.'

'Isn't that dangerous?'

'I'm a very careful man.'

Christ, if Devenish died Christina would disintegrate with the grief. Strong as she was, she had a tremendous vulnerability. Especially with all the loss she had had to endure. She'd been fragile enough in Calcutta with the death of her friend, the clinic burning. If she lost her father, it didn't bear thinking about. She'd go to pieces. He didn't want that. She meant more to him than any woman – even more than Emma – had ever meant. Whatever Tobgye's little scheme was, it would have to come off without any hitches.

Tobgye steepled his fingers below his chin and waited for

Davies's answer with his customary patience and silence. There were so many factors to consider.

Here in Talo, Davies was on shaky ground because of Christina. She had finally met her father. Naturally, she would be distracted by the reunion. And now she had become fascinated by the Shabdrung, too. Of course, she was a Theosophist. Christina's sense of freedom, which was so exciting to him, the freedom that had brought her into his bed, was also causing her attention to drift away from him momentarily. If her father became ill, she'd be worried. But she was a doctor. She could nurse him. It would be something to keep her occupied between Talo and India. She might quickly forget about this fascination with the Shabdrung, which was likely to increase the longer they stayed in Talo. Talo was a sticky pit for all of them. When they got back to Calcutta, he, Davies, and Christina would be on more solid ground. If he agreed to Tobgye's scheme, he would be deceiving her, of course. Ideally, he didn't want to deceive her in anything. But he had to see this as a practical matter. And if working for the Department had taught him anything, it was that deceit often worked for the best. Anything might be soon forgotten, especially after a positive outcome. And if he could get the Colonel out of Bhutan without having to arrest him, that would indeed be the most positive outcome for Devenish, for Christina and for himself. Marshall had said that if the Colonel refused to go, Davies should make a simple arrest at this point. But if Davies managed to get the Colonel out without having him arrested, then Marshall would be happy enough. The Colonel wouldn't have to face charges back in Calcutta. And he, Davies, would not be seen in Christina's eyes as the man who had arrested her father. If Tobgye's scheme paid off, it would be the perfect solution. The sooner they got to Calcutta the better. Davies knew how to operate there. Calcutta was home ground. Calcutta was his domain. And Christina could get back to her real work. She could found another birth control clinic. Get back to doing her real work. God knows there was certainly need for that. The population was growing every day. He could support her while she set it up. He just had to get the Colonel out of Bhutan. But timing was crucial.

'I don't want anything to happen to the Colonel right away,' Davies said. 'I've just had an argument with him.'

Tobgye waved his hand, setting the empty brandy glass down in front of him.

'Don't worry,' Tobgye said. 'I'll arrange everything. The moment you give the word.'

'And for God's sake, Tobgye. Be very careful. I don't want the Colonel dead.'

2

The cloister at least gave Davies some cover as the sleet and rain slanted down into the puddles in the courtyard. The guards on the gate had hardly given him a second glance as he passed within again. He knocked on Christina's door. There was no sound from within her room. A sudden chill shook him and he drew deep breaths to get his nerves under control. He wanted to feel the warmth of her in his arms. He couldn't blame her for her father's stubbornness.

Davies knocked again.

Knock, knock, knock.

A chair scraped against wooden boards and something thumped to the floor.

'Who is it?'

Her voice.

'It's me,' he said. 'It's Owen.'

The bolt rattled back and she swung the door half open to let him slip through. In the dark, her arms slid under his jacket and over his shirt, rubbing across his ribs to his back.

'God, you're soaked,' she said.

'I've been at the bivouac,' he said. 'Last rounds. That sort of thing.'

'I have a dry towel in my trunk,' she said.

He shrugged off his jacket, hung it on a peg behind the door and his hat on another. She moved away from him in the darkness. He took off his waistcoat next, loosened and unknotted his tie, his chill fingers pushing at the damp collar button of his shirt. She lit a candle on the low lacquered table by her bedside. The light of the flame played over her loose and untidy red hair, making copper glints. He caught a glimpse of bare breast and the dark nipple as her white cotton shift swung forward when she lifted the lid of her trunk. She found the towel and he stripped off his wet shirt.

'I wish you hadn't had such an argument with my father,' she said.

The tiny hairs on his neck stood up and he shivered. He took the towel from her and rubbed it over his stippled skin. She seemed a bit distant from him. He wanted to repossess her. Lose himself inside her. Come hard. Sink into some black oblivion.

'I really do want your father's cooperation,' he said. 'I wish we could do this amicably.'

'I'm sorry,' Christina said, 'but he's convinced that Tobgye and the Maharaja mean to do something awful to the Shabdrung, you know that. You can't let them do that, Owen. The Shabdrung isn't a violent man, is he?'

The Shabdrung. Why was she so concerned about what happened to the bloody Shabdrung? She'd only just met him.

'And this business with the Chinese; was Marshall lying?' she said.

Davies hung the towel around his neck and ran his fingers into her crinkly hair. Marshall had certainly been lying.

'I don't believe Marshall would lie to us,' he said, 'but the Maharaja or Tobgye might easily have lied to Marshall.'

She nodded. She was mulling it over. She suspected that there was something off-kilter about what he'd said. Her green eyes glittered with the candle flame.

'I'll do everything I can for you, Christina,' he said. 'You know that, don't you?'

He could feel her father's presence around her almost palpably. It made his gut churn. He had to get her out of this bloody country where everything was upside down. And he had to remember that it was her father who was keeping them here. His stubbornness was undermining everything they had together.

'Are you all right?' she said.

One side of her face was glowing in the candlelight, the other was all angles and shadows. She shivered in the frigid air.

'Come on,' he said. 'Let's get under the covers.'

She turned away from him and slipped beneath the heavy cotton quilt. Davies lowered himself onto the undersheet and the thin felt mattress that hardly cushioned the wooden slats of the bed. He was used to such hard surfaces to sleep on in the Himalayas. Perhaps she was, too, by now. She had her back to him. He hooked his arms up under her armpits and slid his knee along her thigh so that the nightdress rode up to her hips.

'Just hold me,' she said.

She'd trapped his hands under her arms and against her ribs. She was rejecting him. He pulled back away from her, came up on one elbow. The candle flame flickered and his shadow eclipsed the glow in her face. He blew it out, and lay down on his back: thoughts of Tobgye in his head, and this Shabdrung, and her father. He wasn't going to be able to sleep tonight. Already her breathing was slow and deep. Exhausted after the journey, he thought, the reunion, the tension of their invasion of Talo. She had just become oblivious to him.

Chapter Twenty-two

THE BENCHES WERE PACKED. FILES OF MONKS, BONY ADOLESCENTS and hoary, wrinkled old men wrapped in maroon robes, were arranged on the other side of the room from Christina. About ten young nuns, like medieval penitents with closely shaven heads, were seated on her side of the room. Wild-eyed men and women with long matted hair piled on top of their heads and tied with red rags sat in lotus position close to the throne, on her left, at one end of the room. All of these unkempt men and women were wrapped in the same distinctive raw silk shawls: white bordered with broad maroon and black bands. The men were dressed in light cotton tunics and the women in darkly striped *khiras*.

Christina was squeezed in tightly beside a nun on one side and her father on the other. She kept her knees up and together. Her tweed trousers were a little tight but this was the best position against the morning chill of the room. She was surprised to see so many people in the temple. As an Englishwoman, she had expected to have a private audience with the Shabdrung. She had imagined – had hoped for – an initiation into some special relationship with him as if she might emulate the experience of HPB in the previous century with the Hidden Masters. Christina rather suspected that Madame Blavatsky might have exaggerated what had happened to her, dramatised it, because there was no evidence here that this teaching was to be conducted in secretive whispers in a darkened room to specially chosen initiates. This gathering seemed to be part of the normal routine of the monastery. Despite the occupation of the *dzong*, Tobgye seemed to be allowing the Shabdrung to continue his usual duties of ritual and teaching with his monks and yogis. Perhaps the Shabdrung was merely under house arrest, as Owen had said. Or was this Tobgye's way of having her father believe that the Shabdrung was in no danger?

The greasy smelling yellow flames of the brass lamps flickered on the main altar to the right of the throne. The altar was dominated by a twice life-size statue of the tantric saint, Padmasambhava, just as the Maharaja's altar in Bumthang had been. Here it seemed somehow more appropriate. In Bumthang it had been almost blasphemous.

'He'll be here in a minute,' her father said.

This was the world of which her father had only been able to give vague hints in his letter, the world that had so fascinated him all his life even to the exclusion of his wife and daughter. Christina was surprised at herself, surprised that she was so ready to put *that* resentment behind her, and that she was as hungry as her father was to see this Shabdrung again. She glanced around the room to see where the Shabdrung might appear. Scroll paintings of ferocious divinities and protectors, and one of the green-skinned goddess Tara, hung on the walls. Gold-leafed images of various Buddhas and Bodhisattvas, peaceful and wrathful, were arranged along the shelves: some seated tranquilly in meditation posture, others twisted in positions of acrobatic copulation, as if joined in an orgiastic dance. Smoke rose from the slits of long, wooden boxes behind the flickering lamps and laid flat, aromatic strata of incense smoke above the heads of the assembly.

A wave of movement swept across the congregation and they all came to their feet as the Shabdrung entered from a low side door. He was wrapped in a simple maroon robe, long braids falling over his shoulders, and he was crowned with a brocade ceremonial mitre like some bishop. He swept through the congregation, each of its members with head bowed low and holding their hands pressed together at the chest in a gesture of prayer. Christina mimicked them, although it made her even more self-conscious. She glanced sideways at her father. He had his hands clasped loosely in front of him and seemed as graceful and relaxed in that posture as any of the monks or yogis. The Shabdrung pulled up his robe at the knee, mounted the steps to the throne and sat down cross-legged. In front of him, on a shelf built onto the throne, were various religious objects: a narrow-spouted vase decorated with a spray of peacock feathers, a brass mirror on a stand, a golden bell and a small gold thunderbolt sceptre. Wrapped in yellow and maroon cloth covers, two oblong texts, one propped on top of the other, rested on a narrow wooden lectern.

Despite the confined space, everyone in the congregation made three elaborate bows, saluting the Shabdrung with their joined hands at forehead, throat and chest, then prostrating themselves to touch forehead, palms and knees to the ground.

If the gesture of prayer had made Christina uncomfortable, this manner of prostration was impossible. It was so alien for her, a Westerner, to bow down in such a way before any man, even if he was a spiritual master. Equally, she was uncomfortable deciding not to participate, as if, standing upright above these prostrate bodies, she had been exposed as some kind of infidel. The benches rattled as the congregants sat down again, accompanied by hacking coughs and elaborate robe arranging. Christina folded her long limbs down onto the bench again and crossed her arms over her knees. She'd pulled her hair tightly back in a bun so that it wouldn't annoy her during the Shabdrung's discourse.

With everyone seated, a low rumbling chant began, accompanied by strange hand gestures with which her father seemed quite familiar. It reminded her of Catholic rituals: masses and benedictions she had gone to as a child. But still, she was such an outsider here, a bewildered newcomer. Unlike her father she had no idea what the words or hand gestures might mean and her father was too busy doing both to explain them to her. He was absorbed in some interior concentration with which he was obviously very familiar. The chant stopped.

Her father leaned towards her, his breath sweet and unpleasant, rich with the stink of the creamy tea they had drunk for breakfast.

'Listen,' he said. 'My translation is going to be a bit rough. He won't pause very often, but at least you'll get the gist of it. I hope it doesn't come out too garbled. It won't be easy to get it accurate.'

'Don't worry,' she said, 'we can talk about it later.'

Next to the throne, a young monk poured tea into his palm from a kettle. He drank it and then filled a bowl for the Shabdrung. The Shabdrung accepted it in both hands and tilted it up to his mouth to drink. Then he set it down next to his array of ritual objects. From the yellow and maroon cloth covers, he unwrapped one of the texts. The book was about twelve inches long and four inches wide. The Shabdrung turned his startling, lucid gaze on her for a second and there was a melting in her belly that was intensely sexual. The smooth skin of his face had such a warm tone to it. He glanced down at the first page of the text and began to speak in a fast and melodious and rhythmic voice; and in sibilant counterpoint, her father, his mouth close to her right ear, translated for her.

'Our life is very short. Time moves forward. It never goes back. We always need to keep this knowledge present. We can't afford to waste time.'

She was concentrating on the rhythm of the Shabdrung's voice as if she might understand the strange labials and dentals of his unfamiliar language, like a new music in which she might lose herself. But her father's voice was insistent.

'In this life, we have the unique opportunity for our own

discriminating consciousness to discover the real nature of existence.'

The real nature of existence. Was that any different from the discomfort she felt in her back and her legs, squeezed as she was between this young nun and her father?

'The practice of examining the mind . . . discovering the nature of the mind . . . is the way we approach this. This is the practice of meditation.'

One of the Shabdrung's hands held the text, the other moved like a graceful bird above the pages. The fluted rhythms of his Dzongkha invited her to lose herself, while to her right her father's low and breathy voice called her attention back to simple and logical thought.

'We're born through pain. Even as we leave our mother's womb, we feel constriction, suffocation, fear. As the Buddha said, in his first teaching at Sarnath, all beings caught on the Wheel of Existence are subject to suffering. The mere fact that we have a physical body leaves us subject to suffering. This is simple to understand.'

She felt disappointed all of a sudden. She'd heard this fundamental view of Buddhism explained at lectures in the Theosophical Society. She suspected the Shabdrung of being patronising towards her. Giving some generic teaching because she was an outsider, not one of these nuns or monks or yoginis. She had hoped to hear something more esoteric – some extraordinary secret teaching. Then the Shabdrung glanced across at her. She saw real anger in his gaze, as if he had heard her thoughts. She was suddenly ashamed, stunned by that look. His eyes dropped to the text and his voice continued. Had she imagined his sudden disapproval? She tried to concentrate on her father's even-toned translation.

'The cause of all suffering is our dualistic vision. The mind constantly creates tension between subject and object and so we spend our time chasing self-created mirages. We meditate in order to understand the mind. We try to understand how it functions and to discover the real nature of the mind.'

This was what Freud and Jung wanted to discover, wasn't it, the unconscious, the archetypes? Or did he mean something totally different to that? She had no time to analyse it. The discourse kept going forward.

'When we discover the nature of the mind, we understand how everything we experience is like a dream. The nature of the mind is beyond dualism.'

That phrase in her ear – the nature of the mind is beyond dualism – in her father's voice, left her disorientated. She didn't understand it. What on earth was he talking about? And there was an army camped around the *dzong*. How was that like a dream? Inside the folds of those robes, the Shabdrung was all flesh and bone and smooth skin: so obviously fragile and vulnerable to the blades and bullets of the soldiers waiting outside the walls. She glanced at her father. He was intent on his translation: his grey eyes were relaxed and alert and focused on the Shabdrung. The fingertips of his right hand touched the grizzled hair at his temple. His lips were slightly open under the heavy grey moustache. And he kept speaking simultaneously with the Shabdrung's voice.

'At this moment in time, we're living in an age of confusion. We are completely conditioned by illusion. We find ourselves in this degenerate age living in the dregs of time.'

The dregs of time? What was this? She imagined a dream – one of those dreams where you are trying to get somewhere quickly and time is running out and your limbs are weighed down so that you can't move fast enough.

Her father was in full flow now and the Shabdrung hardly paused in his discourse. Her father was reciting a litany of an unlikely cosmic history which began with a Golden Age, when the world was some kind of paradise, where human beings were giants who lived together harmoniously for life spans of around fifty thousand years. And this aeon, he said, was followed by a Silver Age, when beings were not so long-lived, though their lives were still of a duration unimaginable to present-day minds. Christina recognised echoes of the cosmology which Madame Blavatsky had set down as esoteric history in *The Secret Doctrine*. But hearing it explained in this way, from the mouth of the Shabdrung, via the voice of her father, it acted on Christina's senses and consciousness like divinely inspired poetry. The ceremonial litany, the telling of the story itself, was in itself a ritual altering of consciousness whose telling was somehow altering the Shabdrung's own state of consciousness, too. And by this recitation, he was drawing her, and the others in the room, into his own perceptual experience, his own perceptual field which had little or nothing to do with the literal meanings of the words. This was a kind of incantation, perhaps, an enchantment, similar to hypnosis. But she found herself resisting it. She was afraid that she was about to be catapulted into some nightmarish visionary realm similar to her experience with the medium in Bumthang. But this change in her consciousness was subtler than that induced by the medium. The Shabdrung spoke of the degeneracy of the Silver Age into the Copper Age; and on into the Iron Age – the present aeon – which resulted in an acceleration of the perception of time, all-consuming time, that devoured the physical body and the clarity of mind. And this Iron Age, he said, would end in pestilence and confusion and destruction – towards which the inhabitants of the earth were inexorably travelling with ever-increasing velocity, as if he was describing some kind of Buddhist Apocalypse.

Suddenly she experienced a radical perceptual shift that made the colours of the room much brighter. There came the intuition that she shared this state of consciousness with every member of the assembly in this cramped mountain temple, all of whom were experiencing a state of consciousness that was vast and unconfined by the tight press of body against body or of bone and flesh and blood. And this caused to arise within her the intimation of some vast dimension beyond time of which she and they were a part – as if by explaining the passage of mythical time, the passage of perceptual time had disintegrated. This disjointing of the rational and the irrational within her own mind had the bizarre effect of disrupting her perception of the physical world where she sat with her father by her side and the Shabdrung on his throne, conscious still of Owen waiting for her and of Tobgye and his soldiers in the valley below. And the world of her perception was indeed utterly dream-like, as phantasmal as the unfolding cosmology described by the Shabdrung, or the worlds conjured by some wonderful and powerful drug. She was hot and breathing in aromatic incense and the stink of sour sweat from the bodies around her; she could feel an electric prickling beneath the surface of her skin. And she could see each thought pop into her head as if it was some object that had nothing to do with her. And who was it, anyway, observing this thought? It wasn't as if she could see something called 'a Christina' in that vast emptiness of her mind. What was this consciousness?

Whatever it was, now a sudden shadow fell across it and she knew that this world, even if a dream, was about to turn into nightmare because the Shabdrung, just as she did, had a physical body, which was subject to physical laws. That was part of the rules of the particular dream that he shared with her and her father and the monks and nuns and all the waiting soldiers outside. And from the rules of that dream she knew there was no escape. He seemed so fragile: this boy of twenty-six in the hands of the occupying army of the secular government. And still the Shabdrung, through his melodic recitation and her father's translation, continued his prophetic testimony. He predicted the collapse of the Buddhist teaching itself, the teaching of which he was avatar. In the future, he said, these teachings which had once brought its practitioners to enlightenment would be bought and sold in the marketplace, empty symbols devoid of meaning, and useless to those who heard them because unconnected to any surviving lineage of knowledge-holders capable of transmitting the direct experience of them. And she knew that being in this room with someone of this depth of experience of pure consciousness was how this knowledge was transmitted, not through books or dry intellectual lectures delivered from the podiums of learned societies.

'But *we* are all connected,' her father said in her ear. 'All of us in this room have been together before and we'll be together again in future lives.'

And in that moment she was overwhelmed by the whirling perception of space and time, circumstance and physicality, within whose net she was caught. She was in the eye of this hurricane of creation, as if she had caught a fleeting glimpse of the face of some God Almighty between one second and another, a limitless sacred presence full of terror and glory, and the room now appeared to be suffused with a bright and glaring light. Her rational mind kept on working so that she could question herself whether the unfamiliarity of these alien surroundings, the danger to her father and the Shabdrung and his followers, the bizarre circumstances of this confluence of grief, terror and wonder, had caused the underpinning of her rational mind to collapse and allow these photic phenomena to flood through the gaps in thought.

Then the Shabdrung fell silent. Her father was silent while she struggled to make sense of the words, the translation, the reaction of the congregation of which she was part. She was trying to keep a grip on the rational. To be scientific. She was increasingly aware that this thought process was dulling the edge of her perception. And that there was something she could not quite put her finger on, as if whatever understanding she was about to reach with her rational mind kept slipping out of her grasp, just as the Shabdrung was slipping out of her grasp in the physical world. She would have to leave Talo, she knew that. She had travelled all this way to meet him and it seemed as if all those circumstances – the fire in Bombay, Lakshmi's death, meeting Richard and Owen in Calcutta, even her affair with Owen, and the medium's seance – were all necessary to bring her into this moment of time and space where she was flooded with rapture and terror – which she could only describe to herself as a state of grace. All the other people in this room had studied with the Shabdrung for years. She had heard just this one terribly short and beguiling discourse by this young Master, but the key to that knowledge to which he had alluded was in the hands of these monks and nuns and yogis and yoginis, her father among them.

And now the Shabdrung unwrapped from its cloth cover a second small text from which he began to read. Her father whispered the rapid words into her ear, about the mind of discursive thought and the nature of the mind: that ground out of which all creation and perception arose. And then she understood why each colour seemed brighter, each form sharper, each thought clearer, and how, if she persisted in developing this ever-greater clarity, she might penetrate to a more radical understanding of the illusory nature of all that appeared to her five senses and her conscious mind.

'This state of pristine awareness and its connection to the field of perception,' translated her father, 'can be maintained in daily life, outside of formal meditation.'

Truth to tell, from observing the rise and fall of thought in her mind, and the power of emotion that overwhelmed her even now in this temple, she despaired of ever being capable of experiencing or developing her experience of such clarity and spaciousness if no one was with her to point it out like this, even if the Shabdrung could explain it in perfectly clear and simple language how it was done by means of meditation.

His discourse now finished, he wrapped up the text and she

was left stunned and ecstatic in the silence. Then the Shabdrung said a few words directly to her father.

'Tomorrow,' her father translated. 'Come again tomorrow. We'll continue for three days.'

A rush of physical pleasure filled the cavity behind her ribs, filled her skull and descended into her belly. It was visceral. The anticipation that for three days she was going to be able to experience this extraordinary state of consciousness filled her with more pleasure even than any other drug she had taken during her time in London, whether hashish or heroin or cocaine.

Everyone stood as the Shabdrung descended from his throne. As he passed her father, he put one of the wrapped texts into the Colonel's hand, said a few words to him, and made his exit by the small curtained door. She felt covetousness for the knowledge in that book, as if it was a bar of gold that her father held in the palm of his open hand.

Chapter Twenty-three

IT HAD STOPPED RAINING BUT THE COURTYARD WAS MUDDY and puddled, the dirty water stained yellow by disintegrating and fibrous manure. Christina pulled her shawl around her against the damp and misty air and walked across the courtyard of the *dzong* as if her feet rested only tentatively on the ground, reminiscent of that state of dream, close to flight, that had remained with her since she'd heard the Shabdrung's discourse. She passed out through the massive gate to where the army was encamped.

The wide meadow dipped before her to the mist-shrouded pines. Smoke rose into the cloudy air from the flickering campfires as the soldiers prepared their noonday meals. She gazed for a moment at the unreal tableau of an army of occupation laying siege to the open city of Shambala, in which she had become a willing inhabitant. Across the densely peopled meadow, Owen emerged from Tobgye's tent. He was capped and dressed in his khaki field uniform and high leather riding boots against the mud.

He started when he noticed her, as if he had been about some surreptitious errand in the tent of the Bhutanese minister. His hesitation was only momentary and he came towards her up the slope of the meadow and through the bivouacs of the sepoys. Each clank of pot and snort of horse was acute to her ear as if the empty dimension of sound was more substantial to her than that of touch, of physicality. If only Owen could have shared that experience in the temple with her.

'It's finished then?'

He was trying to sound cheerful.

'Yes. I wish you'd come.'

He shook his head.

'I thought we might eat together,' he said.

'I want to eat with my father,' she said. 'I've come so far to see him.'

He looked away over the encampment. She was disappointing him.

'Of course,' he said.

He clasped his hands behind his back. It struck her as a very military gesture.

'How was your audience with the Shabdrung?' he asked.

'Why don't you come to hear him tomorrow?' she said.

Her voice fluted. It sounded too nervous, too enthusiastic.

'It would mean so much . . .'

She cut that off. If he wanted to hear the Shabdrung, then he ought to do it of his own volition. She had no wish to black-mail him. She consciously controlled her voice.

'You might get so much out of it,' she said.

He winced as she said it.

'And time's so short,' she said. 'I know we have to leave soon.'

And that was only going to remind him of her father's intran-sigence.

'Has your father decided he's ready to leave yet?' he said.

'I wish you could find a way to ease his mind on that. I don't know how.'

'Yes,' he said. 'I wish I could, too, for all of us.'

He turned away for an instant as if he had an idea or a desire that he had intended sharing with her but had changed his mind. She was conscious that neither of them was saying what was really on their minds. And there was something strange in his eyes, distant and disturbing, as if some freak electricity was lighting up the synapses in the darkness of his skull. Or was she seeing herself in him, deranged somehow by her overenthusiastic responses to these psychic phenomena that she'd encountered in Bhutan? If her experience with the medium had fractured something between her and Owen, she suspected that this experience with the Shabdrung might set them at odds. There was a way to bridge that gulf.

'Come tomorrow,' she said. 'You know Dzongkha and my father can translate for us.'

She imagined it like some kind of wedding ceremony: both of them entering into that otherness conjured by the Shabdrung's ritual. That's what a wedding ceremony was, even for Christians: a man and a woman entering into some other psychic state together, induced by a clergyman – a representative of God on earth. Owen would understand that – with his 'approximation of grace', his High Church and stained glass.

'I can't,' he said. 'It's too . . . it's alien to me, all this. I couldn't possibly do it.'

His mouth tightened and his eyes narrowed, halfway between regret and irritation.

She could understand that, too. Perhaps she was letting herself get carried away: the mystical wedding of Christian Rosenkreuz and his Soror Mystica with the Shabdrung as the priest. She *was* letting herself get carried away. Her father had offered her something of enormous value. She would only cheapen it by trying to drag Owen into it against his will.

He lifted his cap, ran a hand through his hair.

'I'll lunch with Tobgye,' he said.

There was a resigned bitterness in his voice, within which she detected a large dose of jealousy. He was jealous of her father and he was cutting himself off from a part of her life to hurt her and to hurt himself. There was no need for it – but lovers don't act reasonably. Love wasn't about reason. After that wonderful start – the infatuation and the glorious lovemaking – they start to niggle and irritate each other, each one trying to coerce the other to accept long-held and momentarily suspended prejudices and convictions. She had seen it happen before, and she was very conscious that this was the first time it had happened between her and Owen. She could put a stop to it now. She reached out a hand to touch his forearm, but he stepped away from her.

'Owen, what's wrong?' she asked.

'Nothing's wrong,' he said. 'I just have some difficult decisions to make.'

He raised a hand, gave her a wry smile.

'Go to your father. I'll see you tonight,' he said.

He turned back down the slope and walked away from her. The sight of his broad back in that khaki uniform as he picked his way through the hunched soldiers and the damp tents brought on a mixture of sadness and rage. She would have to be patient. He was struggling to fulfil his duty to the Department, which she knew he took so seriously, and her father was certainly making that difficult for him. To hope that he might share her experience of the Shabdrung was asking too much of him. After all, it was that down-to-earth quality of his with which she had also fallen in love. She pulled her shawl tight around her body and watched him until, without looking back at her even once, he ducked his head and disappeared into Tobgye's tent.

CHAPTER TWENTY-FOUR

HER FATHER REACHED UP TO THE SHELF BEHIND HIM AND TOOK down a clear quart bottle and two wooden cups. A kitchen servant bent over and cleared away their bowls, chopsticks and knives, and the remnants of their evening meal. The servant glanced briefly in her direction and then was gone through the white curtain with a blue cross that hung from the lintel. Her father set the bottle and cups on the ornate lacquer table between him and Christina. The Shabdrung had delivered his third and final teaching that morning and her father seemed to be in the mood to celebrate.

'Let's have a drink together,' he said.

His eyes were clear, bright, and he had a slight smile under the heavy grey moustache. But she was too excited to even think about drinking, and confused and worried. She couldn't help thinking about what Dr Freud would say. Had she indeed regressed into some childhood religious fantasy in the face of circumstances that her conscious mind refused to accept? She didn't believe it. Such an analysis didn't alter her conviction one iota. Owen hadn't wanted to discuss the teaching with her. He'd seemed irritated when she'd brought it up.

During the day, he was busy with the soldiers and with Tobgye, and she knew that he was already preparing to leave. For the last three nights neither one of them had tried to initiate making love. Each of them remained wrapped up in their own preoccupation. She was just as guilty of it as Owen was.

'Why can't I explain it?' she asked.

'Christina, you're too excited by this. You need to relax a little.'

'I've been afflicted by faith. It's like an affliction, isn't it?'

'Faith?' her father said.

'Yes. It's like . . . When he's speaking, you know . . . do you know what it reminds me of? Well . . . like when I went to communion, the first time, as a child, when they put the host on your tongue and it starts to melt. And you are a child so you believe everything they've told you, the priest, the school, so you believe that it's Christ, and he's flooding you with grace. That's what they've told you. So you feel like your whole body lights up inside. And it does. I mean. I'm trying to look at this rationally. You observe yourself, you see. But in there, in the temple, while the Shabdrung was speaking, I felt this sort of grace, do you understand? There was this sense of vastness. Almost terrifying.'

'I suppose it helps to be brought up a Catholic,' he said. 'That way you'll always get the most out of any religious ritual. But what's the affliction part?'

She leaned towards him, her shoulders bent over the table, her red and shiny hands pressed together between her knees. She could talk about this with her father as she couldn't with Owen. She and her father had shared this experience and he could verify the reality of it. He just seemed so much calmer about it than she was.

'When you're ill,' she said, 'your mind and body can't do anything about it. You're simply in that condition. You have a temperature, and you're delirious, whatever. You can't say, "I don't believe this," can you? Perhaps something alters in your body, in your brain, some chemistry that gives you this sense of awe, this light, this feeling of total pleasure in your body, but you're not detached from reality. It's just that the physical world doesn't seem to be so solid somehow, like a dream. How did he do that?'

'Christina, you're raving. Calm down.'

Yes, perhaps she was, but although the line between psychosis and this acute insight into the root of perception might be very fine, she was convinced that she was still on the side of sanity.

He handed the wooden cup to her. She took it from him but held it in both hands just below her chin. The liquid in it was as potent as petrol. The fumes even got in her eyes. He raised his hands, palms flat towards her, as if encouraging her to drink, but she just stared at him over the pool of clear alcohol in the bowl. If he had experienced what she had this morning, he wasn't showing it. He wasn't excited by it in the way that she was. And then she knew.

He's used to it, she thought.

'When did you meet him?' she asked.

'The Shabdrung?' he said. 'Six years ago.'

She needed a cigarette. She reached into the pocket of her tweed jacket for her cigarette case, popped the lid and held it out to him. He shook his head. He rubbed his stomach in a strange way. She tapped a Player's Navy Cut on the silver case, lit it with her petrol lighter, dragged deep, so that a speck of tobacco fell on her tongue. She picked it off and breathed out smoke with her words.

'He said that we'd meet again. In another life. He did say that, didn't he? What do you think, really?'

'You're a Theosophist,' he said. 'I thought you were a Theosophist.'

'Yes, I am . . .' she said. 'Or I'm not . . . I just don't know any more. I mean, I never experienced anything like this at a Theosophy meeting: some things, strange things, at seances. And weird states of mind. With drugs: heroin, morphine, cocaine, hashish.'

If he was shocked by her admission of drug-taking, he didn't show it. He rubbed his eyebrows and temples, head bent, and she thought to ask him if he felt all right, but he replied before she could say anything.

'I thought you Theosophists believed in reincarnation,' he said.

'I don't know,' she said. 'I don't find the transmigration of the soul a very comforting idea, I'm afraid.'

'It's not supposed to be comforting,' he said. 'Just the contrary. But according to Buddhists, and Hindus, if you have a strong connection with a teacher, that connection can be renewed, even in another lifetime, in another body.'

'That's shocking, isn't it?' she said.

Did she really believe that? She had certainly heard about it in Theosophical Society meetings. And she had accepted it in some way as a concept but she had never actually believed it, had she? With the Shabdrung, it seemed to be a real possibility. But how could anyone really count on it? Not unless you could actually remember a past life. And she certainly couldn't.

She breathed out smoke.

'Do you believe in it?' she said. 'Reincarnation?'

He bent forward, shrugged. His face had tightened. He was in pain, she was sure.

'Could all be bunkum,' he said. 'The big question: what's beyond death? Everybody wants to know, don't they? Christians, Hindus, Muslims, Sikhs, Buddhists, Theosophists.'

He had gone pale.

'Are you all right?' she asked.

'Just a little stomachache,' he said.

'Can I get you something?' she asked.

'It's nothing. I expect it'll pass in a minute.'

She nodded. He seemed to be waiting for another question.

'But what about *you*? Really,' she said. 'What do you believe?'

Apart from his physical discomfort, her father seemed a little uncomfortable about having to reveal himself to her. But she wanted him to; this was why she had come all this way to see him, in his world. He owed it to her. She was his daughter. He had to own up to that for once. He ran his hand back through his thick grey hair, held it a moment at the back of his head.

'Are you a gambler?' he asked.

'A gambler?'

'Yes, it's like a gamble, isn't it? I've read all these books. Met all these so-called holy men – half of them not worth the time of day – but if I were to gamble, I'd have to bet on it: something after death. Transmigration of the soul? Why not? I think you're right about grace. It's the experience of grace that makes faith possible, isn't it? For a Christian. Or a Buddhist. Whoever. The Shabdrung can help some people experience . . . can introduce some people to what Christians might call a state of grace. It happens all over Asia among Hindus and Buddhists, but not *all* of these lamas or swamis can help you to see it.'

This was her father who had led her through the bazaars when she was a little girl, pointing out all the anomalies and wonders of India, explained to her the shapes and powers attributed to the gods in the statues and pictures of the roadside temples: Siva the Destroyer; Kali the devourer of time; Vishnu the dreamer of worlds; Ganesha the bringer of good fortune. All those ridiculous forms that never had much sense for her. Until London – and her occultist student days – she had clung more to her mother's Christian view of the world. And after that to anything that would give her a direct experience of the spiritual dimension of being. Theosophy had given her a way to study it without really having to commit to a hard and fast belief. Compared to the way the Shabdrung had opened her perception, Theosophy had merely rippled the surface of consciousness. With the Shabdrung's methods and inspiration, she could go so much deeper. She had an intuition of how it was that the Shabdrung could remain so unperturbed by the nightmare invasion of Talo. He perceived the earth as a dream, a mirage in limitless time, subject to physical laws while the dream continued, but which was merely transformed into some other equally evanescent vision at the moment of death. And this hardly disturbed his state of mind at all.

Her father wrapped his forearm across his lower abdomen.

He *is* sick, she thought.

But when he spoke it was as if he was in tune with her thoughts.

'When you dream every night,' he said, 'it all seems so real, doesn't it? If someone cuts you with a knife, in the dream, you bleed and you feel pain. If you see something horrible, you get scared or you're revolted. And every morning when you wake up, the dream disappears and what you felt was so real has no reality whatsoever. And then it's the world that seems so real and you have the same experiences of pleasure and pain and fear. And you believe in it the same way. Like one vivid dream arising out of another. Why not wake up into some other kind of dream at death? If I were to lay down my money, I would bet on that possibility. And if I were to lose the bet, and all of this quest for knowledge, all this *belief*, just turned out to be a delusion of my own mind . . .' He shrugged. 'I'd lose nothing. I'd have oblivion like everybody else. I'm an old man. I've studied the most extraordinary texts. I've met the most extraordinary men and women. I've travelled in places that few others have even the hope of seeing. I've experienced states of mind that are beyond imagining for most people. What would I have lost? What could I possibly lose? I wouldn't trade a day of my life for anyone else's.'

He shared a certain kind of knowledge with the Shabdrung of which Christina had only an inkling. And he valued the Shabdrung's presence and communication so much that he was prepared to defy the Department or Tobgye to defend it. But, equally, he was bound by the limitations of his physical body and that was what she was conscious of now.

'You aren't looking well,' she said. 'Let me get you some hot water.'

He waved his hand dismissively, irritated, it seemed, at her fussing.

'What do you think is going to happen to him?' she asked. 'The Shabdrung.'

'The Shabdrung? Tobgye was expecting resistance and he brought a bloody great army that the Shabdrung's bodyguard could never stand up against. And they brought Davies to get me out of the way.'

'What will *you* do?' she asked.

'I won't go. They'll have to take me out of here in a box. Tobgye was afraid to harm me without Department backing. And the Department wouldn't give Tobgye permission to eliminate one of their own. The Bhutanese might lose respect for us. It might create problems in the future. The Department will have to remove me in some other way. Davies is their man. Perhaps they thought to get you involved. Whatever he plans on doing, he'll have to act soon. Tobgye is getting anxious.'

She flinched when he talked like that about Owen. And now she was afraid that her father might undertake some catastrophic suicidal action against Owen, the Department, or Tobgye.

'Please don't do anything rash,' she said. 'It won't help anybody.'

'What do you mean?'

'I don't know. I'm just afraid that something awful could happen and I've seen enough in the past month or so to last me a long time yet.'

'I'm sorry, Christina,' he said.

And she saw very clearly now how he had invited her here for this brief moment. He had given her the experience of something that he treasured – before it was lost to him, too. He grimaced again and wrapped both his arms around his stomach.

'God, I feel awful all of a sudden,' he said. 'Better get to the privy.'

His face had drained of all colour. She set down the *arakh* cup and came around the table.

'Let me help you,' she said.

She put her arm around his shoulders.

'Christ, the hygiene in this *dzon*g is bloody awful,' he said.

Then his whole upper body convulsed and his vomit splashed onto the floor.

'Oh my God,' she said, 'lie down.'

'Privy,' he said.

She helped him up. She was strong enough to support his weight leaning on her, and she brushed the curtain aside and got him into the corridor. The flagstones were crooked beneath their feet. She couldn't fall prey to panic. She would let him void his bowels, and vomit more if he needed, then she would need to search out Owen and have him bring the medical supplies: morphine and quinine; cream of tartar. That would stabilise him. Then she could try to find out what it was that was wrong with him. It could be anything. Bhutan, India, Nepal, all over the subcontinent, there was always this infuriating, ever-present chance of falling prey to some tiny germ, like a stray bullet out of nowhere making its sudden strike.

CHAPTER TWENTY-FIVE

I

THE MUST OF THE SHEEPSKIN COVER HUNG IN THE DAMP AND dusty air of her low-ceilinged room as Davies moved on top of her. Her arms were around his back and her thighs were open for him but by the light of the flickering butter lamp, and the shadows in the hollows of her eyes, her drawn cheeks, it was obvious that she was distracted. He pulled her tighter to encourage her, so that he could feel the smoothness and warmth of her skin against his, but her body was limp, unresponsive. He raised himself above her on his hands. At some level, he suspected, something in her cells, connected with his, might divine through a kind of visceral knowledge his, Davies's, part in her father's illness, even though the symptoms were like any common dose of dysentery or giardia or hepatitis. Or was it that she was thinking of this bloody Shabdrung again? She'd become obsessed by him.

'Are you all right?' he said.

She brushed back a strand of hair from her freckled face and then raised her hand to his shoulder. The green eyes looked at him directly now.

'I'm sorry,' she said. 'My father.'

'Worried,' he said.

He got softer inside her, felt himself slide out.

'He's so weak,' she said.

Davies rolled off her, onto his side. This had all been predictable. He'd known, as soon as he'd made the decision to let Tobgye intervene, that both he and Christina would go through an even more difficult time. It had been difficult enough already with this Shabdrung nonsense, but now he had set forces in motion in which they were both embroiled and it would all get rougher before it got better. He just hoped he hadn't made a mistake. She had asked him to ease her father's mind. If it all came off as planned, he could get the Colonel out of Bhutan without having to arrest him, without alienating either Christina or the Colonel, and without the Colonel, in turn, alienating the Department by refusing to obey orders.

Tobgye had explained it all carefully: it was a species of mushroom. In large doses it was lethal. But in small doses, it would look as if the Colonel had simply gone down with a bad liver infection. Tobgye had shown him a dried specimen. It was a common variety, similar to a species found even on the mountains of Wales. Davies knew it as *Amanita phalloides* – the death cap. It was what the Borgias had used on their enemies in medieval Italy, but generally with a more lethal effect than that which Davies intended for the Colonel. A few spores could be given to the Colonel in his food.

Davies had to admit to himself that the audacity of it had been appealing too. But Christ, it was risky.

'I'm sure he'll be all right,' he said. 'It's probably something he ate or drank. We just need to look after him. I do wish he'd agree to get out of here. We could get him to a hospital in India. It's so unhygienic up here. Don't you agree?'

Her hair was a tangled wiry bush on the pillow, her arms folded across her body, those intense eyes staring at the ceiling.

'He won't leave. He doesn't want to leave. The Shabdrung . . .'

'Nothing's going to happen to the bloody Shabdrung.'

He locked his fingers behind his head, let out a hard breath. 'Can we just think of your father for the moment?' he said.

She recoiled from him at that, and from the wild look in her eye and the flush in her cheeks he knew that he had stung her.

'I *am* thinking of my father,' she said.

'It would take us just over a week to get him to a decent hospital in India,' Davies said. 'I'm sure that he'd be all right if we could get him to some proper treatment.'

She pulled the covers around her breasts. He had deflected her anger and got her to draw in on herself. She was mulling that over.

'A week, yes,' she said. 'I wish I knew what he had. There's no laboratory here to get a reasonable diagnosis. You know how these things are. Some virulent germ, I don't know. It does look hepatic. I've given him some of their herbal medicine, too, as well as ours. But every time he eats, he gets sick again. I think you're right. It would be better to get him to a decent hospital but the thing is . . . he doesn't want to go back to India.'

That's it. She was listening to him again. And he, Davies, did want Colonel Devenish to recover. Tobgye must have given the old man a hell of a dose of the fungus. Devenish was delirious. He'd lost a lot of fluid. It *would* actually be better to get him back to India where they could keep him nourished and hydrated intravenously. Davies wasn't going to have Devenish dying on him.

Davies turned towards her, brushed her hair back with his fingers. She stared up at him, her pale freckled face full of fear and ferocity. Up the ante, now. Another risk. Involve their beloved bloody Shabdrung. He felt like such a bastard doing this but he couldn't resist it. He had something inside him that made him want to be cruel to her over this holy man whom he knew had come between them.

'Perhaps the Shabdrung . . .' Davies said.

He paused.

'The Shabdrung?' she asked.

'Your father respects the Shabdrung's opinion,' Davies said. 'We could see what he suggests.'

'About my father being sick?'

Christ, he was on shaky ground. Too late now. Best to go ahead with it.

'In a way,' Davies said. 'Yes. I was thinking . . . particularly about the wisdom of taking your father to India. I just thought. Perhaps he might have some advice. About the best thing to do.'

She tilted her head, her wide mouth open in surprise.

'The best thing to do?' she said.

'Your father,' he said. 'He respects the Shabdrung. And I'm sure the Shabdrung would advise what he thought would be best for your father.'

She was weighing him up.

'You want my father out of here and now you want to enlist the Shabdrung's help,' she said. 'You bastard.'

'Yes, I want him out of here,' Davies said. 'And yes, I think the Shabdrung would help. But believe me, I don't want anything to happen to your father. I think it's the best thing for him. You must believe that.'

She stared at him a moment.

'Tomorrow,' he said. 'I'll ask his advice tomorrow.'

'Jesus Christ, Owen,' she said.

'Do you *not* want me to ask him?'

She might say no. But it was very bloody unlikely. It was certainly tempting to her, wasn't it, to have the Great Master make a pronouncement on the best course of action to treat her father's sickness. Why was he punishing her like this? Her lips pressed together. She looked away from him as if something had appeared at the foot of the bed that needed her intense attention.

'All right,' she said. 'Why don't you?' as if she thought that it might all be going to backfire on him. But it wouldn't. He was sure that it wouldn't.

2

The old grey-whiskered monk, the Shabdrung's personal assistant, led Davies and Tobgye along the corridor to the small temple. The Shabdrung was already there, seated on a low carpeted dais. Behind him on the wall was the ubiquitous painted scroll of the saint Padmasambhava. The Shabdrung was leaning over a small text. From under the brocade hat his long braids hung down around his face. He looked up as they entered the room, that smooth, open and youthful face. The dark eyes were so damned alert. He might be young but he missed nothing. Davies had the horrible insight that the Shabdrung knew exactly what was going on, why Davies and Tobgye were there, what had happened to the Colonel. The monk raised his palms towards two seats that were next to but slightly lower than the dais. Davies let Tobgye sit down first. Davies was confident enough in his command of Dzongkha that he would know what was going on.

The old monk set two cups in front of them and poured steaming butter tea from a metal kettle. Then the monk shuffled out backwards in a half-bow.

Tobgye spoke in Dzongkha.

'Major Davies wants to ask you about Colonel Devenish,' he said.

The Shabdrung nodded.

Davies straightened himself up on the cushioned seat. The Shabdrung was looking right through him. Davies had rehearsed this. He was used to deceit. Used to appearing ingenuous. But he had the awful feeling that he had somehow underestimated the young man in front of him.

'The Colonel is very ill,' Davies said.

He was well aware that his pronunciation was a bit off, closer to the Lhasa dialect of Tibetan than Dzongkha but the Shabdrung obviously understood.

'I thought that I should ask your advice. I think it's better for the Colonel if we try to get him to India, where he might have some hospital treatment. I'm afraid that if he stays here, he won't get better. Perhaps you could do a *mo*, a divination.'

The Shabdrung shook his head.

'There's no need to do a *mo*,' he said. 'There's nothing that the Colonel can do here. It's better if he leaves, I think. Better for him. Better for everyone.'

Davies squeezed his fingers into fists and released them. He had one more request. There was no need for the Shabdrung to grant it – but he would lose nothing by it.

'I'd like to ask you,' Davies said, 'if you'd advise the Colonel of your opinion. It might make it easier for us to have his cooperation when we evacuate him.'

The Shabdrung smiled. When the Colonel was gone the young man would be even more exposed to Tobgye, the Maharaja, and his general, the Paro Ponlop. It wasn't a pleasant prospect. There was no need for the Shabdrung to make it easier for Davies and Tobgye to get the Colonel out of the way. But the Shabdrung also knew that if he refused, the Colonel would either get Tobgye's lethal attention or he would be arrested and taken back to Calcutta in irons.

'Of course,' the Shabdrung said.

He stood up.

'We'll go and speak to him then.'

3

The whiskered assistant led the way down the corridor, closely followed by the Shabdrung, and Davies could feel that strange charismatic presence as he kept close to the Shabdrung's shoulder. The monk lifted a curtain, held it back and the Shabdrung entered the Colonel's room. Davies hurried after him. Christina stood up by the side of the bier-like bed. She looked haggard, with dark diagonals beneath her eyes, her skin, even her freckles, pale. The Colonel was propped up on his cushions. His face was lined and ravaged, cheeks drawn, the skin a deep hepatic yellow and the eyes yellow, wide open now that the Shabdrung had entered, but his mouth was slack under the heavy moustache.

'How is your father?' the Shabdrung asked in English.

'Not very well,' she said.

The Shabdrung sat down on a stool next to the bed. She glanced at Davies and he tried to give her a reassuring smile, all the time mortified that the Shabdrung would reveal all that Davies thought he knew and that it would lead to truly horrendous recriminations. He almost wished it would. And that such a revelation might still work to get them out of the awful future that he was sure was being created right at this moment. But he couldn't stop himself. He was going to go through with his and Tobgye's plan. He knew that the only way to avert it would be to take the Shabdrung with them into India. And that was impossible, wasn't it?

'The Shabdrung has something to say to you, Colonel Devenish,' Davies said.

The Colonel nodded. He was wary. Of course he was wary with Tobgye in the room. The Shabdrung began. Davies translated for Christina.

'You are very sick. I don't think that it's good for you to stay here. If you want to cure this illness, you have to leave Talo very soon. I think it's for the best. You must get to a hospital quickly, in India, where they can take care of you.'

Devenish pushed himself up on his elbows.

'Not going,' he said.

'Settle down, Daddy,' she said.

The Shabdrung continued in Dzongkha.

'I know you're worried about me,' Owen translated, 'but Sonam Tobgye has assured me that the Maharaja means me no harm. The Paro Ponlop will arrive soon; and he's been entrusted by the Maharaja to be Talo's protector. I wanted to tell you that whatever happens we'll always be connected. There are no barriers between us. I promise you this. When you get better, you can help your daughter a little. Help her to understand the text that I gave you. You can translate others for her. I'll be very sorry for you to leave, but you must go back to Calcutta as soon as possible. It's for the best.'

The Colonel's yellowed and bloodshot eyes widened. The uncooperative flesh on his face was wasted but the words came out forcefully enough.

'You poisoned me, you bastards.'

Christina looked from her father to Davies and then to Tobgye.

'Colonel, you are sick,' Tobgye said in English.

'Let's concentrate on a diagnosis and a cure, Colonel,' Davies said. 'I think it's important that we get you to a hospital as quickly as possible. Christina can do an analysis. And the Shabdrung agrees it would be better for you. We have enough solution to give you intravenously for seven days. That'll get us to the railhead at Jalpaigur. With luck, we can get some more supplies there and rush you down to Calcutta by train.'

'I'd rather die here,' the Colonel said.

'Don't say that,' Christina said. 'We can come back. When you're better, when everything's better.'

'These bastards have poisoned me,' he said.

Her pale skin flushed. She turned to Davies.

'I'm sorry, Colonel,' Tobgye said. 'You know yourself what a liver sickness can do. How it can make you feel. We only want the best for you.'

Christina would know that hepatic patients were the worst

patients to deal with. Classic symptoms. They easily get depressed and enraged. She had no reason to suspect. The way her eyes were darting about she was confused and panicked, but she would do whatever she needed to do to nurse her father. The Shabdrung was making it easier for her to leave Talo.

The young Shabdrung leaned over her father, took one of his hands and held it close to his chest. He whispered rapidly in his ear. Davies strained to understand but the Shabdrung was talking too quickly and too quietly.

'This is not right,' her father said in English.

The Shabdrung leaned over and touched his forehead to the Colonel's.

Good then; they were saying goodbye.

Then the Shabdrung stood up and took Christina's hands in his and turned that impossibly bright smile on her. He was looking at her like a lover and she looked as if she was melting with pleasure under that gaze, despite her father's rage and resistance. If he had not slept with Christina the night before, Davies would have been certain that she had made love with the Shabdrung. Had she had time? When he had been with Tobgye, or out at the billet with the men? Or when she had supposedly been with her father, could she possibly have been to bed with the Shabdrung? This was insane.

'We'll set off for Calcutta first thing in the morning,' Davies said.

Christina glanced up at him, green eyes angry. He was putting her through it, wasn't he? And as she looked at him he saw disappointment, rage, worry, relief, a whole range of emotions passing through her eyes and over her face like squalls as she faced the inevitable journey back to India.

And Devenish's eyes were blazing, too. But he kept quiet. The Shabdrung must have said something to stay his anger.

Now the Shabdrung dipped a hand into the fold of his robe

and brought out a pendant on a chain that he held out to Christina. The muscles of Davies's shoulders tightened as she took it on her palm. It was a perfect pearl set in a silver clasp in the shape of a lotus flower.

'This is beautiful,' she said. 'I'll treasure this.'

The Shabdrung took her right hand and he pinned her forearm between his own forearm and his body, drawing her closer to him. Davies had seen her face like that before, when they had first gone to bed together. He pressed his lips together. He couldn't make a scene now. Her eyes filled up.

'Goodbye,' the Shabdrung said in English.

The holy man turned his dark eyes onto hers for a moment. Then he let go of her arm and leaned over her father again. The words they exchanged were in a low murmur. Davies was helpless to understand what was going on between them. The Shabdrung squeezed her father's hand, stood up and then he was gone. Christina knelt down next to her father, and Tobgye grabbed Davies's arm and drew him out of the room and into the low and narrow corridor.

'Thank you, Major Davies,' Tobgye said. 'The Maharaja will be delighted. I'll have two guides ready for you in the morning.'

CHAPTER TWENTY-SIX

THEY WERE FIVE DAYS AWAY FROM TALO AND FIVE DAYS AWAY from the railhead at Jalpaigur. They had followed the course of the Puna-Tsang Chu down valley into thick damp forest. Broad-leafed ferns arched over the narrow trail and dripped moisture onto Christina every time her head or shoulders brushed against them. She was soaked through. While the sun penetrated the gorge during the day it wasn't so uncomfortable, but by mid-afternoon the narrow, heavily wooded valley was in deep shadow and her wet clothes had turned icy against her skin. Hornbills swayed in the branches of the trees above them and the call of beautiful blue-billed birds – *piho, piho* – accompanied them all along the trail. She had lived with an ever-deepening sense of dread for three days. Her father was still terribly sick although her instincts told her that he would pull through as long as she kept him well hydrated and supervised his diet carefully. Their separation from the Shabdrung, too, had thrown its dark and desolate cast over the paradisaical landscape and undermined her nerves. She had awoken three mornings since from a strangely disturbing dream whose images still rose in her mind. She had been with her father in the dream, standing by the side of an outdoor stage awaiting the imminent arrival of some great teacher. In front of the stage were hundreds of Bhutanese monks and nuns and yogis in a state of great agitation, all being kept from swarming over the stage by some burly *gekods*, the monastic discipline enforcers. The crowd let out a long 'OOOh!' when a large stone tower – exactly as she had seen in her vision with the medium in Bumthang – went flying across the sky and they all surged forward. Her father said, 'If they don't settle down in a minute there'll be a manifestation of Choma Lhamo.' She knew immediately that this was the blue-skinned goddess she had seen on so many scroll paintings; she could sense that dark presence lurking on the periphery of consciousness. When she awoke she felt a strange admixture of joy, sadness and loss. All the while, she tried to evoke a sense of the Shabdrung's presence as she took care of her father, and that presence seemed vivid to her while, at the same time, her surroundings seemed ever more empty and desolate despite the increasingly lush and tropical landscape.

She urged her mule on, ducking under the heavy green fronds that overhung the trail. Just ahead of her, her father was being carried on a stretcher slung between two mules. When the path got rough, the soldiers would carry him on their shoulders.

The column came out of the vegetation onto a flat spit of land where a large stream joined the main river. She was relieved when Owen finally called out the order to bivouac for the night. This clearing in the surrounding forest was strewn with washed-up logs, all strung with damp grass and weeds, broken branches and oddly torn rags, the detritus of previous floods. A black-faced ibis strutted along in the shallows, lifting its long legs and dipping its curved red beak into the waters. It fluttered away into the air as Owen and the guide rode close to it. The sepoys unslung her father's stretcher, laid it on the ground and quickly pitched a tent for him.

She got down off her own mule and one of the sepoys took the bridle and led the animal away to picket. She was sore from being in the saddle and she couldn't help but think of the comforts of Calcutta: a soft bed beneath the mosquito netting, a cold gin fizz, a solid meal.

Her father was awake. She knelt beside the stretcher.

'Are you all right?' she asked.

He nodded. His yellowed cheeks were sunken and rough with stubble, the dark folds that ran down from his eyes deeper than ever before. The whites of his eyes were still an ivory yellow.

She unscrewed the lid of her canteen and poured a capful of water for him.

'Here, drink this,' she said.

She tipped the cup to his lips and he steadied it with one hand as he drank. Droplets of liquid clung to the ends of the hairs of his grey moustache. The tent was up and the two sepoys came to lift the stretcher. She stood up and they took her father into the tent. Owen was marking things on a map and scribbling notes down near the confluence of the stream and the river. They had hardly said a word to each other since they had begun the journey. All day she spent in the saddle, close to her father's stretcher, while Owen led the expedition with their guide. And at night, she kept vigil by her father's bedside.

The sepoys came out of the tent and she went in. Her father was wrapped in dark green army blankets on the camp cot. One of the orderlies had seen to the drip to keep him hydrated. She opened her bag and took out a clean spatula.

'Show me your tongue,' she said.

He complied, the coated and pale tongue hanging forward, ridged and close to cracking, yellowish-grey. She depressed it with the spatula and looked into his throat. He gagged. But she had time to see that the membranes were coated with a dark residue and there was still some swelling. She wiped the steel spatula and he let his head fall back on the pillow of the camp cot.

Her father was convinced that he had been poisoned. From strictly medical evidence, it was plausible. Some forms of fungi might cause vomiting and hepatic reaction. Owen had said that the Bhutanese were famous for their poisons. Tobgye? She found that plausible, too. The symptoms of fungal poisoning would look for all the world like hepatitis. If Tobgye had done such a thing, where was Owen in all this? But this had to be hepatitis. All her training told her to look for the obvious first. And it looked like hepatitis. She wanted to take a swab of that residue in his throat and test it when they got to Calcutta but there was no guarantee that she could find the right diagnosis even then.

'I think I'm getting better,' her father said. 'We should go back to Talo.'

He ran his dry tongue around his dry lips.

'You're still weak,' she said. 'We can't go back. Not yet.'

Even if he was feeling better, there was no way he could return to Talo on his own, however desperately he wanted to. And Owen would never allow anyone to go with him. Her father, in effect, was in custody, Department custody, without need of arresting him. Only a few days ago she had believed her father to have the constitution of a pack mule, but whatever it was that had infected him had eaten up all his strength, sapped him, dehydrated him through the diarrhoea and vomiting.

They were far from Talo now. All she could remember were Tobgye's armoured soldiers closing around the Shabdrung as he stood by the gate to say goodbye to them. Her imagination seethed with projected possible futures: of a return to Talo, of the Shabdrung's escape to India or to Tibet, where she might have another chance to meet up with him. Her fantasies ran to passionate nights with him in a room in a Calcutta hotel, or even sailing with him to London.

The mountain wind rattled the sloped canvas of the tent above her, a constant maddening flutter that it was impossible to stop. Christina crouched forward on the stool, looking down at her father, willing him to get better just as she had done with Lakshmi in that hospital in Bombay. The collar of her tweed jacket rubbed her neck under her unkempt red hair. How many times had she been in this hunched and desperate and power-less position? How many beds, how many patients? What bloody use were all those years of training?

The sickness seemed to come in waves but it did seem to her that the waves were coming further and further apart, and were not as strong as they had been in Talo.

She lifted a bowl of tea from the bedside table and brought it close to his mouth.

'Drink a little more,' she said.

She held the tin cup close to his lips.

A half-smile, then, at the corner of his mouth. He drank, but most of his fluids were coming from the bottle hanging above the bed. She prayed continuously – to what? To God Almighty, to the Shabdrung?

Outside the tent, voices were speaking in Dzongkha: two women and Owen. The women's voices were urgent, demanding, Owen's irritated. She sensed the change in her father's body on the cot as the timbres of those voices reached him, and it was as if within this sack of skin and fevered flesh hanging upon the bones he was suddenly animated, a sudden new lucidity in his yellowed eyes.

She rose from the low camp stool and opened the straining flaps of the tent. Owen was there with two Bhutanese women. They were bundled up in heavy striped *khiras*, their heads wrapped in red cotton scarves, bloodshot and teary eyes in wind-ravaged and tightly drawn faces. She recognised them from the Shabdrung's temple.

'They want to see him,' Owen said. 'They've been marching day and night to catch up with us.'

'Let them in,' Christina said.

She stepped aside and pulled the tent flap back for them to enter. They squeezed past her into the tent.

'Have a cook bring some more tea, Owen,' she said.

She closed the tent flaps again and fastened the ties tight to keep out the buffeting wind. The women would not sit but gestured with their palms upwards for her to sit first. She knew that she was obliged to and there was no room in the tent to struggle with them politely. She sat on the camp stool. She was close to her father's head. The women squatted. Her father came up on one elbow. His voice was little more than a whisper but it was obvious how much he wanted to talk to them. To get news of the Shabdrung. She understood nothing. Her father's voice was hoarse and urgent. He seemed to know them well. She didn't interrupt them. There were gestures and tears and supplications. The awful truth had no need for translation. She felt a sick emptiness in the pit of her gut. Then her father turned to her.

'The Shabdrung,' he said. 'He's dead.'

She nodded.

'One of the Maharaja's generals. A big man. Powerful man. He entered the Shabdrung's room in the middle of the night. There were ten men with him. He was holding out a white scarf in offering. He approached the bed. The Shabdrung's bed. Soldiers all around him. The Shabdrung was naked, they said. Had gone to sleep naked. He reached up to take the scarf. The soldiers grabbed him. Held him down. The general . . . the general forced the scarf into the Shabdrung's mouth. Down his throat. The Shabdrung couldn't breathe. He choked to death. Suffocated. Suffocated to death. They threatened to kill all the monks in the same way if they spoke a word of it. These two escaped. Hurried down here after us.'

The real thing, yes. She understood what it meant. She'd found a genuine spiritual master and now he was already dead. And she had been part of the expedition that had travelled all this way to prepare for his execution. She pushed her way past the two kneeling women. The knots of the tent flaps fell open easily under her fingers and she emerged between the sheer crags of the Puna-Tsang Chu gorge that loomed over the camp. She staggered among the desultory soldiers hunched over their paltry fires.

Owen seemed as if he had been waiting for her to emerge.

'You'll have to forgive me,' he said. 'I could hear through the canvas.'

'You were listening?'

'It's not true what they said . . .'

His soft eyes shifted about under the peak of his cap.

'I knew what had happened,' he said. 'I didn't want to upset you. Yesterday, one of Tobgye's men – dispatch rider – brought us news. It seems that their holy man, the Shabdrung . . . he committed suicide three nights ago . . . with a number of his monks.'

'You bloody bastard,' she said.

Every muscle and sinew twisted under her skin and then uncoiled suddenly through her body like an electric shock as she leapt at him, her arms curved, and her nails raking at his face and hair and tearing and gouging, bloody and slippery, and fists pounding against bone. A mingled screech and growl erupted through the tunnel of her throat and her teeth jarred against his cheekbone and dug through skin and flesh and her mouth was blood-flooded and her eardrums were pierced with his shrieks and then hands dug into her upper arms and her thighs and her head was yanked back by the hair and she was twisting in the grip of Owen's soldiers and the weight of their knees and arms pinned her down on the damp earth. Her screams rose above the roar of the waters and echoed around the walls of the dark and devastated gorge. Then Owen's face appeared over her. A shock of dark hair fell forward over his forehead. Blood welled up from a gash about an inch below his left eye and ran down red and copious over his cheek. It dripped on the front of her blouse. He stared down at her. She strained against the arms of the sepoys holding her pinned to the ground.

'You bastard. You *bastard*,' she breathed.

'Christina, please . . . Christina . . . Listen now . . . It wasn't me. I didn't do this. It's not for us to interfere. It's their country. I didn't do anything. Believe me, please.'

There was a real sincerity in those brown eyes of his. She couldn't believe that he would do such a thing. Tobgye, yes. But not Owen. He couldn't do that. Not have the Shabdrung killed like that. He couldn't, could he?

'Listen . . .' he said.

His hands reached forward even as the blood from his face dripped off the edge of his jaw and onto her breast. His fingertips rested on her cheeks.

'Listen . . . Christina . . . I'm just here to take care of you. I'd never do anything to hurt you. You know that.'

She let herself slump back against the damp earth, no longer resisting the restraints of the Indian soldiers who still pressed down on her arms and legs.

'You bastard,' she said.

PART FIVE

CALCUTTA, LATE MARCH 1931

CHAPTER TWENTY-SEVEN

GRIEF WAS LIKE A SUCCUBUS. IT HAD DRAINED HER OF ENERGY even as she slept in the train. She awoke and stared into the shaded compartment, aware that they were close to Calcutta, coming into the station. It was like the recurrence of a dream – past grief, present grief, the visions of the night all too vivid. She had dreamt about the Shabdrung again. Owen had done this. He and Marshall and Tobgye and the Maharaja and the rotten bloody Department had dreamt it all up. She was slick with a hot sweat. She came up on her elbow. She couldn't shut out of her mind the image of the white silk scarves being pushed down the Shabdrung's throat – and she couldn't reverse time to erase the event itself. Perhaps she was being punished for some horrible karmic debt which she had no recollection of accruing. She wanted to sink back into oblivion where she could have no thoughts, no horrible visions like those of the night before when she had dreamt the murder once again. And Owen had been embroiled in it all. There was no way to deny that. She felt contaminated by him. Like leprosy. Somehow she shared in the culpability that was his. She knew that the logic was insane but she couldn't stop this feeling of guilt. It was physical: a chemical reaction in her body. Where was the Shabdrung now? What did she believe really? Was he in some heavenly realm? What would the Bhutanese say? She imagined him floating in some heavenly space somewhere, some other dimension of clear pure light.

A ridiculous image, she thought, another wish-fulfilling construction of the mind, futile and desperate. Or was it like the Hindus said? Atman, the soul, dissolving into Brahman, the absolute? But if that was the case, what was it that would reincarnate? And as for reincarnation, what was the use, even if it did exist? What if the Shabdrung were to be reborn in this world as a baby? How was she supposed to find him? And even if she did, she would grow old and die before he would be able to communicate with her as an adult again. What use was that? And that was the best option for meeting him again. Either that, or die now. The thought of her own death, at this moment in time, was absolutely terrifying. Had it been terrifying for the Shabdrung, too? Had he maintained that state of grace as he died, or had the torture of suffocation completely overwhelmed him? Well, he was dead now. No way to know. Her father believed that it was possible to reunite with the Shabdrung for lifetime after lifetime, but what did he know? And what good was that when she had to live in the present not in the future? Perhaps spiritualism was a means to contact him? She discounted that immediately. She couldn't imagine the consciousness of the Shabdrung speaking through the voice of any of the spiritualist mediums she had ever met. The key to keeping the Shabdrung's presence alive in herself was deeply connected with her father. Her father was alive and recovering from the poison, or the hepatitis, or whatever it was that had racked his body for the past ten days. That in itself was a blessing. She couldn't bring the Shabdrung back to life but she could take care of her father.

She pulled back the stiff and dusty curtain from the window. It was a different city from the one she had left, she could sense that, even as the train screeched and rocked and clattered into Calcutta. She had come around to it again as if her life was on some kind of spiral of grief, bringing her around to the same places while her state of mind was in a different but still elegiac season.

A pall of smoke drifted out of Bangal Babu's bazaar, next to the station. It rolled across the tracks, brown and gritty, and the slanting light of dawn was diffused through it, a dangerous glow, intimation of imminent fires, and the domes of the temples beyond had been darkened from white to orange and ember red as if the air itself had thickened and was spat through with sparks.

Her father was already sitting upright on his couchette in the semi-darkness, his big-knuckled fingers clasped between the bony knobs of his knees. The sickness had withered him so that his quilted clothes hung loose on his body, the flesh wasted on his bones, and the ligaments slack that held those bones together. He looked as if he had been eaten from the inside out: the skin still yellow and deeply scored with wrinkles, the moustache now too big for his face, his eyes sunk in their sockets.

'Kali Ghat,' he said. 'City of Kali, goddess of destruction.'

There was a wry smile beneath the heavy moustache; he was returning to some kind of resilience. His voice still had that rasp in it but at least he found it easy to speak now. On the train journey, he had begun eating again – mostly bananas and the thick white curd that they had bought at railway stops all along the line. He could keep that down easily enough. The bananas would nourish him with minerals and vitamins and the curd with protein, and stabilise the bacteria in his stomach.

She laid aside her shawl and slid her feet off her own couchette so that she sat opposite him, her white cotton dress a little stale from the travel. The pungent smell of sweat rose from under her armpits. The winter was ending and the heat of the lowlands building.

'Richard will be expecting us,' he said. 'Always stay with Richard in Calcutta. Davies will have wired the Department about our arrival. He'll know, Richard will. He'll be there to meet us.'

That time, at Richard's house, with Owen. Hot water, he'd

said. He had been open enough about it all. Not like Owen. Her father trusted Richard.

'You don't mind staying there?' she asked.

'Why should I?'

'Richard,' she said. 'He's in the Department, too. If you're so sure that Owen poisoned you . . . why would you?'

'It's all a game, Christina.'

'A game?'

'Owen, the Department . . . got what they wanted. Richard isn't directly involved. I'm not a problem any more. They won't do anything else to me.'

She was aghast. She couldn't think of anything more monstrous than what they'd just come through.

'They poisoned you,' she said.

'I've done worse.'

'Like killing the Shabdrung?'

He flushed. His eyes hardened, and his lips pressed together. That brought up his ire again.

'From their point of view: realpolitik,' he said. 'I would never . . . but, look, my hands aren't so clean.'

And she saw him then as he had been when she was young: distant, a player in the Great Game from which she and her mother were kept apart. He was still the same man who was capable of seeing the political dimension of the Shabdrung's killing and his own poisoning as something separate from the personal. The difference in him now was that he had chosen something else in front of the Department. The fact that he felt more acutely and passionately the relationship he had had with the Shabdrung than that he had had with his family, exposed a raw nerve in her. This was a man who had absented himself from the life of his daughter and his wife so that he might undermine and manipulate regimes on the frontiers of the Raj. He was so used to these horrible diplomatic games and dirty tricks that he could still stay in the same house as a member of the Department: even if he believed that the same Department had poisoned him and killed his spiritual teacher.

'Did you ever kill anybody?' she asked.

He tilted his head, the eyes tired and wary.

'Not directly,' he said.

'How long ago?'

The muscles of his face hardened.

'Long enough. I went into Tibet with Younghusband. We must have killed about two thousand Tibetans near Shigatse.'

'In a battle?'

'What difference does it make? Gatling guns and rifles against swords and muskets. Bloody mess. I'm not proud of it.'

The anger drained from his face. At least he seemed genuinely ashamed of it now.

'Is that what you thought at the time, or after you met the Shabdrung?'

'What?'

'That you weren't proud of it.'

He looked directly into her eyes. He was completely lucid and present.

'Don't be ridiculous . . . Proud of that? It was awful. Unfortunate. We were facing the Tibetan army, a battalion or so. They'd blocked the pass near Shigatse. We'd isolated one of their generals on the field. No outright hostilities at this point, but the Tibetans were standing their ground and refusing to let us pass. None of us spoke Tibetan that well. There was a misunderstanding. One of the sepoys tried to grab at the general and he went for his sword. Another sepoy shot him. Then the Tibetans shot back.'

He paused for a moment.

'We hardly lost a man,' he said. 'Carried on to Lhasa. Younghusband even got interested in Lamaism. Fancied himself as a bit of a swami when we got back to India.'

He smiled at that.

She was aware of what he was smiling at. She'd seen other Westerners convinced that they held some magnificent spiritual knowledge – Mrs Besant, Oliver Haddo among them – but she couldn't imagine her father announcing himself as some kind of spiritual leader as the others had done. But he valued the knowledge he had gleaned from the Shabdrung enough to bring her all the way to Bhutan to share it with her.

He was going to recover from his illness. He was going to live for at least a few more years, she hoped. But now they would both have to decide where they would go from Calcutta. Neither of them could stay. She was sure of that. But before they left, he might still have to deal with Owen and the Department.

She glanced instinctively at the door of the compartment. It was shut solid. Locked against him – against Owen. He was at the back of the train among the sepoys. She could sense him. He was thinking of her, wanting her, wanting to make amends for the damage he'd done. A virulent amoeba? A tragic suicide? How could Owen ever have thought that he might succeed in hiding such an abomination from her? The filthy hands of the Department were all over it. His bloody filthy Departmental hands. And his bloody filthy Departmental hands had been all over her body. And then her throat and her chest constricted with a tremendous sensation of loss. Owen had made an awful mistake. She suspected that he might even be lacerated by remorse. But his unimaginable course of action had broken whatever it was that they had had together. There was no 'if only'. Owen was like her father had been when she'd been a child: blind to what he was doing and to what he had done.

The train squealed and lurched to a stop.

'Come on,' she said to her father, 'I'll help you up.'

He shook his head and leaned forward, then came to his feet as if every joint in his body had rusted. He swayed, a little stooped between the seats. She hated seeing him like this. A few weeks before, when he'd appeared through the heavy gates of Talo

Dzong, her father had been a hale and robust mountain man. All her life, she'd never known him to be physically weak. He'd always been a powerful man, a dynamic man, even if he had chosen to abandon her. Now he'd been reduced to a shell of his former self; she had had to help him to go to the lavatory and to wash, and to eat, like an ancient baby. He was recovering but now he looked exhausted by the effort of maintaining his balance. His power of recuperation was hardly that of a twenty- or thirty-year-old.

She reached up to the luggage rack for their canvas travel bag. She pulled the bag out of the netting. It was light. The rest of their baggage was in the goods van. She clacked the bolt back and pulled the compartment door open. She stepped out into the corridor. It was full of the blue wispy smoke of *beedees*. Outside the window, billows of steam and smoke drifted across the platform. The turbaned sepoys in the corridor averted their eyes from her and stepped back into their own compartments to let her and her father pass. Rifles rattled against the sides of the compartments. Khaki duffel bags scraped across the littered floor. Her father followed her, still a rasp in his breath, and he reached out one bony hand to the window frame for support. She balanced her canvas bag on her thigh, lifting it forward, towards the carriage door. It was open. No sign of Owen. She descended the steps to the platform in the dim light of dawn. Steam rose towards the cast-iron arches of the roof above. Inexplicably, the dusty platforms were empty of would-be porters, anxious hawkers, aggravating rickshaw-wallahs. Only great bound bales of cotton were piled there, and packing crates, and soldiers to guard them, armed with rifles and bayonets. Well, they were on a military train, weren't they? Perhaps that was the reason that civilians had been kept away.

She reached up a hand to help him balance.

He took her arm.

Then she saw Richard. He was approaching from the end of

the platform where, at the ticket collector's booth, a large, sand-bagged gun emplacement had been built. The ugly barrel of a Lewis gun, with its circular magazine, pointed out from the front parapet towards the station entrance. Behind Richard more soldiers were gathered in front of the ticket offices and at every station exit. All of them were armed with rifles, bayonets fixed. It seemed as if the station were garrisoned for a major siege, as if a war was raging in the streets of Calcutta, through which they had to travel.

And to see her cousin on the platform like this was, once again, like the recurrence of a dream, the elements slightly rearranged since her last arrival in the city. Richard's face was tense, the skin taut over the muscles. She sensed Owen behind her at the far end of the platform. Richard would have brought the car, Owen's Rover, as he had the last time, and he would know about Bhutan, so that he must have arranged something other for her and her father. She couldn't imagine sitting in the back seat of the Rover, as she had done on her last time in Calcutta. What a nightmare to imagine the back seat of the car with Owen on one side of her and her father on the other. She could sense the rage in her father, too. Had her father done similar killings in the past? Arranged poisonings for the Department?

Richard was only ten yards away from them.

'Colonel Devenish!'

Owen's voice.

He hadn't called her name. She stopped and her father stopped. He turned, his arm heavy on hers. Owen strode down the plat-form towards them. The creases on his suit were as sharp as if it had been freshly ironed, his shirt the same. The regimental tie was tight to his collar stud.

'Colonel, Christina, you'll need an escort, the streets . . .' Owen said.

'Richard's here,' the Colonel said.

'They've had riots. A strike,' Owen said. 'No porters or rick-shaw men, you see?'

Owen's voice was strained, the baritone threatening to go uncontrollably higher.

'I've brought the car for you,' Richard said.

'The car, yes,' Owen said.

She could walk but her father couldn't.

'I don't want to drive with you, Owen,' she said.

He nodded curtly.

'Go with your father. And Richard,' he said. 'I'll go back in the Crossley with the escort.'

'Thank you,' she said.

'You can arrange for their baggage, Parker,' he said. 'And, Colonel, I'll arrange for a meeting with General McKeowan to discuss the events in Bhutan. I'll do everything I can for you. I assure you.'

'Thank you,' her father said. 'I won't need your help.'

The train whistle screeched under the cast-iron roof. And in the split second of stillness that followed, she saw into myriad possible futures. All of these men gathered around her at this one moment in time, the confluence of those forces set into motion through space and time . . . All these elements combining, dissolving and recombining like chemical compounds and solutions, sometimes harmless, sometimes explosive, like a piece of potassium dropped into water, its deep lilac flames flaring to light up the desolation of this new Calcutta dawn.

Chapter Twenty-eight

ALREADY THE SUN WAS LOW, DIPPING OVER THE SKEWED geometry of the city's horizon. It was a pleasant and balmy evening, but the sky's evening blue was smudged with pale brown smoke lit by flickers of sporadic fires. There had been riots since Gupta's hanging, outbreaks of vandalism and violence against British-owned businesses, rubbish fires deliberately started to attract the fire brigade and the police so that the gathered crowds might stone them. And here she was, sitting on the terrace in a light floral dress, numbing herself with gin, and separated from the seething city by the high walls of Richard's garden. She looked down on a mass of rhododendrons, bougainvillea and broad-leafed ferns and two palm trees that clicked their fronds over the wrought-iron gate of this little fortress garden of the Raj.

Her father – well on the way to recovery now – sat on her right, and to her left was her cousin, Richard. Both the men, icons of the Raj, were dressed for dinner in linen suits, white shirts and dark ties. Strange the type to which her father returned whenever he spent time in the city. The Calcutta sun and the ebb of his sickness had returned the colour of the Colonel's skin to a healthy tan. Where once he had looked heavy in Bhutan, and then gaunt with jaundice, now there was a wiriness about him, and a new restlessness. She knew that he was anxious to be away from the city again. Richard was tense. He had enough reason to be.

'Look at that,' he said. 'I can't help thinking . . . I had a hand in all that. My testimony.'

He waved at the smoke and glints of flame beyond the wall, his hand movements jerky, exaggerated by the length of his arms and legs as he swayed in his chair.

'What else could you've done?' her father said. 'There had to be a trial. You were a witness. Gupta would have known the consequences before he fired the gun.'

Christina lit a Player's, felt the bite of the smoke in her throat and lungs.

Owen had been a witness, too. She imagined him giving his evidence: an oak-panelled courtroom, a white-faced judge with a plummy accent, and a ridiculous robe and a ridiculous wig with the royal arms behind him, a lion and a unicorn, *Honi soit qui mal y pense*, symbol of alien authority on the soil of India.

She drew deep on the Player's and blew out smoke. Here they were, drinking while Calcutta burned, Christina Devenish, a daughter of privilege, with the overwhelming sense that she – and perhaps her father – was on the wrong side of the wall. She leaned over to grab the neck of a marble-topped bottle and topped up her father's tonic water. Then, from the green earthenware jug, she refilled Richard's gin fizz and her own.

'Bloody awful timing for the trial,' Richard said. 'The independence march tomorrow. It was always going to be big.'

'I know,' she said. 'I'm going.'

'Unwise,' her father said.

'We've already . . .' she began.

'There'll be trouble . . .' her father interrupted her.

'I'm not worried about it,' she said.

She took another quick puff on the cigarette.

Richard smoothed his trousers, took another drink.

'I've got to ask,' he said. 'I mean . . . I know you're pro-independence but . . . they're going to use this march as a protest over Gupta. And whatever you think about independence, he was a terrorist.'

'This march was planned long ago. The government set the trial date. It's as much a government ploy to undermine the march as a terrorist attempt to hijack it. You know that. And the vast majority on that march will be Gandhi supporters.'

'There'll be plenty of troublemakers,' Richard said.

'Yes,' she said. 'Maybe on both sides.'

'Then why go?' her father said.

She brushed ash off the thigh of her floral cotton-print dress.

'After what happened in Bhutan . . . I just feel I need to make a stand: for myself. You understand? Against all the bloody hypocrisy.'

And there was something else pushing her into it, too, some intuition that she couldn't quite put her finger on, some nagging certainty at the periphery of consciousness that she was going to be in the right place at the right time.

She took another sip of gin.

'I'm sorry to embarrass you, Richard . . . with the Department. I'm in danger of overstaying my welcome, I know. But I'll be gone soon. I've decided. Day after tomorrow, I'm going back to Bombay,' she said.

'Overstayed? What are you talking about, Christina?' he said. 'Major Davies insisted that I take good care of you.'

Her whole body contracted at hearing Owen's name. And Richard was irritated with her. It would be better if she went, and soon. They were getting on each other's nerves in this house.

'You can stay as long as you like,' Richard said.

'I'm sorry, Richard,' she said. 'You've been so kind to us.'

He turned to her father.

'I wish *you'd* stay, Colonel,' he said. 'You've always been welcome here, you know that.'

He sounded rather desperate. As if he would miss her father's company. She couldn't help but think that Richard was such a lonely man. Her father and Richard seemed to have a peculiar understanding of each other. Richard was far more comfortable with him than he was with her. He and her father shared some sort of knowledge, or way of being, as Department men, of which she had no idea. It was a world that was closed to her. Although her father had now resigned from the Department, he had still been part of its inner sanctum. That experience could never be cancelled out by mere resignation. In the past two weeks, neither Richard nor her father had mentioned the possible poisoning or the Shabdrung's death: at least, not in her presence. It shocked her that her father seemed to be able to compartmentalise his emotions in such a way. But she was privy to her father's darker moments, too: the dread in his eyes when he awoke in the morning.

She still thought that Richard was a bit too close to bloody Owen for either of them to be really comfortable, no matter how much Richard and her father got on.

'I'm much better already,' her father said. 'Calcutta doesn't agree with me. You know that. I'll be happy to get away to Darjeeling.'

'I wish you'd come with *me*,' Christina said.

'Don't belong in Bombay either,' her father said.

'I suppose not,' she said.

Partially it was selfish, her wanting him to come with her. Now that he was recovering so fast, she was certain that if she stayed with her father he would teach her the exercises to explore and deepen those expanded states of consciousness to which the Shabdrung had introduced them. But it was also difficult for her to accept her father as some kind of spiritual guide. She needed to get away from him for a while to absorb, on her own, all those bizarre experiences that she had lived through during the expedition to Bhutan.

Be that as it may, it was still tempting to abandon her plans for Bombay and the demonstration and go quietly with her father to Darjeeling.

He must have translated hundreds of texts while he was in Bhutan, and she was anxious to study them. Perhaps it wouldn't be so difficult to get the same texts in Darjeeling. But she was convinced that it was possible – essential – that she learn to achieve that extraordinary state of being that was so open and unperturbed whatever the circumstances, even if the most ordinary circumstances in India in these times seemed to be political and social turmoil. She couldn't help but think of the Shabdrung's example. He hadn't run away from involvement in politics, even if it had led to his death. He'd renounced nothing. He'd maintained his extraordinary presence in the middle of total political chaos. That was the challenge she wanted to face herself. And her father had given her a gift. Over the previous five days, he had meticulously translated the small book of the Shabdrung's for her. He had written it in beautiful calligraphy on thick rice paper and wrapped it in a cloth from Talo.

'This book,' he'd said, 'it's a kind of key.'

She would need that book if her father weren't there to talk with her. She wanted to see if she was capable of repeating that experience she had had with the Shabdrung on her own. That was the essence of scientific experiment after all. That it could be repeated. And she wanted to see if it could be done under more normal circumstances – if there was any such thing as normal circumstances in India at that moment.

She felt that she had to get the clinic re-established as soon as possible. It was where she belonged. But there was no reason to lose all contact with her father again as she had in the past.

'I'll come to visit you just before monsoon,' she said.

He stroked one end of his heavy moustache.

'Good,' he said.

She took another drag on her cigarette, blew out smoke, sipped her gin. She brushed away a bead of sweat on her left eyebrow. Her hands were shaking a little. She stubbed out the cigarette. She was nervous about the demonstration, too. Out in the city another fire flared close to the Nakhoda mosque, the flames clawing at the deeping blue of the dusk sky, and flickering on the tall distant tower of the minaret.

Time to go home, she thought. *Home? Home?* Where is *home* exactly?

This was Richard's home in Calcutta. She had a home in Bombay. Her father? He would simply rent a bungalow in Darjeeling. Home wasn't a country, was it? You couldn't say that the British were at home in India. Then there was Owen out there in the city somewhere. What did Owen Davies call home? He was rootless. She couldn't imagine him going back to the Welsh valleys any more. The Political Department was his only home now – more so than it had been for her father. Owen had become a dweller in a different darkness. He'd reinvented himself. Looking for a new family. Like a monk. The Holy Order of the Political Department. And she had been the same. No real family to speak of. Her father always on expeditions, her mother in Ireland, and she was little more than a girl when she'd been shipped off to that cold grey motherland in the North Atlantic. That's what she'd been looking for in Theosophy: a new identity, another family, a link to the past and India. And was that what she was trying to do with the Shabdrung: to join her father's surrogate family? All of them – her father, Owen, herself – they were rootless creatures. They had all simply wanted to invent a new home for themselves here on this subcontinent. And the place where they belonged was not a place but a state of mind that a place supported: India, Bhutan, the Himalayas. And all those Hindus and Muslims and Buddhists who were born here and lived here, and died here, whose ancestors' bones were ground up in the earth and stones of the place, this was their home, wasn't it, even if they all thought it a temporary one? For them, this world was a brief span on the way to millions of other reincarnations in other worlds, other universes for the Hindus and the Buddhists; or to heaven or hell for the Muslims.

'You have to go to Bombay,' her father said. 'It's where you belong.'

She had a moment of dread as she imagined the burned-out ruin of the clinic. But she didn't want to run away from anything. Had to face it. She had work to do there. No one said that home was a place in which you had to be safe or comfortable. Not when the country was like this, in a war zone. She was a doctor in a war zone. And she had suffered her losses.

'But you must visit me in the summer,' he said.

'God willing,' she said.

He gave her a wry smile.

Yes, she would get the clinic construction underway but take a break just before the monsoon, and join her father in Darjeeling for a time. One thing at a time: the demonstration tomorrow, then to Bombay; then Darjeeling.

She sipped at her drink, quinine, sugar and alcohol bubbling on her tongue.

Richard leaned forward, his fingers tapping on the glass in his hand, staring at the space between their feet.

'You do know that . . . Major Davies,' he said, 'Owen . . . he wants to talk to you.'

This had to come up. She reached for another cigarette and then stopped herself.

'I've got nothing to say to him,' she said.

'He asked if he might come over to see you. I said that I'd ask you.'

She shook her head.

'He sent a note. I have it here,' Richard said.

He reached inside his jacket pocket. He handed her the envelope: a heavy, creamy vellum. She turned it over in her hands. She glanced at her father who sipped at his tonic water and then pointedly looked away over towards the smoky and burning cityscape.

Richard settled back in his chair, cradling his glass in front of his face.

She broke the seal of the envelope, slipped out the folded paper.

Dearest Christina,

I need to talk to you. I don't want to risk making a scene by coming to Richard's house without your agreement and arranging a time to meet with you. I've missed you terribly since we returned to Calcutta. I can't stand being without you. I miss your touch, your beautiful green eyes, your strength, your presence, your love.

I'm so sorry the expedition to Bhutan turned out as it did. I was hoping that it would have resulted in you and I sharing common ground in an often hostile world. I wanted so much for us to share a life together. We live in such troubled times that everything we do seems to be permeated with violence and the threat of violence. I would dearly love to separate all of us from it but I am a soldier and I think like a soldier, and my duty brings me into situations of violence and conflict every day.

So much went on in Bhutan that was beyond my control. Losing you was the worst thing that was beyond my control. Time is unforgiving. We can never turn it back but I beg you to forgive me any wrong I might have done you.

You must believe me that I had nothing to do with your father's sickness or the death of the Shabdrung. I had hoped that sharing our lives would somehow have lessened the burden of these troubled times for both of us. The times I spent with you were the most blissful of my life. I have never loved a woman as I love you. I know that I have so much more to discover in you. Whatever you feel about rekindling the love that I know we felt for each other, please consent to meet me before you leave for Bombay, at least so that we might say goodbye.

With all my love and affection,
Owen

She folded the letter and slid it back into its envelope. Her muscles and nerves seemed to be twisting and knotting under her skin. There was so much they could have shared together. But even now, he was lying. She didn't know whether he honestly believed what he had written or not. Perhaps he was incapable of seeing the truth. Incapable of seeing his own lies. Had the Department done that to him?

She tucked the envelope under the ashtray with its still smouldering cigarette.

'I've got nothing to say to him, Richard,' she said.

Richard glanced across at her father who continued to look at the smoke-smudged, deepening colours on the city's tumbled-down horizon.

She got up from her chair.

'I'll tell him in the morning,' Richard said.

'I'm going to my bedroom, now. Do you need anything, Daddy?'

She wanted to put distance between herself and the letter as if it might contaminate her.

'No, I'm all right,' he said.

'Good night both,' she said.

'Good night, Christina,' her father said.

'Good night,' Richard said.

From the door to the veranda, Christina glanced back at her father.

'I shan't wake you tomorrow,' she said. 'I'm going out early, to the demonstration.'

'Christina . . .'

Her father leaned over the back of his chair, the linen suit loose on his big-boned frame.

'Do be careful in the morning,' he said.

CHAPTER TWENTY-NINE

ACRID SMOKE DRIFTED BETWEEN THE BUILDINGS AND OVER THE rooftops in the early morning. Davies and Parker sat in shadow in the back of the Rover. The roof and windows were up against the irritating smoke. The rubbish fires of the city streets flickered on the corners where the white-wrapped and listless beggars had gathered for the night; and now, just after dawn, the lathi-wielding policemen rousted them out of their charpoys to break up the groups of possible troublemakers. The independence demonstration was due to start in two hours. The car would be at Curzon Gardens within twenty minutes. The inside of the car was still cool in the early morning. Govinda, as ever, was in the driver's seat. Everything was as usual but for the black emptiness caused by Christina's absence that was consuming him from the inside out.

'Christina's going to be there, you know, at the demonstration,' Parker said.

And the mention of her name was enough to make him feel as if Parker had torn some vital organ out of him.

'Christina?' Davies said.

'Not even her father could put her off,' Parker said.

'Jesus Christ. The city is in a state of near riot and she wants to be on the street with these demonstrators.'

'She knows what it's like.'

'We should have forbidden this bloody march,' Davies said.

'Congress would have defied the order, as you well know . . . I dare say.'

'I've got to talk to her,' Davies said.

'I'm afraid she doesn't want that,' Parker said.

'No, she doesn't, does she?'

He could picture her now at the railway station – walking away from him down the platform. She hadn't looked back once. He could imagine her in the tent with him that first night they had made love: the feel of her body in his arms; the rasp in her voice as she told him to enter her; the flush that rose like a mask across her face the more aroused she became; the way she shuddered when she reached climax. He couldn't bear it that he had lost all that. It was the Shabdrung who had taken it all away from him.

'How could they both have fallen for that Shabdrung nonsense, Parker?' he said. 'Believe that some spiritual master could offer them all the answers. It's like they left the rest of the world behind.'

'No, they're still in the world,' Parker said. 'They're just convinced they've penetrated to the heart of the illusion. That's how they'd put it anyway.'

'I can't help thinking she allowed herself to be hypnotised or some such thing. I just don't understand,' Davies said.

'If you're not on the inside of that spiritual business, I don't see how you *can* understand.'

'I'm not,' he said. 'And I don't.'

Parker shrugged. He obviously didn't give a good damn how Davies felt about Christina. Parker was a colleague. He wasn't a friend.

Davies looked out of the window at the gaudy shop fronts and the open sewers. The sun was coming up over Calcutta and heating up the streets. Men wrapped in *dhotis* were washing themselves by the side of the road. They were hacking up phlegm and spitting into the ditches. And here he was, Major Owen

270

Davies, stranded here in this city on this subcontinent pendulant to Asia. He was in the heart of the military and political machinery of the Raj, where he belonged. Christ, the things he'd done. Didn't bear thinking about. Fight fire with fire. That's what he'd done. He'd hoped that Christina might have . . . Christ, he might as well admit it to himself: it had always been impossible.

He had gone to church. He had prayed: for survival, for forgiveness. He believed in order. But God for him was present by His absence, too. She and the Colonel believed in that basic heresy of the presence of God in everything and they believed they were privileged enough to experience that presence directly – day in, day out. It was the sin of pride. It denied the mystery of God. It allowed Devenish to defy the Department as Gupta's belief had allowed him to shoot Simpson. Not that he could imagine Christina and the Colonel going quite that far.

And now Christina was out there, on the Calcutta streets, demonstrating for Indian independence and he, Davies, was in the back seat of the Rover, his staff car. The Rover moved more slowly now. The streets north of Curzon Gardens were full of squads of soldiers with rifles, and policemen with lathis, getting ready to deploy close to the Maidan on the arrival of the demonstration.

He had chosen this way of life, hadn't he? There was a certain integrity in that. Right and wrong. He hadn't been born into the upper echelons of the Raj like the Colonel or Christina. But he had chosen to serve it. He believed that what the Government was doing in India was fundamentally right. And the Colonel and Christina felt themselves privileged enough to be able to betray it. But that was democracy, wasn't it: the best of a bad lot for everyone? And he was there to protect it. By fair means or foul.

And still Davies wanted to see her. Even if his rational mind told him that it was impossible, had been from the beginning impossible, to make her his wife, still there was something in him, something visceral, that made him want to see her again, to talk to her. Even if she utterly rejected him, cursed him as he stood in front of her, he couldn't stand the total exclusion from her thoughts, her feelings, of knowing what she was doing after he got so close to her on the way to Bumthang. And then at Talo. The Shabdrung.

And it struck him that Tobgye, by killing the Shabdrung, had frozen Christina's image of the holy man in time. Of course, she might have been struck by the charisma, by some spiritual experience, by the apparent saintliness of the man. But by Tobgye killing him, she had had no time to be disillusioned by him, or to let her mind clear of whatever smoke in mirrors he had conjured up for her. Tobgye had made the Shabdrung an immortal saint for her, and now that he was dead it would be impossible to tarnish that image. Davies could never win against the rivalry of this saint in his Buddhist heaven, he knew that. The Shabdrung would be enshrined in her memory for ever. And he, Davies, would always be the Judas Iscariot who had betrayed him.

The car had slowed to a crawl. Govinda honked the horn, hoping to get the companies of soldiers to move aside to let them through. The demonstration. He was there to command a sizeable contingent of the military and police. Govinda honked the horn again and the Rover moved forward. He hoped to God that nothing terrible was going to happen to her.

CHAPTER THIRTY

SHE TURNED INTO THE MOWLA ALI BAZAAR. THE STREET WAS crammed with demonstrators, both men and women, banners bobbing and swaying, in carnival chaos. All these brown faces stared at her with suspicion as she pushed on through the bazaar, marked by her skin, part of that conquering race – *parare subjectis et debellare superbos* – merciful to those beneath the yoke and ruthless to those who resisted it. She pulled back the long sleeve of her navy cotton dress and checked her watch. Almost nine o'clock.

She picked her way through the crowd to the gateway at the end of the street. Two Congress security guards stopped her, big Sikhs in turbans and dusty brown, Western-style suits.

'Where are you going, madam?'

'Theosophical Society,' she said. 'I know they're here. I'm looking for a Mrs Commander.'

One of them motioned with his bearded chin, and they let her through into the garden of the townhouse, where Congress tricolours waved at each corner of a carefully manicured and well-watered lawn. Close to the house was a large group of European women and a few men. Christina was certain that she would recognise Marjorie Commander from Richard's description. Sure enough, the grand dowager was seated in a large wicker chair. Her voluminous white cotton dress covered her rather like a diaphanous sail upon an ancient catafalque. She was in her late sixties at least. Her dyed auburn hair had been tightly curled by her hairdresser and was plastered to her temples. Her eyes, nose and mouth gave the impression of being daintily painted on a large white egg. She was surrounded by a whole gaggle of young women as if she was mother hen to them. And next to her was a young Indian man in a grey *khurta*. He wore round glasses and had trimmed his beard somewhat in the style of the Russian revolutionist, Leon Trotsky. He had a large Kodak camera in his hands and he was pointing it at the Theosophist group. There was a pop and flash and a cloud of acrid magnesium smoke drifted towards her. The photographer looked her up and down.

'Mrs Commander, I'm Christina Devenish.'

The egg-shaped face lifted and the old lady squeezed Christina's hand.

'Oh, Richard's cousin. Welcome, my dear. We'll be moving off soon. Before it gets too hot, I hope. Pity you just missed the photograph. This is Mr Lal.'

The young photographer nodded to Christina.

Mrs Commander stood up.

'Mr Lal is writing an article on British dissidents.'

'Oh really,' Christina said.

'Yes,' Lal said. 'It's very heartening that not all the British in India are trying to block the Independence movement.'

His head waggled in that Indian style, the eyes big behind the lenses.

'Take care today,' Mrs Commander said to her.

'Do you think we'll have trouble?' Christina asked.

'There are a lot of police and soldiers close to the Chowringee Road,' Lal said. 'I saw them on the way here.'

'We'll have a few hotheads in the crowd, too, I expect,' Christina said.

Mr Lal smiled broadly.

'No doubt,' he said.

'Mr Bose, the mayor, has personally delegated some ushers to keep an eye on our group,' Mrs Commander said.

She didn't seem in the slightest bit perturbed.

'Madam, madam, we are ready to go.'

The leader of their escort, another burly young Sikh, respectfully gestured a palm towards a group of Indian dignitaries.

'That's Mr Bose over there,' Mrs Commander said.

It was easy to pick him out. Bose was dressed in a Western-style suit and tie. Tall, dignified and intense, he had all the charisma of a born leader and those corporation members around him had the air of acolytes, even Jalalauddin Hashemy, the Muslim leader, and Mrs Jyotirmoyee Gangulee, the education secretary. They seemed to hold Bose in awe. Christina knew of Bose's reputation, too, from Owen. Owen claimed that Bose was 'hand in glove' with the terrorists. She wondered how true that was.

'Fall in behind the council party, please,' the escort said. 'You'll be safer close to the mayor.'

'Stay near me,' Mrs Commander said. 'Nobody will bother to harm an old lady.'

'I'd be honoured,' Christina said.

'Must go,' Lal said. 'Pictures . . .'

He waved the camera.

'Of course, of course,' Mrs Commander said.

She gripped Christina's elbow. Christina glanced about at the other demonstrators, and tried to steer Mrs Commander closer to the Sikh escort. The crowded street parted for the mayor's entourage. Stewards from the mayor's office called out orders in Hindi through white metal megaphones.

'I know everybody here,' Mrs Commander said, leaning into Christina. 'Nothing to worry about.'

All these protestations from Mrs Commander were making Christina nervous.

With a series of signals and shouts from the ushers, the mayor's group marched down along the Mowla Ali Bazaar. Another group of Sikh bodyguards immediately closed behind the dignitaries and then the escort ushered Christina, Mrs Commander and the Europeans into line. The mayor and his group moved at a brisk march and then they turned right into Corporation Street. The crowd in the bazaar surged into place behind the Theosophists and the noise was suddenly deafening all around Christina.

Jai Hind!

Ban-de Mataram!

Jai Hind!

Ban-de Mataram!

Mrs Commander gripped Christina's forearm more tightly as they followed the march around the corner. On each side of Corporation Street there was a line of policemen nervously tapping their lathis against the pavement. The wiry Indian Leon Trotsky, Mr Lal, was up ahead with his camera, hurriedly changing a plate. The street narrowed as they approached St Theresa's Church. The technical school was about fifty yards ahead and more tricolours were flying next to the gate where a crowd of young students were cheering the approaching marchers. Mrs Commander still gripped Christina's forearm as they passed by the YWCA building. They were in a sea of silken colour and swaying bodies and rhythmic chants. Then they came level with the heavily guarded headquarters of the Calcutta Mounted Police. The marchers seemed to veer away from the front of the building automatically. Christina's skin prickled, but other than the twitching of the horses' tails, and the idle swing of the lathis in the hands of the horsemen, there was no movement from the police. The slogan chanting grew louder and the column of demonstrators surged ahead with their banners and tricolours.

'We're going to be all right,' Mrs Commander said.

And Christina wished that she would just shut up.

The head of the procession approached the crossroads with

the Chowringee Road. Across it, and to Christina's right, mounted troopers had lined up between the north side of the road and the south side of Curzon Gardens. Opposite Curzon Gardens, the faint noise of the fast-paced tramp of soldiers marching double-time drifted across from the open space of the Maidan. A company of Gurkhas in khaki uniforms and slouch hats approached with all the power and precision of an express train across the Calcutta Football Ground, the soldiers' rifles held diagonally across their chests.

'They're in a hurry,' Christina said.

'Gurkhas,' Mrs Commander said. 'Light Infantry always marches double-time. First in, last out.'

'Frightening, isn't it?'

'It's meant to be,' Mrs Commander said.

The column of Gurkhas came to a halt and fanned out in a line below the Cenotaph which was about a hundred yards away. The mayor planned to hoist a tricolour there. The officer's next order echoed across the Maidan, not at all muffled by the chants of the demonstrators.

'Fix . . .'

There was a clatter of metal.

'. . . bayonets.'

A shimmer of movement and another clatter of metal.

'What are they doing?' Christina said.

'It's just for show. For effect,' Mrs Commander said.

But Christina didn't believe her for a second.

A large black Rover drew to a halt behind the cavalrymen on the crossroads. Something caught in her stomach when she saw Govinda, Owen's driver, get out of the car and pull down the canvas top. Then Owen stood up in the back of the car. If he happened to look in this direction, he might have been able to see her among the marchers, but it was unlikely unless she tried somehow to make herself known to him. Owen got out of the car, followed by Richard. It was disconcerting to see her cousin with him. Both of them were in pale khaki uniforms, and peaked officer's caps, as if trying to blend in with the other policemen. Owen saluted a mounted officer who appeared to be in charge of the massed forces of the Raj. He continued on towards two smaller squads behind the main lines of mounted and foot police. He made some sort of hand sign to one of the squads and they surged forward to block the north exit of the crossroads adjacent to Curzon Gardens. He made another gesture and the second squad ran across the road to take up positions to block the south exit close to the Continental Hotel. Then he got back into the open-topped Rover and, with binoculars, observed the crossroads from the slight elevation the car gave him.

She and Mrs Commander – still clinging to her arm – were almost at the crossroads, marching faster as the demonstrators became more agitated the nearer they got to the Maidan and the Gurkhas and massed police around Curzon Gardens. She was close to the line of horsemen that separated Owen and his Rover from the marchers. The noise of the slogans was thunderous.

Jai Hind!
Jai Hind!
Inclub Zindabad!
Inclub Zindabad!
Inclub Zindabad!

The noise and the colours and the electric anxiety of the crowd and the tension of the policemen exhilarated and terrified her. '*Inclub Zindabad*', 'Long live the revolution', sure to excite the crowd and provoke the police. Now, on both sides of the procession, the policemen began to march in step with the demonstrators, just a few yards of space between the uniformed officers and the crowd. Christina stumbled as Mrs Commander was jostled into her. The protesters in front and behind them pressed together as if to get away from the policemen, and she was crushed up against Mrs Commander and one of the Sikh ushers.

'Sorry,' Christina said.

Mrs Commander simply shook her head.

'Don't let go of me,' Christina said.

Up ahead, pushed by the crowd of bodies behind them, Subhas Bose and his group of Congress party dignitaries surged forward towards the open space of the Maidan. In front of Christina and Mrs Commander, the main body of the procession suddenly widened and the policemen at the edges were forced to give ground. For a second, Christina had room to breathe and held up Mrs Commander by her forearm. She twisted towards a harsh shout and she saw a lathi swing up and, in a sudden instant of silence, she heard the whistle in the air before the crack against the head of a protester and the man's scream as he dropped to the ground.

'Oh my God,' she whispered.

Mrs Commander's fingers dug like claws into her forearm.

A great yell rose from the crowd, a demonstrator jabbed at a policeman with his placard and suddenly all the policemen were flailing their lathis. Mrs Commander made frightened cooing noises as they were crushed together again. Christina's arms were pinned against her sides by the bodies all around her.

'I'm falling, I'm falling,' Mrs Commander cried, and Christina tried to hold her up and balanced. The other European Theosophists behind them yelled in useless protest at the police. Beyond the marchers, she heard an officer shout out orders.

A squad of foot policemen charged at the head of the procession. Six of them beat Subhas Bose to the ground in a flurry of lathi blows. Christina screamed as a burly policeman kicked the legs from under Jalalauddin Hashemy. From within the awful crush of protesters, she could make out Subhas Bose on the ground, legs curled up, his arms trying to protect his head, while the six policemen around him thrashed at his squirming body.

Mr Lal swung up his camera and took a photograph and then he was backpedalling into the crowd trying to change the plate.

A flash of green and orange silk reeled through the scattering demonstrators and a flurry of lathis fell on Mrs Gangulee as she tried to get herself between the policemen and the mayor.

'Come on,' Christina said.

She grabbed Mrs Commander's arm and began to squirm out of the crowd, dragging Mrs Commander behind her in the only direction the crowd had thinned, which was towards the prone Subhas Bose and Mrs Gangulee. Surely the police would stop the beating in front of two white women witnesses.

'What are you doing?' Christina screamed at them.

But the beating went on and a surge in the crowd pushed her and Mrs Commander away from it and into the middle of the crossroads. The crowd suddenly scattered in front of them.

'Are you all right?' Christina said.

'Yes, yes,' Mrs Commander said. 'Look, there's Mr Lal.'

Lal was caught between a knot of demonstrators and a squad of lathi-wielding policemen. He swung his camera up to get a picture just as four policemen raced towards him. One of them slammed the camera back into his face.

'Stop!' Christina screamed absurdly. 'He's a photographer.'

'Let me go,' Mrs Commander pleaded. 'They won't touch me.'

The open ground of the Maidan was close by.

'Get out of here,' Christina said.

Mrs Commander nodded.

'Help her,' Christina called to one of the Sikh escorts.

The Sikh looked helplessly at Lal and then back to Mrs Commander.

'This way, madam,' he said to her.

He took Mrs Commander by the arm and steered her towards the Continental Hotel.

'You too, madam,' the Sikh called.

'No,' Christina yelled.

She ran towards Lal and the policemen. She bumped into one of the policemen's backs. Lal lost his grip on the camera and clutched desperately at his glasses. The camera cracked and shattered. The policemen were all around him. Christina hammered on their backs and then she was whirled backwards and crashed to the ground. She sat, stunned, in the middle of the road, putteed boots stamping close to her hands, khaki-clad legs shifting around her, not knowing which policeman had flung her down. Through the legs and the flailing arms and lathis, she could see Lal bent over, but still standing, his arms up to protect his head. She had to get to him. The knees of her stockings tore as she twisted on the ground and regained her feet. A heavy blow cracked against Lal's ribs. The four Indian policemen jabbed and thrashed at him and he flailed with his arms to ward them off. She lost one of her black pumps and reached down to get it back onto her foot. A surge in the crowd spun her away from Lal among the bumping bodies of the demonstrators. She could still see him writhing away from the blows of the policemen, about twenty feet away now, but she couldn't push through the crowd to get to him. The end of a lathi thudded into the side of his head and his knees buckled and he sprawled forward on the ground.

She screamed and tried to pull people out of her way but they pushed her back.

As Lal reached for the camera with his left hand, a stamping foot crushed his fingers.

'You bastards,' she yelled.

And then blows slammed down on him again and again and she was crying now, please stop it, please stop it, and clawing at shoulders and arms in front of her and he was curled up into a tight ball and finally she lost sight of him as the policeman dragged him away to a Black Mariah and the crowd swirled her away, and she felt hands clutch at her breasts, pinch her buttocks, a hard slap on the side of her head that sent her reeling. Faces full of hatred swam past her face and screamed at her in Hindi or Bengali. Foul words in English. Then it stopped as the crowd around her suddenly scattered. Then all she could see were the policemen who swarmed around her like a protective phalanx. This was insane.

'Dear God, Christina, what on earth do you think you're doing?'

Richard leaned in towards her and he gripped her arm tightly. The policemen around them moved across the crossroads and lashed out at the crowd of protesters between them and Curzon Gardens.

'Let me go, Richard,' she yelled. 'Let me go.'

Her cousin loosened her arm. His eyes were shocked, staring at her as if she were mad. Beyond the phalanx, other policemen dragged more limp or struggling bodies towards the open backs of the Black Mariahs. The main body of the demonstration had retreated down Corporation Street, back the way it had come, and was streaming into the side streets.

Christina's knees were scraped and burning. Her breasts and buttocks bruised. Her head throbbed above her ear where the blow had landed. Her legs were wobbly but she moved away from Richard and tried to keep her balance as she walked towards Owen. He was standing at the bottom of Curzon Gardens, now, in front of the cavalry. He waited for her to get to him, her gait wobbly as she approached him.

'Why don't you stop it?' she said flatly.

'Stop it?' he said.

'Yes, yes. Stop it.'

He shook his head.

'What are you talking about? Not even Gandhi could bloody stop it.'

'Damn you, Owen.'

'You saw what happened,' he said. 'I had nothing to do with this. It's a full-scale bloody riot.'

'It was the police,' she said. 'It was the police . . . And you bloody ordered them to do it.'

It was useless to argue with him, here on the street like this. Owen took her by the shoulders, head slightly tilted.

'Are you hurt?' he asked.

'It's nothing,' she said.

'We'll have a doctor take a look at you.'

'I am a doctor,' she snapped.

She turned away from him, back towards the debris-strewn crossroads. No sign of Mrs Commander or Lal or Bose or Mrs Gangulee. Mrs Commander must have got away, the others had probably been arrested.

Owen grabbed Christina's shoulder from behind and she spun around to face him.

'Let's get you somewhere safe, for God's sake,' he said. 'Get in the car. Let's get you away from here.'

'I'm not getting in your bloody car.'

She pushed away from him and ran towards Corporation Street.

'Christina,' he shouted behind her. 'Where are you going?'

She spun around and swung an open palm at him and he swayed back to avoid it.

'And don't have anybody follow me,' she screamed.

'You can't go down there,' he said.

'Don't try and stop me,' she said. 'Just don't. All right? Just don't.'

She turned away from him. Her whole body ached. She staggered over the crossroads and away from him. Her hair had come loose and hung wiry around her face. Her navy blue dress was covered in dust, her stockings torn, her knees scraped and dirty. The sick and empty feeling in her stomach was worse than all the burns and aches and sharp pains that she felt in her muscles. The whole street was full of broken placards, trampled banners, torn tricolours, discarded clothes, rumpled shawls. Everywhere groups of policemen stood about laughing and joking, excited after the rout.

'Christina, stop!' he called.

She glanced back. Bloody Owen was following her. He was running across the street towards her. She just wanted to get away from him, didn't want his hands to touch her, to hear his voice, to have him anywhere near her, and she ran in a panic down Corporation Street. She heard more shouts from the wounded and the small knots of protesters helping their comrades away from the processional route.

She looked back. He was gaining on her. She turned into a narrow alleyway. It was full of more demonstrators trying to get away from the scene of the riot. Already piles of rubbish had been set alight on the street corners and the fleeing crowds panicked as the flames flickered up and the smoke choked the alleys.

She jostled her way through the crowd and she could hear him call to her and when she looked back the riot-shocked Indians were instinctively clearing out of his way as if his uniform were some kind of talisman that forced them out of his path. She had to lose him. Maybe in the Raja Bazaar which was like a maze. Most of the city had shut down for the march but as she raced through these alleys, close now to Sealdah Railway Station, she saw that food sellers had stayed open to feed the marchers who had strayed off the route. Vats of oil smoked in front of the stalls, and *puris* still sizzled; they were piled up in brown and glistening mounds beneath the awnings. The vendors were calling to one another, hurrying to pack up their sacks of flour and spilling vegetables.

Still she could sense him behind her, coursing her like a dog after a hare, gaining on her. She turned right into another narrow lane. Chicken feathers swirled in a downy dance around her feet. On the corner there was a small shrine, an image of Kali, the city's patron goddess, the blue paint of her body crusted black and brown, and her feet bright red, blood-bathed, from that very morning's sacrifice. Christina glanced back but she couldn't see Owen. She just knew he was there. Christina turned into the alley beside the makeshift temple and she found herself in the butchers' market.

On both sides of the alley, the stalls were heaped with freshly killed meat from the morning's slaughter in front of the corner's shrine. Unplucked chickens, and goat haunches, some unskinned and cloven-hoofed, hung from bloody stanchions. On the closest stall, a horned and slit-eyed head rested on a pile of pink lungs and dark brown offal. Pale strings of emptied intestines swam in an enamel bowl of water frothed with a pale brown scum. All around the stalls the fat dark flies buzzed in a frenzied dance. She ran on.

Butchers yelled at her as she hurried deeper into the market. Twenty yards ahead of her, at the end of the alley, broken protest banners were stacked against the wooden posts of a dirty canvas awning of a corner *chai* shop. A group of unshaven *chai*-shop wallahs got up off their benches as they saw her approach and when one of them stepped into the alley more than ten others gathered behind him.

Oh Christ, she thought.

The lane was blocked in front of her.

'No, let me by,' she called.

A wall of butchers from the market, and bruised and angry men from the demonstration, all glared at her. One of the men, covered from chest to knees by a bloody leather apron, stepped out in front of the others. A sliver of steel dangled by his side. His greasy hair was dishevelled, and he was slightly wall-eyed. The fingers around the haft of the knife were stained a dark brown.

'Memsahib,' he said. 'What are you doing here?'

'I'm trying to get home,' she said.

Richard's house – her father was there. She wanted to be

within the safety of those walls. It was just about a mile north-west of the Raja Bazaar.

'Please,' she said. 'I've been at the march, let me go by.'

'The march,' the butcher said.

More men, some bandaged or bloody – from the demonstration, she thought – had come out from under the *chai*-shop awning, and they stood in a semicircle around her, gawking at her, this tall white woman lost in a district in which she didn't belong. And then the butcher with the steel was looking beyond her with those uncoordinated eyes of his. All of the men now looked past her, down the alley of the meat market. She turned around.

Owen stood close beside the corner shrine to Kali. The khaki uniform seemed to be lit up but the peak of his cap laid a shadow over his eyes. Like some Trojan hero, he seemed to believe that he was invincible, that nothing and no one could touch him. He held himself in that soldier's manner of his, shoulders wide, that easy flow of his limbs as he continued towards her and the wall of men now behind her.

'Christina,' he called.

Oh God, stop, she thought.

She turned back to face the butcher and it was as if someone else had put the words into her mouth.

'I'm just trying to get away from him,' she said and immediately regretted it.

'Don't worry,' the butcher said.

More meat sellers from the market had gathered near the corner shrine, curious to see what might happen. There were so many of them. They had blocked the alleyway behind him. Some of them swung cleavers and meat axes.

She was the only one between Owen and the butcher.

The butcher leaned to one side and spat out a bright red stream of betel. Then he eased her aside and walked towards Owen and she was lost in the jostle of the crowd again as the *chai*-shop wallahs pushed past her.

But Owen just kept coming towards her, looking at her from under the peak, ignoring the butcher and the mob between them. He didn't even reach for the flap of his holster to take out his revolver. And then the *chai*-shop wallahs, and the butcher, and the beaten demonstrators all closed upon him and he was occluded behind the wall of their backs.

I'm free to go, she thought. To walk north towards Richard's house.

Owen shouted something in the middle of the crowd and then he screamed.

'Owen!' she called.

She saw arms lift and fall in the boil of bodies. She ran towards the second high screech as if she might pull off the now yelling and frantic crowd. She touched a sweat-stained back and the man wheeled away from her but there were yet more sweating bodies in front of her. There were shouts in Hindi and then the crowd suddenly scattered from around Owen as if she had mirac- ulously flung them all aside.

He was seated on the cobbles, as though slumped, and some curious rigour in his muscles and bones had stopped him from falling splayed. His military cap was gone. His matted head was titled at a hideous and impossible angle and his eyes were half closed. The khaki uniform was shredded in places, torn and stained a deep red where they had cut him. Blood still welled from the gash in his neck where the skin was torn and bubbles of fatty tissue had folded back from the deep wound.

There was no life in his face. His cheeks were streaked with blood. The lashes of his half-open eye were dotted with tiny red droplets. He sat in a deep red pool that was still spreading dark and slick on the cobbles around him. They had cut him some- where below his Sam Browne belt. His wrists rested just above his knees, his fingers curled. His ankles, in puttees, were crossed, and his boots shone a lucid black with parade-ground absurdity.

All the butchers and demonstrators had disappeared off the

street, and two bold pariah dogs already had their front paws on the edge of a stall and were pulling at slabs of abandoned meat. She knelt down beside Owen's lifeless body. The blood was only weeping out of the wounds now, not pumping, clear matter running over the bubbles of fat tissue at the slashed throat.

She rested her hands on her own scraped and stinging knees.

Oh Owen, she thought. Look at you.

For a moment, she had the deranged sense that she was only alive due to some divine protection – and that Owen's corpse was evidence of equally divine retribution. But the memory of the Shabdrung's death made a mockery of that delusion. If anyone had deserved divine protection it had been the Shabdrung of Bhutan. And he had been choked to death, with Owen's undoubted collusion.

Christina knelt in awe beside Owen Davies's torn body, that once intact miracle of flesh and bone and nerve and ligament, heart and consciousness that she had lovingly held in her arms, had taken into her own body. She was afraid to touch it now, the carrion that was left of it. The British would bury it.

Better if they cremated it, she thought.

She heard the tramp of feet and looked up.

It was Richard, leading a company of uniformed soldiers, rifles at port arms, who trotted behind him along the alley, deserted now but for the pariah dogs that slunk off dragging pieces of bloody goat carcass behind them. Richard knelt down beside her. His eyes were wide with shock. His bottom lip was quivering. He glanced at Owen's corpse and then at her.

'Are you hurt?' he asked.

She shook her head and she smiled. And it was as if a sudden flower had bloomed in her skull, as if a barrier had been torn down that had stood between her and that India of centuries of civilisation and spiritual passion that was beyond the endless struggle of good and evil. And there was nothing between her and all the gods and demons of the Mahabharata, or of the

Himalaya, those creatures of dream and nightmare that moulded the actions of men and women, and drove them to ecstasies of art and frenzies of slaughter. Nothing between her and all the whirling atoms and suns and constellations within whose web her body was trapped–while in her mind she was dancing, dancing over the body of this rootless man, this murderer of god-kings, this poisoner of her father, this torturer who would never be buried in the land of his birth, but whose fate was such that he had died at the mouth of the Ganges like the most blessed of Hindus, and the sun above her was a perfect red orb, blazing with a fiery red light.

Acknowledgements

I first heard the story of the Bhutanese Shabdrung in 1979 and since then have dug through the British Political Department's secret files that have been downgraded from classified under the fifty-year rule. I am indebted to Michael Aris's *The Raven Crown* for his citation of the India Office Library's references which led me to the papers. Other books, including the present queen of Bhutan, Ashi Dorje Wangmo's *Of Rainbows and Clouds*, were also useful, as well as *Memoirs of a Political Officer's Wife* by Margaret D. Williamson. The story of Dinesh Gupta can be found in many books on the Bengali independence movement of the 1930s. What was once Dalhousie Square in Calcutta is now named after him and his two fellow guerrillas.

Thanks are due to: David Doughan of the Fawcett Library for pointing me in the direction of *Shtri Dharma*, the journal of the All India Women's Federation, which provided useful background information for Christina Devenish's life; the staff of the India Office Library in London, the New York Public Research Library, and the library of Columbia University in New York; Devi Laskar and her parents for their information on the city of Calcutta; Dai Smith of the University of Glamorgan; Dan Franklin at Jonathan Cape for his clear, insightful and meticulous editing; Kate Jones and Amanda Urban of ICM for their work for my wellbeing.

Thanks to Helen for her careful readings of every draft and her loving support.

Information regarding the cosmology of the succession of the aeons came from discourses given by the late Dudjom Rimpoche in London in 1979, from an interview with Yangthang Tulku conducted in Boston in the mid-eighties, and from a meeting with Hotu Sempa in Tibet in 2000. Thanks to Namkhai Norbu Rimpoche for his clarification of certain historical details pertaining to Bhutan, and for his elucidation of Buddhist view, meditation and action, I can't thank him enough.

Also available in Vintage

Desmond Barry

THE CHIVALRY OF CRIME

'Gritty, powerfully alive...*The Chivalry of Crime* is a *tour de force*, deserving of every accolade that comes its way'
Peter Carey

'Barry shows an extraordinary talent for creating historical characters who inhabit a convincing past...This is a great, galloping, delightful read that will rope in even readers who are no fans of the Western'
Independent

'Wow...Well, here's a history of the James gang wrapped round a novel that sure ain't for the faint-hearted. Imagine a combo of Cormac McCarthy's *Blood Meridian*, Charles Frazier's *Cold Mountain* and Dylan Thomas, and you've got it – slaughter in luscious prose, a cracking debut'
Brian Case, *Time Out*

'With prose as sharp as a pistol shot and a flow like that of some mean cavalry, Barry maps out the smoky moral world of gunslingers...Number one with a bullet, *The Chivalry of Crime* marks an audacious and compelling debut'
Sunday Tribune

VINTAGE

Also available in Vintage

Desmond Barry

A BLOODY GOOD FRIDAY

'An unmissable writer'
GQ

'A skilful tying together of the viewpoints of a disparate range of characters...great dialogue and a vividly evoked setting'
Scotland of Sunday

Good Friday, 1977. Merthyr Tydfil. At twenty to midnight a dozen different forces converge – Macky, just out of jail; the gippos and their knives; the Shop Boys, fifty or sixty skinheads in fanatical pursuit of recreational violence; P.C. Phillips, the young copper with something to prove; Mohan Singh, proud owner of the Taj Mahal curry house. The result: mayhem. 'RACE RIOT ERUPTS IN VALLEYS TOWN'. And witness to it all, Davey Daunt, a spazzy with a leg brace, the only one who knows what *really* happened.

'This action-filled novel also contains its fair share of lyrical moments and saddened contemplation'
Sunday Times

VINTAGE